Seize the Day

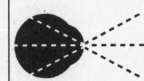

SEIZE THE DAY

CURTIS BUNN

THORNDIKE PRESS

A part of Gale, Cengage Learning

GALE
CENGAGE Learning·

Farmington Hills, Mich • San Francisco • New York • Waterville, Maine
Meriden, Conn • Mason, Ohio • Chicago

GALE
CENGAGE Learning®

LIBRARY OF CONGRESS CATALOGING-IN-PUBLICATION DATA

Names: Bunn, Curtis, author.
Title: Seize the day / Curtis Bunn.
Description: Large print edition. | Waterville, Maine : Thorndike Press Large
    Print, 2016. | © 2015 | Series: Thorndike Press large print African-American
Identifiers: LCCN 2015044725| ISBN 9781410486165 (hardback) | ISBN
    1410486168 (hardcover)
Subjects: LCSH: African Americans—Fiction. | Large type books. | BISAC:
    FICTION / African American / General.
Classification: LCC PS3552.U4717 S45 2016 | DDC 813/.6—dc23
LC record available at http://lccn.loc.gov/2015044725

Published in 2016 by arrangement with Strebor, an imprint of Atria Books, a division of Simon & Schuster, Inc.

Printed in Mexico
1 2 3 4 5 6 7 20 19 18 17 16

To my late grandmother,
Nettie Royster aka "Mama."
Your love and wisdom are missed,
but remain in my heart.

ACKNOWLEDGMENTS

God, the Almighty, Ever-Present, Omnipotent, continues to bless me in ways beyond measure. All things start and stop with Him. Thank you, Lord.

It's been thirty-five years since the death of my father, Edward Earl Bunn, Sr., and yet I still dream of him and I pray that he knows his name will always live through us, his family. My mother, Julia Bunn, has been my closest ally all my life and my friend and traveling partner as an adult. Her beauty, inside and outside, illuminates my life. My brothers, Billy and Eddie, and my sister, Tammy Beck, are my first and everlasting friends that I love through and through.

Curtis Jr. and Gwendolyn (Bunny) are my children, my lifeblood, my heartbeats. They make me proud and humble. Gordon, my nephew/second son, makes my chest stick out. I love my niece, Tamayah (Bink Bink), a college student, and nephew Eddie Jr.,

7

who I expect big things. My cousins, Warren (Button) Eggleston and Greg Agnew are really my brothers. Ditto for my brother-in-law, Deryk Beck. And I am grateful for my loving cousin Carolyn Keener and uncle Al and aunts Thelma and Barbara and Ms. Brenda Brown.

My wife, Felita Sisco Bunn, is the love of my life, my "whole-mate," closest friend and proof that true love exists. I'm grateful for my mother-in-law, Shirley Jordan, and Larry Jordan and father-in-law, Ted Baker, Cecilia Baker and the Baker clan.

The Strebor Books family, led by Zane and Charmaine Roberts Parker, mean more than any typed words can convey. Thank you!!!

I enjoy listing by name the supporters because you all mean so much to me: My ace, Trevor Nigel Lawrence, Keith (Blind) and Delores Gibson, Darryl K. Washington Kerry and Loretta Muldrow, Randy and Flecia Brown, Sam and Maureen Myers, Ronnie and Tarita Bagley, Tony and Raye Starks, Darryl (DJ) and Wanda Johnson, Lyle Harris, Monya M. Battle, Tony Hall, Marc Davenport, Tami Rice-Mitchell, Brad Corbin, William Mitchell, J.B. Hill, Bob & La Detra White, Tamaira Johnson Kent Davis, Andre Johnson, Wayne Ferguson, Tony

& Erika Sisco, Karen Turner, Betty Roby, Leslie Neland, Kathy Brown, Venus Chapman, Monica Harris Wade, Tara Ford, Christine Beatty, Greg Willis, Al Whitney, Brian White, Ronnie Akers, Jacques Walden, Dennis Wade, Julian Jackson, Mark Webb, Kelvin Lloyd, Frank Nelson, Hayward Horton, Mark Bartlett, Marvin Burch, Derrick (Nick Lambert), Gerald Mason, Charles E. Johnson, Harry Sykes, Kim Mosley, Angela Davis, Ed (Bat) Lewis, Shelia Harrison, David A. Brown, Rev. Hank Davis, Susan Davis-Wigenton, Donna Richardson, Sheila Wilson, Curtis West, Bruce Lee, Val Guilford, Derek T. Dingle, Ramona Palmer, Warren Jones, Deberah (Sparkle) Williams, Leon H. Carter, Ricky K. Brown, Clay Dade, Zack Withers, Kevin Davis, Sybil & Leroy Savage, Avis Easley, Demetress Graves, Anna Burch, Kevin & Hope Jones, George Hughes, Sandra Smith, Sheila Wilson, Mary Knatt, Serena Knight, Joi Edwards, Sonya Perry, Daphne Grissom, Denise Taylor, Diana Joseph, Derrick (Tinee) Muldrow, Rick Eley, Marty McNeal, Nikita Germaine Houston, D.L. Cummings, Rob Parker, Cliff Brown, D. Orlando Ledbetter, Garry Howard, Stephen A. Smith, LaToya Tokley, Angela Paige, Clifford Benton, Len Burnett, Lesley Hanesworth, Sherline Tavenier, Jeri Byrom, Carla Griffin, Liketa Morris, E. Franklin Dudley, Skip Grimes, Christine Beatty, Jeff Stevenson, Billy Robinson, Jay Nichols, Ralph Howard, Paul Spencer, Jai Wilson, John Hollis, Garry Raines, Glen Robinson, Dwayne Gray, Jessica Ferguson, Carolyn Glover, Kim Royster, Erin Sherrod, Mike Dean, Sheryl Wesley, Dexter Santos, Chastity Austin, John Hughes, Sherri Polite, Mark Lassiter, Tony Carter, Kimberly Frelow, Michele Ship, Michelle Lemon, Zain, Karen Shepherd, Carmen Carter, Tawana Turner-Green, Marilyn Bibby, Sheryl Williams-Jones, Jewell Rollen, Harold Rose, Danielle Carrington, Nia Simmons, Cheryl Jones, Kiesha Pough, Karen Marie Orange, Ashley Nicole, Yvonne Young, Barbara Hopkins, Vonda Henderson, Danny Anderson, Shauna Tisdale, Melzetta Oliver, April Kidd, Keisha Hutchinson, Olivia Alston, John Hollis, Dorothy (Dot) Harrell, Aggie Nteta, Ursula Renee, Carrie Haley, Anita Wilson, Tim Lewis, David Dickerson, Sandra Velazquez, Pam Cooper, Regina Troy, Denise Thomas, Andre Aldridge, Brenda O'Bryant, Pargeet Wright, Mike Christian, Sid Tutani, Tammy Grier, Regina Collins, Roland Louis, April Tarver, Penny Payne, Cynthia Fields, Dr. Yvonne Sanders-Butler,

Alicia Guice, Clara LeRoy, Calvin Sutton, Denise Bethea, Hadjii Hand, Fred Gore, Bernadette Brown, Petey Franklin and The Osagyefuo Amoatia Ofori Panin, King of Akyem Abuakwa Eastern Region of Ghana, West Africa.

Special thanks and love to my great alma mater, Norfolk State University (Class of 1983); the brothers of Alpha Phi Alpha (especially the Notorious E Pi of Norfolk State); Ballou High School (Class of '79), ALL of Washington, D.C., especially my beloved Southeast.

I am also grateful to all the readers and wonderful book clubs that have supported my work over the years and to my literary many friends Nathan McCall, Carol Mackey, Linda Duggins, Terrie M. Williams, Kimberla Lawson Roby, Walter Mosley, Monica Michelle, Nick Chiles, Denene Millner, Leslie Neland and Nhat Crawford.

I'm sure I left off some names — it was not intentional. If you know me, you know my mind is going . . . but not my imagination. ☺ I appreciate and I am grateful for you. #LiveLife

Peace and blessings,

— Curtis

CHAPTER ONE:
LIFE

I'm about to die. Doctor said so. Maybe not today. Perhaps tomorrow. Whenever it's coming, it's coming soon.

Cancer.

But I'm not scared. I'm a little anxious, a little curious, to be honest. Curious about how it will happen. Where I will be at that moment — the place and where will I be in my head, my mind. Will I get scared when I feel it coming? *Will* I feel it coming?

Well, those are thoughts for another day, a day that, truth be told, should not come for a few months or so. That's how long it will take the cancer to totally ravage and deplete my body and put me to sleep. Forever. That's what the doctors say. And they know everything.

So, here I am. In the prime of my life . . . waiting on death.

Can't cry about it. Not anymore. When I said I wasn't scared, I was talking about now. A month ago, when Dr. Wamer gave me the news, I was scared as shit.

Do you have any idea what it's like to be told you're at the end of your life's journey? At forty-five? With a sweet daughter? With so much more to do? With so much undone?

I was so overwhelmed that it took me two days to pull myself out of bed, to turn on the lights in my house, to eat an apple. Then it took me another two days to tell my father, who took it as if cancer was eating away at his existence.

"Why can't it be me, Calvin?" he said. "Why you? You've lived a good life. The best thing I ever did was marry your momma — God rest her soul — and contribute to your birth. The rest of my life, I can't say I'm that proud of. Except you. You've made me proud."

And why did he say that? I bawled like a freshly spanked newborn, and my sixty-eight-year-old dad and I hugged each other at the kitchen table at his house for what seemed like an hour, two men afraid out of their wits.

Since then, I have pulled myself together — what's left of me, that is. Doctors say they can't do surgery, but I can try radiation and perhaps chemo. But there are no guarantees. That's code for: "it won't work."

And I have seen how debilitating those treatments can be.

It never made sense to me that you go to the doctor for a checkup feeling fine. Then he tells you that you have cancer or some hideous disease and starts firing chemicals into your bloodstream like you shoot up a turkey you're about to fry on Thanksgiving. Almost immediately you feel like shit and before long you start looking like shit. You lose your hair, you lose your energy . . . you lose who you are. And eventually you lose your will to live.

For some, for most, that's the route they chose and I wouldn't dare begrudge them that.

Me, I would rather live whatever time I have left instead of having my insides burned out and become so drained that I cannot live, only exist . . . until I die.

Maybe it's me, but that doesn't seem like fun. Haven't had much fun since I went to the hospital for my annual checkup, feeling good and looking forward to a date that night with a nice lady I had met. Next thing I know, they tell me I have some form of cancer I can't pronounce, much/less spell. "Sarcoma" something or other. Attacks the blood cells, organs, bones . . . you name it. When they said it was fatal I lost interest in any more specifics.

I will be forty-six in four months . . . if I make it that long. I have a twenty-three-year-old daughter and a zest for life that is as strong as a weightlifter on steroids. Staying laid up in a hospital, withdrawn and diminished after chemotherapy or radiation does not qualify as living to me.

When I finally was up to eating, I ended up at the National Harbor, where I could see the Potomac River run from Maryland into Washington, D.C. It was an interesting spot with good sandwiches and nice desserts, which fulfilled my sweet teeth. Yes, I enjoy cakes and pies too much to limit my attraction to "sweet tooth." That's why I said "sweet *teeth.*"

Anyway, I sat alone, at a high-top table near the bar — a dying man with a plate of food and his thoughts. Ever since learning I would die, I was able to slow down my thinking. Everything was on express.

People walked right by me, some spoke to me or smiled at me. None of them realized they were in contact with a dead man. That's how I saw myself — walking dead. I was like a zombie, a creature moving about the earth but already departed. I just didn't look like one . . . yet.

I saw everything differently, too. Like, it

did not matter if my favorite football team, the Washington Redskins, won another Super Bowl. I didn't care much anymore about my wardrobe or purchasing that Mercedes CLS550 I had been eyeing or even if my 401(k) flattened out. It all seemed so meaningless to me after the diagnosis.

Still, I was not sure what I was inspired to do or how to live out my life, other than to *not* let doctors turn me into a bed-ridden slob before my time. I didn't ask anyone else's opinion on it. I just went with it.

My daughter, Maya . . . I couldn't tell her. It was hard for me to even say her name without getting choked up. That's how daughters are to their dads; we live to their heartbeat.

My father told her. "She deserves to know," he reasoned. "Maybe not everything going on with you. But this? She deserves to know this."

Maya did not call me about it. She showed up at my house one Saturday afternoon, right before I was about to get in a round of golf, in an attempt to free my mind of the burden. The garage door went up and there she was, pain and sadness all over her soft, lovely face. I knew my daughter and that look made me cry, without her saying a word.

"Daddy," she said, hugging me so tightly. Every time we embraced I smelled baby powder, like I did when she was an infant. It was my imagination or just how badly I wanted my little girl to remain my little girl.

"I'm OK, Maya," I said. "It's going to be all right."

She sobbed and sobbed and I held her as tightly as I could without making her uncomfortable. It broke my heart. My job as her father was to protect her. It crushed me that I was the cause of her anguish.

"You didn't have to come here, sweetheart," I managed to get out when I finally composed myself. "See, this is why I didn't want to tell you right away. You are all upset over something you can't control. It's out of both our hands right now."

Maya wiped her face and looked up at me with those eyes that were the replica of mine: brown and piercing.

"Daddy, we can't control it, but you've got to let the doctors try," she said. "I spoke to an oncologist from Johns Hopkins on my way here. He said nothing good will come out of doing nothing."

I had to break it down for her so—as, Isaiah Washington said in the movie *Love Jones* — "It will forever be broke."

"Let's go inside," I said. I wiped away her

tears and kissed both sides of her precious face. She turned me into mush. We were both a mess.

I called my friend, Thornell, and told him I had to renege on golf. I hadn't told him the news, either. That would be another tough call. But nothing compared to that talk with Maya.

"Sweetheart, about two months before I went to the doctor, I spoke to an old high school classmate at Ballou. His name was Kevin Hill. Yes, your godfather. Great guy, as you know. Do you know how we met? We played basketball against each other in junior high and became friends when we ended up at Ballou High School together. When Kevin got sick with multiple sclerosis, it slowly but surely ravaged his nervous system over the years until he was unable to do anything but lie in bed to die.

"I visited him at Washington Hospital Center. We reminisced and I was able to make him laugh and take his mind away from his plight, at least for a few moments. But the whole time I was looking at him and feeling so sorry for him, there was so much more for him to do in life. I thought I didn't convey that, but he sensed it. And he wrote a letter to me that means more to me now than ever."

I pulled out the folded sheet of paper with the letterhead that read: "Kevin Hill . . . Remember Me."

And then I read it to Maya: "Calvin, don't feel sorry for me. The things I did in my life, I enjoyed them. I could have done more, but I learned and accepted that God's plan was different. But all this time laying around in bed, I have had a lot of time to think. And I have a lot of regrets. I regret not traveling and not mending my relationship with my sister and not learning Spanish and so many other things. You know what I should have done, but makes no sense to do now? Cut off all my hair. I saw how some bald guys looked so cool with a shaved head. Even Samuel Jackson looked cool with a bald head in *Shaft*. I should have done that a long time ago. Now, if I do it, no one will see it.

"Anyway, my point is: Don't live with regrets. Live your life. *Carpe diem.* You know what that means? It means: seize the day. Seize it. Take it. Own it. Make it yours and get the most out of it.

"Nothing is promised. Yeah, you've heard this before. We all have. But we go about a day as if it's no big deal to make the most of it because we can do it the next day. Or the next. That's not the right approach. I'm forty-four. I got this disease from bad luck. If I knew it was coming, I would have done a lot of things I planned to do later. You and I have done a lot together and been as close as two friends could be, so I can say this to you without you getting offended: Get off your ass and live your life."

Maya got it then. The fear and hope left her. Reality settled in. She knew, at that point, I was done. No amount of radiation, chemo, Tylenol or anything else could help me. My days had been finalized. It had to be about what I did with those remaining days that mattered.

"Daddy, what can I do to help you?" she asked.

"Love me, baby," I said. "Your love means everything to me. And pray for me. Pray that I'm able to make my last days here meaningful and fun and that I live them as if I'm alive, not waiting for death."

My daughter cried. "I can do that, Daddy," she said softly while hugging me.

We corralled our emotions after a while and I walked her to her car. "I feel so much better," I told her, and it was the truth. I didn't realize how much of a burden it was not having had that conversation with her. I finally was prepared to live my final days, to "seize" them as my friend Kevin said I should.

Problem was, I didn't know how or where to begin. I actually did not have lofty dreams of travel or glory. I didn't have a "Bucket List." I was an ordinary man with few extraordinary ambitions. I didn't like to travel much because I didn't like to fly and riding too long in a vehicle made me carsick.

I ate when necessary, but did not have exotic tastes. I had a group of friends, but I spent the most time with Kevin. I had but one vice: golf.

My first thought was just to play golf every day . . . until I collapsed on a lush fairway. Kevin would have appreciated that. He and I were so close that we had become like brothers. For sure, we had a connection that was rare among people: I carried his kidney in my body.

When one of mine was damaged in a bad car crash and I needed a new one to avoid a life of dialysis, I was amazed by two things: Kevin was willing, without hesitation, to go through tests to see if we were compatible; and that he *was* a match. I had no siblings and my father's kidneys were not healthy enough to share.

If Kevin had any reservations about doing it, I never saw them. If there was any fear, he never revealed it. And he never expressed any ambivalence about donating an organ to his friend.

For all I had done with and for him in the thirty years we knew each other, there was nothing I could do to repay Kevin for his deed for me. And as I read his letter as I had each day, something occurred to me the way an idea comes to a prolific author: As a way of honoring Kevin, I will live out some of the things *he* never got to do based on what he wrote me in that letter.

That was the least I could do, considering the kidney transplant saved my life. Doing things he wanted to do would extend my life and give it more purpose. And I decided I would throw in some of my own unfulfilled ambitions, too.

CHAPTER TWO:
ALL OVER THE PLACE

Ever since my diagnosis, my sleep had been interrupted almost every night by weird dreams about death and Kevin and people chasing me and other things I couldn't remember. But I woke up terrified.

At the same time, I could not hold a thought when I was awake. It was hard to concentrate. My mind flared off to someplace I was not, someplace I wanted to go or someplace I feared. It was a strange existence.

It was a relief to wake up this particular morning feeling refreshed and somewhat inspired. I dreamed about Kathy Drew, my first love. We broke up when she took a job in San Francisco, leaving me behind in D.C. We were twenty-five then. I understood her decision; we didn't have a life-long commitment and the opportunity was too good to refuse.

But I didn't realize I would love her all

my life. The distance made our relationship fizzle, but the fire always burned within me. I dated and even loved some good women since Kathy. But she always was the pinnacle. Strange thing was, I couldn't figure out why . . . until my life changed with death pending.

Knowing you're going to die did something to my thinking. We're all trained to know our time will come at some point. But my case was different because I knew death was near, even though I felt fine. I didn't have any headaches or stomach discomfort. I had some X-rays that show a growth in my stomach that shouldn't be there. And the docs said it would kill me.

And because I knew my time was near, my senses seemed sharper. I saw things clearer. So I could see Kathy for who she was to me: a love that was not on the surface, a love that was not driven by sex or a need for companionship or youthful exuberance. It was simply real love that was almost tangible and unconditional, even at that young age. Now I know: True love was not that complicated.

It irked me that it took this long for this realization. I had twenty years to try to make something out of what we had. Instead, I played the tough, so-called manly

25

role, the "There are many fish in the sea role."

The dumb role.

Look at me now: understanding I could have had the love of my life when I have little life left.

"Why do you think it's too late?" Thornell said. He was one of my closest friends and golf buddy. When I told him I was going to die, he held it together, held me together. He was predictably stunned and looked me up and down and wondered, like I did, if the doctors knew what the hell they were talking about. He talked about getting second and third opinions. But by the time I told him, I had already made those rounds.

"It's too late because I don't have any time to really have something with Kathy," I told Thornell.

"That's the reason you should contact her," Thornell said. "Do the things that make you feel good."

It made sense to me. Shit, whom was I trying to fool? Anything would have felt like a good reason. I wanted to contact her, to hear her voice. The problem was, I didn't know where to begin in trying to locate her. We hadn't spoken in seven years. But Thornell had an answer for that, too.

"Facebook," he said.

And he was right. Kathy was the type of person who would thrive on that social media site. She loved people and communicating and sharing . . . all the hallmarks of what made Facebook what it was. Or was supposed to be. It morphed into something much broader than the original idea, in good ways and bad.

In any case, I had signed up long ago, but hadn't even posted a photo. I was a voyeur. Saw some interesting stuff and learned a lot, too. I also recall people posting about losing loved ones and thinking how sad that was. One of the few times I commented on something was when one of our classmates posted about Kevin's death. I wrote:

"This man was the best friend anyone could have. To lose him is to lose a part of myself."

And I meant it. I never thought at the time that someday I would die and be the subject of posts from friends. That made me feel strange. Almost everything made me feel strange. My emotions were all over the place.

Anyway, I resisted the urge to post about myself on Facebook because I heard a lot about the drama that came with being on it if you connected with nosey people, messy people, critical people, people who would

27

put their personal business out there for all to see, people who would be jealous of what you posted and on and on.

I always thought that was an exaggeration . . . until I set up my Facebook account. I saw a lot of the bickering and wondered who those people were. I read about people's drama. One guy was critical of seemingly everything in his life; he never posted anything uplifting. Women called women names and exposed their business, at the same time making themselves look silly. It was a mess.

But it also was enlightening. I learned about history and news events and little-known facts and heartwarming stories and stories that showed the compassion of people.

I also read where Facebook was among the new top reasons for divorce. And I knew through some friends that it could be a place to find people of your past. Out of all that could be gleaned from Facebook, *that* was my ultimate mission: to find Kathy Drew.

Thornell and I sat at my kitchen table with my laptop and started the search. He was as excited as me, a real friend hoping I'd find something, someone, to make my remaining days brighter.

Problem was, there were a *lot* of Kathy Drews on Facebook, and none of the photos looked like the Kathy I remembered.

"What about her?" Thornell suggested.

I looked at the photo closely. Her privacy settings did not allow multiple views of her profile images. But the face was similar, from what I could tell. So was the smile, which always made me smile. It was sort of an "I have a secret kind of smile."

You always had to say, "What?" when she flashed it because you felt like she knew something you didn't.

"The smile makes me think this could be her," I said to Thornell. "But the face is a little wider."

"That don't mean shit," he said. "You ever been to a reunion? Women who were thin turn fat real quick."

"Men, too," I said. I always tried to be fair. "I could be wrong," I continued. "But I don't have her gaining a lot of weight. She wasn't vain, but her appearance meant a lot to her. I have her being close to what I saw about twenty years ago."

"Yeah, well, I think you should prepare yourself for the worst," Thornell said, laughing.

"I'm trying to find the woman, not marry her," I said. And in that moment, I wondered what finding her would accomplish. Sometimes, a lot of times, battling the strange emotions that came with *knowing I'm going to die . . . soon* had a depression component that was difficult to manage.

I learned to not get mad at myself about not being able to handle the realization of it all. How many people could? It was the reality of all realities. There were times, when I was on the golf course or absorbed in a good book or movie that I didn't focus on dying. But it didn't last; it was fleeting.

When the toll of it all burst out — that's what it did; it didn't seep out, it flowed like water out of an opened fire hydrant — my mind and disposition went various places, depending on the day. The psychologist the doctors recommended I visit said this would last for a while, but could get better as time progressed.

I wanted to say, *Really? Just how much time do you think I have? It's not like I'm on a three-year plan, doc.*

But I let it go because what would have been the point? But that was how my emotions fluctuated: I'd wake up depressed, hardly able to get out of the bed, paralyzed with fear and sadness. Or I was angry and lashed out at the person in front of me. Other times I would shut down and say very little. Still other times I would cry — no, *bawl* — until I would almost become breathless.

Trying to find Kathy on a social media website gave me a new emotion, though. Hope. Momentarily, I was down about it — what would finding her actually do? But that passed when I looked at the bigger picture. I needed to find this woman. I needed to tell her that I loved her.

"Maybe that's not what you should say right off the bat," Thornell said. "I mean, you haven't seen the woman in a long time. Maybe a 'hello' would be a good place to start."

I laughed. That's the meaningful thing about true friends — they treated you the same no matter what.

"I'm dying," I said. "But I ain't braindead."

Thornell laughed loudly. I took a swig of the bottled water I had next to me and kept my eyes on him. When he stopped laughing, his face made a remarkable transition to sadness in a nanosecond. What I said was funny . . . but it was sad, too.

"Let's concentrate on finding Kathy," I said. "This woman isn't her."

But there was a profile that was mysterious and gave me hope. The person's listed name was Kathy Drew-Turner. There was no photo, however. But she listed San Francisco as her current city and Washington, D.C. as her hometown. There was not much more I could see about her without being her Facebook friend.

"Why are you excited about this?" Thornell said. "There's no photo. And this person is apparently married."

"Kathy *would* be married," I said "She deserved to be married to someone who appreciated who she is. Plus, what do I care if she's married or not?"

Thornell seemed uncomfortable, one of the rare times in our friendship. "Well, I'm sorry, man," he said. "I know you just said what you said, you know, about dying. But I had forgotten that quickly. It's hard. It's hard to put my head around this. It's hard to believe.

"I look at you and you don't look sick. You don't sound sick. You don't act sick. And, most of all, I don't want you to be sick."

I was determined not to fall apart, to hold it together so he could hold it together.

"It's been about more than a month since they told me . . . told me the news. I'm good with it. Not like I'm ready to go. But what can I do? It is what it is. I just want to do some things my boy, Kevin, never did and a few things I never did. If I can do that, when the time comes, I'll be OK . . . I think."

We didn't say much after that. I sent the friend request to that person I hoped was Kathy.

"But how are you feeling?" Thornell asked. "I mean, you went to the doctor for a physical and he told you you had cancer. But you were feeling fine. Do you still feel good?"

"I do." That was true but with a gray area. A few days before, I started to feel pain in my stomach. It wasn't so bad, but with my condition I was panicked. Before I knew it, in my mind cancer was running wild, eating up my organs like Pacman.

The fear was almost overwhelming. I convinced myself that this was it. That notion of believing I was about to die extracted much of my soul and all of my faith . . . for a minute. Somehow — and it could only have been the Lord — my mind became clear enough for me to reason with myself: "God is here."

I didn't know if I actually heard the words or if the thought was thrust into my head amid all the chaos. But it hit me and it calmed me down. I was not overly religious. My parents made sure I went to church and

I established a relationship with God as I got older. I prayed daily and I sure enough lifted my head up to him after learning my days on earth were limited.

It turned out that the pain in my stomach was just a stomachache. But I learned from that frightful experience: I had to trust in God through all this. I did not have a church home. I visited numerous churches to get various views on life and God and religion and spirituality, etc. I looked at it like joining a golf club. Why join a country club and be compelled to play the same course over and over again? Golf was much more enjoyable for me when I experienced different courses.

Doing so, I got to see various course layouts and scenery. I was challenged differently on different courses, as no two are alike. Visiting churches allowed me to experience many pastors' styles and teachings. I heard different choirs and met different people. The variety helped me from becoming jaded about religion and religious leaders. The way things were, that was not so easy to do.

CHAPTER THREE:
THE POWER OF PRAYER

When the time came to get some spiritual, Godly advice, I called on the Reverend Davis Henson. He was the pastor of a mid-sized church called New Covenant Baptist in Southeast, D.C. I refused to try the leader of one of those mega-churches with five layers of people to go through before you got to meet with the pastor, who sat on high, like that Creflo Dollar guy in Atlanta who asked his followers to pay for a $65 million private jet. The nerve of some so-called religious leaders . . .

I chose Rev. Henson because during each of my four visits to his church, he never asked for a love offering or new building fund offering or a fuel my private helicopter offering. They passed around the plate, but there was none of the guilt that some churches tried to make you feel about not contributing your electricity bill money to their cause. Rev. Henson seemed to be committed to offering the Word and helping people, as best I could tell.

"Brother Calvin, the note says you had an urgent need to speak with me, so I made sure we scheduled this right away. How are you?"

"Pastor, thank you for your time. I know you're busy. I'm here because I went to the doctor and I got some bad news . . . I'm going to die. Terminal cancer."

I kept my eyes on Rev. Henson; I wanted to see if he would flinch. He didn't. He said, "Let's pray."

I was not expecting that. I was expecting, "Oh, I'm sorry to hear that, brother," or something to indicate sorrow. But he called on the Lord. We bowed our heads.

"Father God, our brother Calvin has been told he will receive his wings soon. That's what the *doctors* say. We know that You control all things. And as believers in You, there is no fear now. There is only faith that whether his days number one or one thousand that they be lived out in God's will. We pray that You cover Brother Calvin in strength and courage and that he honors You and honors himself as he walks in his daily life, looking ahead to glorification and nothing else. In the precious name of Jesus, we pray, Amen."

I was impressed. To utter that prayer with no warning was amazing. I felt his anointing. When he was done, all I could say was, "Amen."

"So, you're here to do what?"

"Well, we already did one of the most important things, which is pray. I guess the other thing I'm trying to do is make sense of this. How did this happen to me? Why?"

"Is that really the question to ask?" he said. "I have a question for you: Why *not* you?"

Again, he stunned me. "Why not me? Because I want to live."

"Then live," he said without hesitation.

We looked at each other a few seconds. I figured he was trying to let sink in what he meant. Finally, he added: "Brother Calvin, we do not know what is promised to us. We all will get our call home at some point. We all know that. Mine could be tomorrow or some time before yours. We just don't know. That's why it is important to live our lives uplifting God, doing for others, praising His name.

"It's natural for you to ask 'Why me?' and to be scared. Would you want it to be someone else? Would you wish death on someone else? I'm going to say you wouldn't. The diagnosis has been made about you, and I would say to look at it as a call from God to touch people. You have time to do that. He could have had you fall dead on the ground where you stand. He has not cursed you by taking your life; He's blessed you with an opportunity to make a difference in *other* people's lives."

I had not even remotely looked at it that way. I always considered this some sort of punishment or just plain old bad luck.

"Listen," Rev. Henson added, "you're going to continue to have moments of despair and fear. It's natural. I'm not saying to leave here feeling like you're never going to have issues with this. But you're in a unique position. An enviable position, believe it or not. You can spend your last days uplifting God, telling people you love how you feel, making a difference. And when the down times come, pray this prayer:

"Father God, I know You have called me home. My time is coming. Give me strength and courage to walk in Your path in these final days. Thank You for the blessing of life. And thank You for the blessing of death, for I know the greatest gift is coming home to You."

Tears seeped through my closed eyes and down my face. For all I had attempted to resolve in my mind, the spiritual peace gave me a strange mix of fear and stability. I was scared but I felt a new sense of purpose. My borderline depression surely would get me down at times. But I now had something to hold me up when those occasions arose. Before meeting with the pastor, that was my underlying fear: How would I bounce back from the inevitable bouts of feeling sorry for myself?

"So, what kind of cancer is it, if you don't mind me asking, and what treatments are you taking?"

"It's a rare form of stomach cancer called intra-abdominal desmoplastic small-round-cell tumor," I said. It was one of the few times I was technical about its name. "It's a soft-tissue sarcoma that grows in the stomach. It's rare and usually is detected in kids and young adults. I'm forty-five, so it's even more rare.

"Researchers are stumped by it. There's a five-year survival rate in only fifteen percent of the cases. They give me only a few months, up to six if I'm lucky."

The pastor shook his head. "And the treatment?"

"Well, the treatment is chemo, chemo, chemo . . . to extend your life a little — *maybe*. It's a cancer that can't be beaten, I'm told. Had more than a few opinions on it. So, I watched my aunt die of cancer. She was less than a hundred pounds by the time the chemo burned through her body. She 'lived' probably an extra week, a month or something. But she was not really living. She was in bed, sick, weak, barely conscious. She was not herself. And that's what the chemo did to her.

"I can't be that way, Pastor. I've got to try to live my life, what I have left of it."

"Are you saying you're not getting any treatment?"

"I'm not. I'm going to pray on it and live, as you said earlier. I can't do that in a bed, sick and weak."

"You're obviously a smart man and know what you want. I hope you've exhausted your opinions and explored all the options."

"The doctors don't agree with me. My daughter didn't agree with me. But after I explained to her that I have to live and not just exist, she understood . . . said she did, anyway."

I started to cry then. Not for me, but for my child. I breathed to her heartbeat. If anything hurt me through this mess, it was knowing I wouldn't be with her and knowing how devastated not being here would be for her.

"Maya is everything to me, pastor," I managed to get out. "I can't think of her now and not get upset."

"Our children are like appendages, extensions of us," Pastor Henson said. "I understand how devastating this can be for you . . . and her. Be an example of courage and strength for her. I think you're already doing that, but I had to say it anyway. You have to live your life as you see fit. I cannot argue against not getting chemo if there is not real evidence it's going to make your more comfortable. I've seen how it can debilitate. But you've got to pray, see a therapist and have you considered natural, holistic remedies? There are people you can see who have what doctors consider radical treatment options because they are not medically approved. But many have found better results that way, at least from a comfort level standpoint.

"If it is God's will that the disease takes over, then so be it. But, for the sake of extending your life and remaining able to function, the holistic method might be an option to research."

"Interesting you bring that up because I learned about someone in Atlanta who has an all-natural, holistic program. My daughter found her. I don't know the specifics, but it's about cleansing the body of toxins.

My Obamacare insurance — which I love, by the way — does not cover it. No insurance does. It's pricey, but I have 401(k) money that I can dip into."

"I think you should try something," the pastor said. "I understand how harsh chemo can be on the body. Maybe the natural option can be more effective and not as invasive."

We exchanged pleasantries for a few more minutes before I rose from my seat. Pastor Henson moved from behind his desk, came over and hugged me.

"You're a strong man and you've done the right thing by praying to God and placing your faith in Him," he said. "I'm here at any time to help in any way. Here — these are my home and cell phone numbers. Use them at any time. Any time. God be with you, Brother Calvin. God be with you."

I left there feeling like I had nourished my soul, if not extended my life. I thought about my friend Kevin, and something led me to the barbershop.

As I lived the life I wanted, I also wanted and *needed* to do some of the things Kevin wrote that he never got to do. First thing was to get a haircut. Excuse me: a shaved head.

I hadn't even thought about what I'd look

like bald. When you know you're going to die, appearances hardly mattered much anymore. Instinctively, I shaved and ironed my clothes and made sure I looked my best. But it was pure force of habit. I didn't have a woman — got rid of one about six weeks before the diagnosis because she brought drama every other day. And what good was it now to meet anyone? My desire for intimacy was close to zero, which saddened me because I had been quite amorous since I was a teenager. And who would want to get involved with a dying man anyway?

So cutting off all my hair didn't matter to me as much as it did honoring my friend. I went to my barber, Kevo, over at Iverson Mall and he looked at me as if I asked him for money when I told him, "Cut it all off. Shave it."

I didn't have that much, but what I had was distinguishable and was a part of my appearance that helped shaped my physical image that people saw when they looked at me.

"What?" Kevo asked. "You mean lower than usual?"

"I'm going for something new. All of it. A bald head worked for Kojak, Jordan, Ving Rhames and just about anyone else. Maybe it will work for me."

"So you're serious? OK, if you say so. But this is cool. Your hairline was starting to run away from you, anyway. Plus, it'll take some years off your look."

I laughed with him, but he had no idea that I didn't have years left. I learned to laugh to fend off crying, which was interesting because before the "news," the only time I recalled crying was at the news of my mother's death from an aneurysm more than a decade earlier. I found crying episodes to be signs of weakness and pitiful, especially from a man. Tears were for women.

When I told my father my position on that, he held himself back from smacking me. "Son, don't be stupid. What are you, a caveman? You cry if you have a heart. It has nothing to do with strength or being a man. It has everything to do with having compassion, having emotions, having a heart."

I heard him, but I didn't really understand at the time. I got it later, though. The number of people who burst into tears at just the mere notion that I had cancer showed me they had compassion for me, compassion for life. And, when I was alone, I cried. Every day. I cried because I had compassion for myself. I cried because I was scared. I cried because it was OK for men to cry.

I didn't tell Kevo, my barber, what was going on with me. He was so emotional about the Redskins or President Obama, I could just see him making a big scene out of it right there in the shop. So I kept it to myself, thinking I'd tell him at some point.

Meanwhile, he took his time cutting off my hair, as if he were savoring the moment, cutting me down in layers before getting to my scalp. Then he ran the clippers from front-to-back, slicing as low as he could get. Finally, he covered my head with shaving cream, adjusted the chair so I was reclined and, with a razor, carefully, almost surgically, swiped away every strand of hair on my head. I closed my eyes as he did and I thought of Kevin. Funny thing was, I thought of how hard he would laugh at me with a bald head. And it made me smile. If it were funny enough, Kevin would laugh so hard that he would bend over and point at you and stomp his feet. He'd move away from you but not too far that you couldn't see tears streaming down his face.

His laughs were a performance. Kevo caught me smiling as he was wiping down my head with a warm towel.

"What's so funny?" he asked. "You haven't even seen yourself yet."

"No, I was thinking about what Kevin would do if he saw me."

"Oh, man, you know he'd be all over the floor laughing at you. He laughed so hard that I thought he would choke. That was your boy. But I miss that dude, too. Do you know he told me one day he'd like to get a bald head?"

"What? I didn't. That's why I'm doing it now. He wrote me a letter. Said there were some things he didn't get to do and one of them was to see what it was like to have a shiny bald head. So, I thought I'd try it out for him."

"That's all right, Calvin," Kevo said. "That's all right."

He raised the chair upright and when he finished wiping away the leftover foam, he cupped some witch hazel in his hands, rubbed them together and covered my now-bald dome with it. Then he handed me a mirror.

I looked at Kevo before I looked into it. He smiled. "Too late now," he said.

I placed the mirror in front of my face and I was alarmed by what I saw. My heart dropped at first because the initial thought was that I looked like I was a cancer patient who had lost his hair from chemotherapy.

I stared at myself and tried to find me in

this hairless person. But my eyes would barely deviate from my head.

"What you think?"

"Gotta get used to it. From the eyebrows down, I look like myself. But the whole picture, that's something else."

"You look younger," Derrick, a barber working across the shop, said. "With that gray gone, you dropped about six or seven years."

That was it. I was prematurely gray, since my twenties. The gray gave people, especially women, this idea that I was older than forty-five, even though my face was wrinkle-free. I still played basketball and as much golf as I could and I ate right . . . for the most part, to keep my weight down. I did have a soft spot for bread and desserts. But I controlled it for two reasons: one, I had a kidney transplant and staying healthy through diet and exercise was a must; two, I liked to be presentable.

I never considered myself a "ladies man," but I loved women and went through my share. Maybe I *was* a "ladies man" and just felt bad about labeling myself as one. In the end, it didn't matter that much.

"You have the kind of head the ladies will like," Kevo said.

"I have to like it. And, as Derrick says, I

look younger. But I look strange, too. This is gonna be interesting."

I usually hung around the shop for a while to participate in the loud conversation about sports and women, mostly, or current events. But I was not in the mood for much laughter. That was a hurdle I really wanted to get beyond. I wanted to get back to laughing, and I just didn't know how because I couldn't find humor in much.

CHAPTER FOUR:
HEADED IN THE
RIGHT DIRECTION

Sporting a new bald head, I made my way toward Northwest D.C., where my daughter was to meet me for an early dinner at Ben's Next Door on U Street. I didn't tell her about my new look. I figured a surprise would make her laugh, which would make me feel good because I felt guilty about all the tears I had caused her.

I was glad she picked that spot, but going there made me sad. The Fourteenth and U Street corridor had been a stopping post for blacks in D.C. for decades. At one time, in the 1960s, it was a bustling, happening section of town. Bill Cosby had taken his wife on dates at Ben's Chili Bowl, next to where we were meeting. Over the years, prostitution became the area's biggest business and the community crumbled. In the last few years, as white developers came in and turned rundown or abandoned buildings into out-of-sight-priced condos and apartments, the black residents were forced to move while whites came in.

It was equal parts astonishing and sad to see white women pushing babies in carriages and their husbands jogging in a neighborhood once important to a lot of blacks. Gentrification was real, and seeing it in "Chocolate City" bothered me.

I hadn't had much of an appetite since the world came crashing down on me, but I took advantage of any opportunity to spend time with Maya. She worked at the State Department after two summers of internships there. We vowed to have dinner at least twice a week after work.

When I walked into the restaurant, she was at the bar. She looked right at me and turned away; didn't recognize me. Instead of coming over to her, I watched her from a distance and lost myself in all she meant to me.

The longer I stared at her, the more she looked like her mother, which caused even more emotions in me to rise. Skylar was an enigma, especially for a woman. I couldn't trust her and I grew so angry that I could not even speak to her. Maya's beauty and temperament were similar to her mom's. But she was made of something pure inside that was all her own.

With those thoughts in my head, I finally went over to my daughter.

"Well, hello there," I said.

Maya looked up at me and had this confused look. She recognized the voice, but the bald head threw her off. I couldn't quite remember seeing the expression her face wore.

"Maya," I said.

She burst into tears. I immediately hugged her. But I wasn't sure why she was so upset.

"What's wrong?"

She composed herself and leaned back to look at me. "Dad, what happened? Did you get chemo? I thought you weren't going to do it."

"No, honey, I'm fine," I said. "I just came from the barbershop."

"The barbershop? You got all your hair cut off? Why?"

"Remember I told you I was going to do some things Kevin wrote that he did not get to do? Well, getting a bald head was one of them."

She took a deep breath and placed her hand over her heart. "Daddy, I don't know what I thought when I realized it was you, but it scared me. It's bad enough I'm scared every time I call you or you call me; I hold my breath to hear the tone of your voice. I brace myself for you to be in pain or panic.

"For some reason, seeing you with no hair made all kind of bad thoughts race through my mind. Oh, God. I need a drink."

"A drink? I heard in this movie, 'Never drink to feel better. Only drink to feel *even* better.' "

I enjoyed a glass of wine from time-to-time, but gave up alcohol after the transplant. "I was just saying that," Maya said. "I'm not drinking."

"Come on, let's get a table — unless you want to sit here at the bar," I said.

"OK, we can stay here," she said.

"I'm sorry. I guess I should have warned you about the bald head. I thought the surprise would make you laugh."

She ran her hand over my head. "It does make me laugh now. But when I first saw you . . . I'm sorry."

I rubbed her back.

"It looks good on you, Daddy. You look younger. You look hip. Probably all the ladies will be all over you now."

"They always were; ain't nothing changed," I said, and we laughed. It felt good to laugh with my daughter, more than it had in the past. Every experience felt like it could be the last experience. It was never that way before.

"I have some more information about the holistic treatment in Atlanta," she said. "She has a track record of success."

"What does 'success' mean, though?"

"It means some clients who have been told that the cancer was fatal made full recoveries," she said. "Some started it too late or after having already had chemo, but had a much more comfortable life. We don't know if it's too late, but I don't want to wait any longer to get you down there."

"There's no one in the whole D.C. area with holistic treatments?" I asked. I was going to go to Atlanta if need be. It was summertime and I was off from my English teaching job at Ballou High School, so time off from work was not an issue.

"I'm sure there are," Maya said. "But I was referred to this one person."

"OK, I'm in. I haven't been to Atlanta. Heard a lot about it. I look forward to seeing the city."

"This isn't a vacation, Dad. This is . . . I don't know what to call it. But you're going to be on a serious regimen and you have to follow it."

I hadn't seen her so serious about anything.

"Do I have to take some time off and go down there with you?"

"Maybe you should come for a few days," I said. "We could hang out. We haven't done a trip since we went to New York around Christmas two years ago. We can catch the bus next week and —"

"The bus? Dad, you're kidding, right? Why would you get on the bus? That's not a good idea."

"You can meet me down there then. I want to get on the bus. I thought about it. I can be among the people and absorb more. I feel like I need that. Not that interested in flying."

"What are you going to do on a bus, Dad? Come on, now. I'll buy your plane ticket. The bus takes too long and anything can happen. You don't need to be traveling through fourteen stops that will take fourteen hours when you can be there in less than two hours. That doesn't make any sense."

"It doesn't make any sense that I have cancer and have been told I have a few months to live when I feel just fine. So I don't pay that much attention anymore to things that do and don't make sense. I do what works best for me."

Maya wanted to say more, but she didn't. She could tell it wouldn't do any good. I had made up my mind.

"OK. Fine. But I think you should go this weekend. I have your first session scheduled for next Monday."

This child of mine was something. She was taking over.

"Excuse me?"

"Dad, please don't argue with me on this." Her eyes started to tear up. And all my resistance went *poof.*

"OK, baby. Thank you for looking after me. I appreciate you."

She sipped her water and then reached down and pulled up a Whole Foods bag. In it was Alkaline water, purported to slow disease. Then she handed me a brochure.

"Read it."

"I will."

"Now, Daddy. Please read it now."

I was not in a mood to read about cancer treatments, but I could not help but please my daughter. And so, I went through it as fast as I could.

It read: "Some patients are hesitant to try alternative therapies because there is not a large body of evidence surrounding their efficacy. However, many alternative procedures–including acupuncture, Reiki and aromatherapy–have played a significant role in cancer treatment for hundreds or even thousands of years.

"Holistic therapies are palliative in nature, meaning they focus more on relieving symptoms than treating a singular tumor. They are typically used to relieve symptoms and side effects of traditional treatment as well as improve a patient's quality of life.

"Another effective treatment is coffee enemas. It is important to remember that coffee enemas work in conjunction with juicing in healing the body of cancer. Coffee enemas work exceedingly well in detoxifying the liver by the removal of body waste thereby beginning the process of reversing cancer."

That's when I stopped reading.

"Enemas? Am I reading this right?"

"I knew you'd have something to say about that. Yes, enemas. What's wrong with those? People get them every day."

"You don't expect me to stick something up my butt. I know you don't."

"No, I expect Dr. Ali to stick it up your butt, Daddy. You don't have to do anything except what she says. You might not like it, but it's going to help you get that bad stuff out of your body. That's all you have to focus on. Forget about any hang-ups you have about your butt. Your butt's gonna be just fine."

And then she laughed, prompting me to

laugh. "You promised me that you would do whatever I found outside of chemo. This is it."

Who would I have been fooling to say I was not going to do what I needed? I was not happy about it, but if it did what it said it would do — relieve me of the toxins in my body — then I had to close my eyes, grit my teeth and let it happen.

As strong as I had been feeling, the last few days had been marked with the kind of sharp, debilitating stomach pain that the doctors warned would come. They said it would be infrequent flashes of pain for a while and then more frequent and intense over the next months.

I didn't tell my dad or Maya about the shooting pains that were more than the worst stomachache. They were like piercing knife wounds that drove me to bend over hoping for relief. It also all but killed my appetite, which really concerned me because I loved to eat. And if the sight of me with a bald head alarmed Maya, what would she feel in the coming weeks if I started dropping weight at an alarming rate?

And then, sure enough, she asked at dinner: "How are you feeling, Dad?"

To prevent her from worry, I felt forced to lie. "Good. I get a little tired, but other than that, good."

She looked at me as if she knew I was lying. Your children know you as well as you know them, and trying to act like all was fine was a tell that all was not fine.

"Dad . . . ," Maya said.

"You look nice, baby. Did I tell you that?"

"Nice try. Again, how are you feeling?"

It was amazing, the progression of my child. She looked to me for everything when she was young, got sassy when she became a teenager and thought she ran things when she became a young adult.

"Maya, I'm good."

She stared at me for a second or two and let it go. Sort of.

"Well, I'm looking forward to Atlanta," she said. "I think these treatments will help you feel even better. I will look at flights when I get home. I can't believe you want to catch the bus."

I was too busy trying to eat something to not alarm her that I didn't even hear her. She called me out.

"Oh, I'm sorry. I was all into this food," I said, again trying to be convincing. Didn't work.

"Usually you devour food so fast I worry about you choking. But you're taking your time. Pacing yourself. Maybe my complaining is finally paying off."

I jumped on that. "Yes, it is. I've been reading up on healthy eating and one of the things I'm trying to practice is to have many — I think, six — small meals of fruits and vegetables a day instead of three big ones. That's what the experts say is the best way to eat."

That led to a conversation about weight gain and away from me, which was what I wanted. When we were done, I walked Maya to her car. She held my hand, which she hadn't done in years. Then she pulled out her cell phone and we pressed our cheeks together and took a "selfie."

"I'm sending this to Mom," Maya said. "Once your scalp darkens to the color of your face, you'll look really great. Put some olive oil on it and stand out in the sun."

I laughed. "You want me to fry my head? That's messed up."

We laughed a good laugh as we walked U Street.

"I want to honor Kevin. He said he thought it would make him look cool."

"I miss Uncle Kevin," Maya said. "But he'd look like a big mushroom with no hair. His head was too big."

"See, you're wrong for that. What will you be saying about me?"

59

"I can't even think about you not being here, Daddy. I won't think about it. And you shouldn't either."

I wished I could let go of my prognosis. But the reminders were frequent. What I came to was that my focus had to be on life, not death.

I took that thought with me after I hugged and kissed my daughter at her car and headed to my co-worker Walter Williamson's house in Clinton, Maryland. He had texted me during dinner to come over. I didn't feel like it, but I had turned down two invitations for fight parties he held and didn't want to refuse him again.

He was a history teacher at Ballou and we became friends when I learned he loved to golf. That led to a lengthy conversation on the game and us playing several rounds together. Golf is a great revealer. You learn about a person because he usually was inclined to talk about his life over four-and-a-half hours on the golf course. You also learn about someone's character, how he held up under duress, how he bounced back from adversity and definitely his honesty.

After a dozen years playing golf with Walter, I learned that he had a great heart, but was ultra-sensitive and did not manage pressure well. All I had to do when he was about to attempt an important putt was to put into his head that it was a pressure putt, and he'd miss most of the time. But he was a good man who showed great poise when I told him I had terminal cancer.

"No matter what the docs say, cancer has been beaten," Walter said. "You can beat this. Don't give in to it."

It was encouraging to hear him speak with such force. I liked to be around him because he seemed flawed and was not afraid or ashamed to express his weaknesses. I also learned pretty quickly that he did not have a lot of friends.

That's why I made the long journey to Clinton to see him. When I got there, he did not answer the door, which happened most of the time. He was usually in the back or in the basement, so he'd leave the door open for me. This time, I went in and the place seemed eerily quiet. The TV, which seemed to always be stuck on ESPN, was not on. There was no music.

He was not on the patio in the back of the house and he was not in the basement. Walter did not answer when I called out his name. I figured he left and would be back soon. So I sat down in the living room and turned on the television and waited. After about five minutes, it struck me to call him.

When I did, I could hear his phone ringing in the house. I silenced the TV and quieted myself to hear where the ring was coming from. It stopped before I could locate it. So I called it again, and it led me to the garage. When I opened the door, I was knocked to my knees.

Walter hung from one of the garage door rails, strung up by a belt around his neck. A kicked-over chair was on the concrete floor. It looked like a suicide. I was mortified, scared, hurt, confused. But I couldn't take my eyes off him. I pulled myself off the floor and slowly moved closer to my friend. He was lifeless, his eyes not quite closed.

I pulled out my cell phone and called 9-1-1. The operator told me to not take him down, to not touch anything, that it could be a crime scene. I knew the only crime committed was by Walter. He ended his own life.

And that realization sent angry vibes through my body. *How could he do this? Why would he do this? Here I am, struggling to hang on to my life . . . and he ends his?*

CHAPTER FIVE:
FAMILY MATTERS

I sat on Walter's front steps in tears and in shock as the Prince George's County coroner drove off with his body. None of his neighbors came by to see what had happened. They stood in front of their houses looking, pointing. They were curious but not concerned enough to come over and find out what happened. And that's what drove Walter to hang himself — he didn't feel anyone cared.

He felt alone. He felt vulnerable. He felt he had no purpose. I was not guessing those feelings. He wrote them to me in an e-mail that I discovered as I sat there at his house. Knowing I was the one he chose to write his final words to, the one he chose to find him, made me feel creepy and proud at the same time. I read the e-mail on my cell phone more than once:

"Calvin, the first time we met, I wasn't that nice to you. I'm sorry. It was at a teacher's meeting and I said, 'Yeah, good luck with that,' when you said you wanted to make a difference in our students' lives. I was sarcastic because I had the same ambition but didn't feel like I had accomplished anything close to that. And when I'm off my meds, everything seems worse than it is. That's what I'm told by psychiatrists, anyway.

"I'm bipolar, they say. Not many people know it. It's not an easy existence. Meds all the time or there's no telling what I will do or say when I'm not on them. I hid it from the school; I was good at that. I hid it from you. But I wasn't good at hiding the reality from myself. And right now, I just don't feel like there's a reason to be here anymore, you know? I'm no good to the kids I taught, even though I loved every one of them and I hope they make it in this unfair world.

"My family? Well, my parents are gone and my brother, Donovan, lives in California with his girlfriend. He never calls me. Never visits. Haven't see him in almost ten years and haven't talked to him in seven years. My son, Junior, he lives right in Alexandria, but he doesn't call or come to see me. If I'm no good to my own brother and son, then who am I good to? What am I good for? I'm just tired of it all, tired of feeling this way. It's tiring. It hurts. It's best I rest. And I don't deserve to be here longer than you. Who decided that you should die? That's not fair. Live your life, brother. Thank you for being a friend to me."

I was frozen there, unable to really process all I had read, what I had seen, what I felt. I was hanging on to life and Walter took his. That was hard for me to fathom. I viewed life as a blessing. To give it away spoke to how messed up his head had to be. Worst of all, I had no idea he was in so much turmoil.

It never showed. He was quiet mostly but engaging when we played golf and when we spent time together at school. He talked about meeting women and going on dates, which made me think his social life was active. He never mentioned a brother in California or his son; never knew he had a child. I'm guessing he was too embarrassed to bring them up when they didn't communicate.

Ironically, I had just read an article about Lee Thompson Young, the young actor from the TV show *Rizzoli & Isles* who shot himself and how he had been diagnosed as bipolar. His father in the paper talked of the dramatic mood swings he suffered when not on his medication. And here was Walter saying the same thing in his e-mail to me.

Processing it all made my head spin. The image of him hanging there, lifeless, will always be in my head. I told the officers who arrived what happened. They looked at my cell phone to read my exchange of texts with Walter. They questioned me about his attitude, his mindset. Did he have enemies? I told the officer: "You know, it never occurred to me that he never talked much about friends. And he didn't say anything about enemies. He didn't say anything about anyone, really. He would mostly listen when we played golf and laugh. He'd mostly talk about school or students and sports. That was it."

The cops stayed there for hours. They eventually roped off the garage and left me there alone with my confused thoughts. I didn't know what to do. Going home didn't seem right. But neither did staying there.

The last thing I needed was to worry about someone else with all that was going on with me. But Walter needed a proper burial. I realized that. I needed to contact his brother in California and his son. It seemed I was the only one to do it.

Thornell had met Walter a few times on the golf course. I gave him a call first while sitting on Walter's front porch. I was relieved he answered; it was close to eleven o'clock at night.

"Man, you're not going to believe this."

"What? The doctors said something?" Thornell said, assuming my news had to be about my condition.

"No, dog, it's my man, Walter, who played golf with us a few times."

"The history teacher who works at your school?"

"Yeah, him," I said. "So, he texts me to come visit him at his crib. And I got here and he was hanging from the garage rail. He killed himself."

"What? What are you talking about?"

"Yeah, crazy. He killed himself, man. He was hanging there, his neck snapped and his eyes were half open. On top of that, he sent me an e-mail saying that basically he was bipolar and didn't feel a need to be here anymore."

"I can't believe this," Thornell said.

"*You* can't believe it? Imagine walking in and seeing your friend hanged, dead. I'm not even sure what to do with myself. What to do about this whole situation?"

"What do you mean?"

"He said he has no family other than a brother in L.A. and a son right over in Alexandria that he hardly speaks to. No woman. Parents passed away. He e-mailed me and texted me so I could find him. He deserves a proper burial. And looks like I'm the only person to do it."

"Call his brother. Call his son. Let them know what's happened. Maybe they'll step up. And why didn't they talk anyway?"

"Not sure. He didn't say. But, I mean, do I go and look through his stuff to find his brother's and son's info? I don't want to violate him, even if he is dead."

"If you're the only one who is really his friend, then you have to take charge. I know that's probably the last thing you want to do right now . . ."

"You damned right. I don't even know where to begin. But I'm going to see if I can find his brother's info. I'll start right there. Let me go back into his house and see what I see. I'll call you back."

After the police wrapped up their investigation, which took much of the night and some of the next day, I went back into Walter's three-bedroom home in search of . . . I wasn't sure what to search for, actually. The police took his cellphone as part of their investigation. And because I viewed privacy as something sacred, it was hard for me to rummage through his belongings.

But if I was going to do what needed to be done, I had to do it and get out of there because I suddenly felt spooked out. I turned on every light I could find. I stood in his kitchen and after a few minutes, I finally decided to start in a bedroom he seemed to use as an office. It had two bookcases, a file cabinet and a desk and chair. On the desk were self-evaluation forms he started but did not complete. Everything was so neat. It was as if he cleaned up before taking his life.

Next to a pile of books that included a dictionary and a Roget's Thesaurus was a stack of AT&T phone bills. I was hesitant to go through them, but maybe he had called his son and brother and their numbers would be on the bill. I was grateful Walter resisted technology and did not receive his bill online. So I opened the most recent bill. There were calls to Gardena, California, which I knew was very close to L.A. And there were calls to Alexandria, Virginia. I didn't want to take the bills with me, so I wrote down the numbers and hoped that they were the ones I needed.

Before I left the house, I was glad I found Walter's keys on a hook in the kitchen. I didn't want to leave his door open, knowing I'd likely have to return. I picked up a photo Walter had of him and his parents. They all looked so happy. The smile on his face was as wide as the picture frame. He looked to be about eighteen. I wondered if he'd ever been more content.

I set it back down, turned off the lights and made it to my car. I was not sure whom to call first, but chose Walter's brother, Donovan; he lived in California, so it was only about nine at night instead of midnight like in D.C.

I dialed the number without knowing what I was going to say. And instead of hanging up, I figured I'd come up with the right words if he answered. He did.

"Hi. Is this Donovan?"

"Yeah. Who's this?"

"My name is Calvin Jones. I live in Washington, D.C. and I'm friends — was friends — with your brother, Walter."

"Yeah. And?"

"Well, tonight, I'm sorry to say, Walter killed himself. He hung himself in his garage."

"Really?" Donovan said. There was not any shock in his voice. Worse, there was no sorrow. I refused to say anything.

"OK, well. Thanks for calling me," Donovan finally said.

I was immediately angry. "Wait, that's it? I tell you your brother killed himself and that's all you have to say?"

"Walter had problems, OK?" he said. "I haven't seen or spoken to him in years."

"That doesn't mean he's not your brother. Did you know he was sick, was bipolar?"

"Of course I knew that. Listen, I don't mean to sound uncaring. Walter was fine on his meds. When he did not take them, he was irrational and hard to be around. And most of the time he didn't take them. So, it was best to just stay away from that behavior."

"Best for you, not for him. Not being in his life contributed to his troubles. You said you haven't talked to him in years, but he's been calling you, as recently as last week. I looked at his phone bills. So he tried to let you know he was troubled, but you didn't call him back?"

"Who are you again?"

"I'm Calvin. Walter and I worked together; we taught at the same high school. We played golf together. And he asked me to come to his house tonight. I found his body hanging in his garage. He wanted me to find him."

"Well, I don't know what to say," Donovan claimed.

"Are you going to come here and give him a proper burial?"

"Ah, when? I'm not sure. What's his insurance situation?"

"I don't know. But a family member should be taking care of this, not me."

"He has a son, you know?"

"I found that out tonight. But what are you saying? You're not going to be a part of this for your brother?"

"I'll talk it over with my wife and my nephew and we'll figure it out. Is this a good number to call you back?"

"It is. So you're going to call his son?"

"Yes, I'll call my nephew right now. Thanks for calling. I'll call you tomorrow."

I continued my drive home, but did not quite recall the ride. That had never happened before when sober. Too many times I had too much to drink to be driving, but made it home safely and did not remember much of the ride. This was different. After hanging up with Donovan, the magnitude of what happened occurred to me as if in a dream.

A man was dead. My friend. I found him hanging like a pig on the back of a truck in New York's Chinatown. That image haunted me.

It made me think: What were his last thoughts before kicking that chair to start his hanging? How tormented was he to end his life? Why do so many who suffer from bipolar disorder refrain from staying on their meds? Lastly, I thought, what could I have done to prevent this tragedy?

That last question haunted me as much as the image of Walter dangling by his broken neck. Did I see but ignore warning signs? Did he send me signals? The last time I saw him, we met for a round of golf at Landsdowne Country Club in Northern Virginia. Thornell could not make it, so it was just Walter and me. We had lunch in the grille before our round, and . . . now that I think about it, he talked more than usual. He talked about the challenge of teaching today's kids and how it had made him feel less and less effective.

"Our purpose is to teach, you know?" he said. "But when you have these parents who seem to be working against you, it makes the job harder than it has to be.

"Listen, this kid was graduating and needed a B in my class to maintain his GPA to get into Virginia. I talked to the kid the whole semester about getting work in on time, coming to class consistently, the whole thing. His mother came to school midway through the semester and had the fucking nerve to get mad at me for the C-minus he had at the time. It took everything in me to not slap the shit out of her.

"And it wouldn't have been because she was yelling at me in front of her child, my student. But I wanted to slap her because she was doing her son a disservice. He needed to hear her say, 'Son, you have to do better. It's your responsibility to raise this grade. Your future is in your hands.' Instead, she yells at me as if I've done something wrong.

"I pulled out my grade book and showed her that he missed one quiz, scored a seventy-two on one test, seventy on another and had missed three classes. He actually averaged out to a D, but I liked the kid and gave him the benefit of the doubt. So, when he does almost exactly the same in the second half of the semester, what am I to do? I don't want to hold a deserving kid back. But, at the same time, he's got to do the work. Now I'm morally compromised. That shouldn't happen — and wouldn't have happened if the mother just did her part instead of coddling the kid."

"So," I asked, "what'd you do?"

"I gave the kid a B," he said. "I sold out to the mother. That bothers me a lot. I . . . I don't know. It makes me feel unworthy of the job."

"No," I said, "you didn't sell out to the mom. You did what you thought needed to happen for the kid to succeed. That's what sometimes happens with us. You had a tough decision and you chose the kid, not the mother."

"It feels like I gave in to her foolishness," he said. "I've been struggling with it ever since. These parents put you in a bad a position. I didn't want to punish the kid because of the mother. But am I really helping him by letting him slide by? Man, you just don't know — this is a real struggle for me. If I can't do my job without worrying about hurting the child with potential or worry about a mother not doing her job so I have to make up for it . . . it's too much of a burden."

I wonder if that was a hint of his mental struggle. I told him in the grille: "We've had this internal struggle from the beginning. It's always there. I've failed kids and it pained me to do it because they have so many obstacles in front of them. I did what I thought was right. That's all you can do. But it's hard when it's not just about the grade or the work. With our kids, there are many times other dynamics that come into play.

"If you could make a decision without considering them, you'd be less than human. You're struggling with the same thing all teachers, especially in public schools, do . . . all teachers who care, that is."

"Yeah, but you did the right thing," Walter said. "You didn't give in. You held true to your ethics."

"It's always a judgment call," I added. "I could say you held to your ethics by doing what you thought was right for the kid. That's our goal — to do right by them by preparing them for the next level. You've done that. He's a kid from Southeast D.C. who will go to Virginia. That's a great thing."

He didn't respond; he looked off through the window for several seconds at the lush golf course. I finally broke the silence by suggesting we go to the driving range before our round. But that was the most he'd ever talked and he seemed genuinely pained by his issue. Recalling that put everything came into question: Was that a reason for a sick man to take his own life? Was he going on and on to signal me to help him?

I decided I had to let it all go before I drove myself crazy. But it wasn't easy. When I took a shower, however, I had reason to forget about everything. With the hot water running down my back I was taken away from all the drama — and then something happened.

A pain so severe and sharp and penetrating shot through my stomach and drove me to my knees. I was more scared than I had ever been. I felt like Redd Foxx on *Sanford and Son:* This was it. The big one.

The doctors told me I would experience occasional pain, but they lied. This was something beyond pain. I couldn't stand up. I couldn't move. I could only curl up and hold my stomach and pray harder than I ever had for relief. But it did not come. I began sweating, from fear and excruciating pain. I felt like I was going to vomit. My body began to involuntarily shake. What other recourse did I have but to think I was dying?

The water built up in the shower; my foot covered the drain. And I could not move it an inch to let the water flow. I was paralyzed in pain. All that and I'm not accurately describing the otherworldly discomfort that ravaged my body. The stomach was where all the pain was coming, but it rendered the rest of my body immovable. I thought I was going to pass out. Actually, I hoped I would pass out. I could not take the pain.

And I did. I had no idea how long I was unconscious, but apparently I moved enough to unclog the drain before or while I was passed out, relieving the water and preventing me from drowning. I came to with the water, now cold, bearing down on me as if I were lying under a Costa Rican waterfall.

The pain was still there, but far less devastating. I realized I hadn't died, and slowly pulled myself from the shower floor, all the while holding my stomach, feeling like my hand provided some support. I was scared to remove it.

Fearful the debilitating pain would return, I slowly, cautiously moved to pull myself up, turn off the water and wearily make my way from the bathroom to the bedroom. I didn't even consider drying off. I made it to the bed and delicately crawled into it. I curled into a fetal position. Naked and soaking wet, I cried until I fell asleep.

Chapter Six:
Pain & Gain

I awoke feeling slightly disoriented and scared. I believed the doctors. I believed I had cancer. Before that episode, there was nothing beyond the X-rays and their prognosis that really indicated I had it. I didn't *feel* like I had cancer. I knew it after that episode in the shower. I *felt* it. And I was even more scared than when I was first told. That's why I cried.

Stomachaches from food poisoning or cheap liquor or a bad mix of alcohol was nothing compared to what I experienced in the shower. This was something altogether different. It was like the lining of my stomach was laced with acid, while being stabbed with tiny razors. It felt like how I thought cancer might feel. Only cancer could be that excruciating.

My stomach was sore in the morning, as if it had been punched repeatedly. With a pipe. I was able to stand upright and move about enough to grab my heating pad from a hall closet, plug it up and delicately place it across my midsection. As it heated up, I relaxed and eventually dozed off to sleep.

I dreamed that I was on the golf course with Walter and after making a hole-in-one, he told me he was thinking of killing himself because he was depressed. I asked: "How can you be depressed after making a hole-in-one?"

He didn't answer. So, I made him agree that if I got a hole-in-one, too, that he would not kill himself. Then I hit a 7-iron one hundred seventy-six yards over a lake and into the hole. I jumped up in celebration of my ace. I turned around to face Walter and he had a rope around his neck and was hanging from a tree.

I forced my eyes open. My heart was pounding. I lay in bed, looking at the ceiling, thinking about Walter's death and about my life. Neither made me feel good.

My cell phone rang, but I couldn't figure out where it was. That's when I learned I was a little disoriented. I couldn't determine where the sound was coming. Finally, I decide I didn't care who was calling. I was too scared to care.

Feeling like I had cancer was different from being *told* I had cancer. Now it was real, tangible, and I was petrified. I tried to call on Reverend Henson's prayer, but I couldn't remember it. I thought about Walter and figured it was better to be alive than in the ground. But that did not offer any comfort.

After another indeterminable period of sleep, I woke up with a different mindset. I was no longer so scared I couldn't move. I was scared. But I was going to use that fear to my favor and challenge myself to press on.

With the pain minimized, I could think without distraction. I found my phone. And then I found the most powerful pain-killers I could get my hands on. I knew I had to at least attempt to manage the pain. I knew it would come again, and maybe worse, and that was not something that appealed to me. So I would make sure I would have a bottle of oxycodone handy at all times.

When I looked at my phone, I noticed the missed call came from area code 703. That was Northern Virginia, where Walter's son lived. I checked my voice messages, and sure enough, it was Walter Jr.

"Hi, my uncle Donovan called me about my dad. I wanted to call you to talk about getting into his house and searching for insurance information, his will, bank accounts, whatever. Please call me back at this same number."

I was uncomfortable. There was no sense of remorse that his father was dead. He was as a matter of fact as one would be about ordering a pizza with particular toppings. I wanted to call his ass back immediately and let him know how I felt. But it struck me that I did not know the nature of their relationship . . . and that it was none of my business.

So I, instead, gathered myself and went into the bathroom. I was startled that the shower curtains had been pulled off the railing and that water was all over the floor. I could not recall how I got out of the tub or even turning off the water. I was in that much pain.

I grabbed a few towels and placed them over the standing water. The shower hooks were broken, so I would have to replace them — and a new shower curtain, too.

When I got to the mirror, I scared myself. I had forgotten that I had all my hair shaved off and the image I was not expecting jolted me. I rubbed my head as I stared at myself in the mirror. The bald head would look better on me once my scalp's color caught up with my face. But I was OK with the look. Significantly, I felt different with no hair. A little more free.

It took a while for me to clean up the bathroom and to get dressed, but I did and it was a relief that my stomach was pain free. I thought better of telling my daughter about that stomach episode. It would only make her more worried and I couldn't bear that. Not even my father would know. What would be the point of telling them? They'd just get upset. I had caused enough drama.

Finally, I sat down on my living room couch and returned Walter's son's call. I was hoping he'd be dejected to know his father had passed. But I didn't detect a strain of sadness. And that made me angry.

"So, what are your plans for a funeral?" I asked. "Will you and your uncle work it out? You're his only relatives."

"That ain't got nothing to do with me," he said. "I ain't involved."

"But you just asked about the insurance money, his will, his bank accounts. Above all that, he's your father."

"In name only. Man, you seen him more than me in the last five years. I ain't complaining. I'm just staying out of the picture."

"But he's your father. And he loved you. I don't know about issues you all had. But he's your dad. He helped raise you, right? How can you just stay out of the picture?"

"The man killed himself. That tells you everything you need to know about him right there."

"But you want his money? How can you not want to give him a proper burial but at the same time talk about getting his money?"

"Because I'm owed at least that."

"Walter is owed a proper burial by his family."

The kid and I went back and forth for another minute or so without him budging off his stance. Eventually, we agreed to meet at his dad's house later that evening.

I called Walter's brother back to see where he stood on the funeral. His phone went straight to voicemail. I was sort of glad it did; I wanted to be a good friend to Walter, but I had my own issues to figure out. First was what to do about preventing or minimizing another attack.

I called Maya about going to Atlanta for the holistic treatments. The strength of the treatments was that it would release much of the cancer or whatever was in my body through the enemas. Whatever hang-ups I had about enemas before my episode disappeared after it. I would do almost anything to prevent going through that again.

"Why are you so eager to have the treatments now?" Maya asked. She was keen. She knew me and knew that I could be stubborn. "Why the change?"

"I don't know. I can sense that I just need to get this stuff out of my system. My stomach doesn't feel right. I'm scared to eat much; I feel like I will get sick if I do. So I'm hoping the treatments can make me at least get my appetite back."

She bought what I was selling, but not totally. "Yeah, OK, Daddy. If you say so. That's all the more reason for you to fly instead of riding the bus for fourteen hours down there. Your first appointment is in six days. So you have to leave soon."

I told her about Walter's suicide. "Oh, no, Daddy. I remember him. He was a nice man."

"I'm surprised you didn't see it on the news."

"I haven't turned on my television in two days."

"When did you meet him?"

"That time at school when you were honored for Teacher of the Year. He was quiet at first. I sat next to him at the ceremony. But when he learned I was your daughter, he opened up. I'm so sorry to hear this. This is crazy. Why would he do that?"

I told her about the e-mail to me and that I felt obligated to attend his funeral. "I understand. Anything I can do to help, let me know, Daddy."

Another call came in; it was Donovan. I told Maya I'd call her back.

"I'm at the airport. I'm on my way there."

"Really? Good. That's a big turnaround from last night."

"I talked to my nephew and, well, I just need to be there. We've got some papers to go through."

My instincts told me it was about money. He was coming to D.C. for the money, whatever money Walter had. I wasn't aware of any, but that didn't mean anything.

"Papers? You mean insurance?" I asked.

"Insurance, checking account, savings, investments."

I shook my head. "So, what time will you be here? I can meet you at the house to let you in."

"I arrive around eight tonight. Do me a favor? Don't tell Walter Jr. I'm coming."

"Why?"

"Because I need to see those papers before him."

"I really don't want to be in the middle of whatever you all have going on."

"You don't have to be. Just let me in and

you can go on about your business."

It was astonishing that it took Walter killing himself to get his brother to visit. Money: the stimulus of the greedy.

I decided I would tell Walter's son about his uncle coming to town. Why should Donovan get the money, if there was any to be gotten? But that call to Walter Jr. was equally disturbing.

"My uncle is a trip. He thinks he should get something before me? I'm his son."

"What about a funeral?"

"Who said he deserves a funeral? He offed himself. I don't think he wanted a funeral. Who would come anyway? He didn't have any real friends — except you, I guess."

"You really don't know your father — didn't know your father. He touched a lot of young people's lives over the years. Dozens and dozens. Hundreds. He was loved by his students. He taught them and helped lead them on the path to success. That's a big deal, Walter. You can't deny that about your father. That would be wrong."

"What's wrong is that he didn't do that for me. He was there. I mean, there were a lot of times when he didn't take his medication. And that's when he wasn't a good person to me."

"What did you do to help him? You abandoned him, from what I can tell. His e-mail said you would not return his calls. He raised you. And then you get to a certain point and instead of helping, you abandon him? That's wrong."

"Easy for you to say; you weren't there."

"What I know is that when people you love are in need, you don't abandon them. Worse, all you — and your uncle — are talking about is his money. I don't hear any grief in your voice. No plans to remember him for the good man he was when he was healthy. It's all about money for both of you."

I thought I made some inroads with him because he didn't respond for a few seconds. But then he said, "What time can you meet me at his house?"

I knew then that I needed to go to Walter's place and search for paperwork before either of them did. Wasn't sure what I would find, or what I would do with whatever I found. But I was going to look. Walter deserved that.

And so I went. Even though it was daytime and the sun was out, entering his house felt like walking into a horror movie. A man, my friend, was found dead here . . . by *me.* I could almost hear creepy music as I entered the house. The hardwood floors cracked and the door hinges squealed. My heart pounded as if I were a kid walking into one of those haunted houses.

Cancer and dying from it was not on my mind. All I could think of was Walter jumping out from behind a wall, walking dead, and scaring the wits out of me. Finally, once I entered the kitchen, I got a grip.

Come on, man. Stop trippin'.

I gathered myself, took a deep breath and got it together. And although I was finally poised enough to do what I came to do, I still had mixed feeling about going through Walter's belongings. I felt like he was watching me.

Then it hit me: *If he's watching me, then I need to do right by him.*

And my fear and discomfort vanished and I started poring through his stuff. The kitchen drawers were full of utensils — except one closest to the refrigerator. It was one of those "junk drawers" that most people had, a space filled with a mix of bills, letters, scissors, pamphlets, Chinese restaurant delivery menus, coupons and any other thing that did not merit its own assigned place.

A lot can be learned going through peoples' things. I learned that Walter had a Macy's credit card that he hardly used; he was up to date on his cable bill, but late on his gas bill. He wrote checks for $300 six times to Candice Mattison, a secretary in the Main Office at our school. That told me Walter was a good man, as I suspected.

Candice had fallen upon hard times after she got a divorce from her husband of seventeen years. She was convinced he had money to provide her alimony. But she could not prove it, and so she eventually lost her house. She never said anything about how bad things had gotten, but we all noticed that she began bringing her lunch to work and that she became more withdrawn.

I found a letter from Candice to Walter. And it confirmed my suspicions:

I cannot thank you enough for your help. I would never ask you (or anyone) for money. But your blessing has really helped me get back on track. For you to do this for me, I just can't believe it. But you're amazing. I don't know what I can do for you, but if there is anything, please let me know. THANK YOU!

Walter never told me he had helped Candice. But when I thought about it, I wasn't

90

surprised. He was quiet and almost shy at times, but anyone paying attention could tell he had a good heart.

After going through the drawers downstairs, I went to his office, which was about as neat as a work area as I have seen. If there was something to be found in there, I should have been able to locate it. Everything was filed alphabetically. It was so orderly that I took a seat and took my time going through the paperwork because I didn't want to disturb too much how Walter left things.

I learned pretty quickly why his son and brother were seeking information on his money — Walter was independently wealthy. He had stock holdings worth more than a million and real estate valued at close to that. You never would have guessed by his attire, the modest home he lived in, the 2006 Toyota Camry he drove or the unassuming nature he presented.

I was floored by the numbers. Why would he teach at a tough school in Southeast D.C. when he could have lived a life of luxury?

I found the answer in a letter from Candice to Walter.

I'm amazed that you do what you do — for me and for your students. You have every right to move to the islands and relax. But when you told me that only helping people gives you fulfillment, I was blown away. I just hope you focus on that and not the negative things that come up in all our lives.

You have too much to offer to consider "going away," as you put it. I only hope and pray you mean leaving the school and finding others to bless with your mind and generosity. I know you're troubled at times. Thank you for sharing that with me, by the way. But you're a good man with a good heart, no matter what anyone says or how anyone might make you feel. Remember that.

It became clear to me that Walter had shared more about his life and condition with Candice than me. I hadn't spoken to her since I found Walter hanging in his garage, but surely she knew about it because it was one of the lead stories on all the local news broadcasts. I refused to speak to reporters . . . out of respect for Walter.

As I picked up Walter's last will and testament, I heard a noise downstairs. It was not my imagination. I quickly gathered the will and other documents, folded them vertically, slid them into my back pocket and covered them with my shirt.

"Hey," I yelled out as I approached the top of the steps.

"Hey," a voice yelled back.

I became frightened. I had no idea why, but my first thought was that it was Walter, back from the dead, coming to get me for going through his belongings.

My fear did not prevent me from moving slowly down the steps. I tried to mask my fear.

"Who is that?" I yelled in a demanding voice.

"Who are you?" came back the voice. It sounded like Walter's voice, and I could tell he was moving closer to the stairs.

Before I could get to the bottom, he slowly emerged from around the corner, and my heart pounded so hard I literally could hear it. I saw his foot first — a brown loafer, to be exact. I held my breath as he came into view. And I almost passed out when I saw him.

It was *Walter* . . . or at least that was my first impression. He looked just like him and it jolted me so that I took a step back up the stairs. How could this be? I was so scared I could not move another inch.

Our eyes met for several seconds before he said, "You're Calvin, right?"

My lips would not move. I was looking at a ghost and if I could have mustered the strength to run through a wall I would have.

"I'm Donovan, Walter's brother," he added, and a relief came over me that was so strong I had to sit down on the steps.

"Man, what the *fuck*? You didn't tell me you were coming this morning. And you didn't tell me you looked just like Walter. You just scared the shit out of me. I thought you were Walter."

"Oh, man. I'm sorry."

I placed my head into my shaking hands. Without lifting my head, I said, "What are you doing here?"

"I came to figure out the financial situation," he said. "I wanted to get here before my nephew."

I slowly raised my head then. I was angry. His brother was dead and he flew from California so he could "figure out the financial situation."

"There is no financial situation to figure out. What needs to be figured out are his funeral arrangements."

"Yeah, we'll get to that. We'll get to that. But there are other matters to tend to first."

"I don't understand you — or your nephew," I said. I did not care if he was offended or thought I was out of line. What

94

could he do to me? I was already dying.

"This seems like nothing but greed to me. You didn't talk to your brother, even though he tried to communicate with you, and even though you knew he was ill. And now that he's killed himself, instead of feeling bad about not being there for him, you rush out here to find out about money? What kinda shit is that?' "

"Man, this is none of your business," he said, obviously angry, but a little embarrassed, too.

"Guess what? It sure the hell is, because I found him. He wanted me to find him. And he e-mailed me. He reached out to me, probably because the brother he helped raise and his son that he *did* raise abandoned him. So based on Walter reaching out to me, I very much have something to do with everything."

I didn't really believe that. It was family business and I wasn't family. But I was there and I believed Walter did not want his brother for sure and maybe even his son to benefit from his hard work. I was anxious to read his will; it would tell the story. But I was not going to do it in front of Donovan. I wasn't even going to let him know I found it.

"The bottom line," he said, "is that he was

95

my brother and his son and I are his only surviving family. So, whatever he does have is left to us. It's just a matter of how much it is."

He spoke so coldly and dispassionately. There was no compassion for his brother. It was a business trip for him.

It made me angrier. "Don't you have any shame? Don't you feel any sadness for your brother? Don't you feel at least a little guilt for not being there for Walter? Don't you feel a little responsible for him hanging himself?"

"Don't put that on me!"

I had regained my composure and stood up — it was more a show of manhood than it was anything else. I wasn't going to take his shit sitting down.

"You should take some responsibility," I yelled back.

"You don't know what the hell you're talking about," Donovan responded. "He was sick. He took his meds a lot, but he needed to take them all the time. When he didn't, he was a different person. He could become violent or totally silent or just so strange you didn't know what he would do."

"But he wasn't a different person. He was your brother."

Donovan turned away and took a seat at

the kitchen table. "You don't understand," he said.

"All I know is what I've seen. And all I've seen and heard from you is that you want money, your dead brother's money. There's no remorse that he was so distraught — medication or no medication — that he killed himself. You haven't asked any questions around his death. It's like you've been waiting for him to do this."

Donovan lowered his head, and right away I was convinced I was right. He couldn't even fake it. And I didn't want to be around him anymore.

"I'm gone. You can look around and see what you can find. Your nephew should be here in a little while. You all can scavenger hunt together."

I made my way to my car and drove off. In my rearview mirror I saw another car pull up. I stopped and through my mirror saw that it was a younger version of Walter . . . his son. He, too, arrived earlier than he had indicated he would, obviously seeking to get a head start on his uncle. I wanted to keep going, but I felt like Walter's spirit told me to go back, to meet his son and to gauge his mindset.

So I put the car in reverse. I parked up against the curb just as Walter Jr. was getting out of his. He waited for me to get out.

"You're Mr. Calvin?" That surprised me. That was a show of respect to call me "mister." It made me immediately feel better about him.

"Yes, Walter, right? I was just leaving; you got here just in time."

"But we were supposed to meet in like an hour from now."

"Well, your uncle is in there and so I figured you all were good."

"Uncle Donovan is here? See, this is what I'm talking about. He told me he was coming later today."

"And you told me you were coming later, too," I said.

He didn't respond. "I don't know what's up with either of you, but he's in there and I'm gone. Lock the door when you're done. Call me later and let me know what you find — and the funeral plans."

"No, wait. You should come in. If it gets ugly, I might need you to pull me off of him."

"You think I want to be in the middle of your drama with your uncle?"

"You *are* in the middle of it, remember?"

Maybe I wanted to see them beat each other up, so I went in. Donovan was upstairs, rifling through his brother's belongings as if he were in a panic. He was startled when his nephew and I walked in.

"You scared the hell out of me."

"I was trying to leave, but your nephew wanted me to come in."

"Uncle Donovan, you told me you were coming much later today. How you get here so early? *Why* are you here so early?"

"The same reason you're here earlier than you said you'd be."

I saw a family resemblance in the two men, but no family connection. No family love. Walter Jr. did not show any sadness that his father was dead, either.

"So what's going on here?" I asked. "Neither of you really cared about Walter. That's obvious. If you did you would have shown some semblance of remorse about all this. But you're here looking for his money?"

"Uncle Donovan, you really should not be here. You haven't talked to my dad in years. You claim it was about his behavior off his meds. But I ain't stupid. You thought your wife liked him so you stayed away."

"Where you get that from, boy?"

"Boy? Boy? I'm a man. And I got it from your wife, that's who."

"What?"

"Yeah, at the family reunion about three years ago. She said she felt responsible that you and my dad were not talking. I asked her why and she said you came up to them while they were on the dance floor with an attitude at some party years before. But the reality was that she had her arms around my father. She said she was drunk and flirting and you held it against *him,* not her."

Donovan threw onto the desk a pile of papers he had in his hand. I could tell Walter Jr. had been waiting to share that bit of news for a long time.

"My dad didn't want your wife. He introduced you to her. If he wanted her, he probably would have tried to get her instead of introducing you to her."

"My wife is my wife. That did happen, but Walt and I were already having issues. That just sealed it for me."

I couldn't help but interject.

"I don't get people," I said. "If your wife was flirting with Walter, why were you mad at him? You should take that up with your wife, don't you think? If you know your brother wouldn't try to get your wife — if he introduced you to your wife — why would you be angry at him to where you don't communicate with him?

"On top of that, you knew he was bipolar. So when he's reaching out to you for the last few years and you're just ignoring him, don't you think that affected him?"

"Walter Jr. is as much at fault as me."

"What are you talking about?"

"You didn't think I knew, did you? I know you went to rehab for cocaine use about two years ago. I know your father paid for it and he was worried about you. I know you broke into this house and took his flat screen TV and sold it for money, that you took his Apple desktop computer and sold it. That you robbed your own father to get money for drugs.

"And after you got arrested, my brother bailed you out and sent you to rehab. He didn't press charges and you did not have to do jail time. But you broke his heart. You know Walt was a do-gooder. He taught you the same thing. But you became a crack head and broke his heart."

I thought I was standing inside a soap opera. I didn't know what to say.

"My dad and I made peace with that. We talked it out and made peace."

"If you made peace, why weren't you seeing him or in contact with him for the last few years?" I asked. I figured that since I was in the middle of it, I might as well get clarity.

"My wife didn't want me to. She believed my dad was a reminder of a bad time in my life and that to move on. I needed a fresh start."

"You're joking, right? The man who brought you into this world, who bailed you out of jail and sent you to rehab to get your life in order . . . that's the man you need to stay away from? How weak is that? How weak are *you*?"

Ordinarily, I would not speak so candidly. But my life was coming to an end and I knew it. I had no time to be subtle.

"You can't judge me; you don't know me or my life."

"Man, look: I can give you my opinion based on being here right now and what you just said. Why you think you're entitled to your dad's money after being so wrong to him — both of you — is sad."

I turned and walked away. I could hear them talking then arguing with raised voices and by the time I got to the front door, I heard rumblings upstairs, as if they were fighting. I didn't bother to look back or go back. I had seen and heard enough.

CHAPTER SEVEN:
WHEN THERE'S A WILL . . .

Walter's brother and son made me think. They made me think about what's going to happen when I die. Who will be upset about me being gone and who will be searching for money and things?

That's what the doctors said: "Get your affairs in order."

I didn't do as well as Walter. I didn't have millions in investments to leave for anyone. I had a $400,000 life insurance plan that was earmarked for my daughter. That was about it. But it was more than enough to pay for the funeral, any bills I would have remaining and leave her with some money to live relatively comfortably.

When I got home, I was convinced I needed to lay all that out in a will. Reading Walter's last will and testament gave me shivers . . . and direction. He knew exactly what he wanted. It was dated almost three months before he hanged himself. He had planned it for a while.

There is enough in my savings to bury me. The account information is in my nightstand next to my bed, under The Bible. I don't need or want a grand funeral. I don't deserve one. But put me in the ground at Lincoln Memorial Cemetery in Suitland. I have already paid for the plot and name plate. Keep it simple. Nothing fancy. I would like Candice Mattison of Ballou High School to arrange the service. Candice is smart and organized and would keep out people I don't want there.

Seventy-five percent of the money that I have earned through investing is to go to research of the bipolar condition. My lawyer, Randolph Watson, has all that information and knows what my desires are there (minus his fifteen percent). My realtor, Monica Cooper, is to sell my properties, with the earnings going to Ballou High School for students who graduate and need money for college. Set up the fund and call it: The Ballou Graduation Fund. Mr. Watson has started the paperwork.

Of the remaining money at Fidelity Investments, which should be around four-hundred-thousand dollars, my son, Walter

Jr., is to receive five thousand a month for eighteen months — unless he fails random drug tests I have arranged with a private company through my lawyer. Any failed test would end any contributions forever.

My brother, Donovan, whom I used to admire, will receive a one-time payment of one hundred thousand dollars to be used only for his son Everett's college education. Those monies will be disbursed by Mr. Watson to the school Donovan identifies as Everett's college of choice. The checks will be sent to that college by Mr. Watson or someone in his office only. No check will go directly to Donovan.

Candice is to receive a lump sum payment of two hundred thousand dollars for being genuine and kind to me — and everyone. Calvin Jones, I wish I could give you more life. You deserve it. You don't even know how much it meant to me for you to invite me to golf or to dinner or anywhere. With my son and brother turning their backs on me, you picked up their slack and kept me going. The best part is that you didn't know I was hurting or sick. I didn't tell you because I didn't want you to worry about me when you have so much to worry about with yourself. Wherever I am, I'm glad to not be conflicted anymore with my feelings and what I was doing. Thank you for . . . everything. Two hundred thousand dollars goes to Calvin Jones to help you live out your life.

And that was that. I was not struggling for money but Walter set me straight. Not just with the money, but with how I had to get my affairs in order. When doctors told me I was dying, all I could think about was living.

I had to get busy so my daughter would be financially all right when my time came. I had to make sure the drama Walter Jr. and Donovan were going through did not happen with her.

I decided I would draft all that on my bus ride from D.C. to Atlanta. I would have about twelve hours to kill and I couldn't sleep them all away. In fact, I wanted to stay up most of the time, and look out of the window and appreciate what God has created, stuff I did not pay attention to in the past.

Funny how you change when you know you're gonna die. Everything matters. And nothing matters.

I called and left a message for Walter's attorney, letting him know I had the will. I also told him I wanted to be there when he read it in front of Donovan and Walter Jr.

When I checked my voice messages, I had one from Johns Hopkins telling me to come in for a checkup and asking if I had seen a therapist. I appreciated that they followed up with me, even though I told them I was going another route for treatment. I didn't call back.

Instead, I called my daughter, Maya. I wanted to get my visit organized to Atlanta so I could meet with the holistic specialist. I felt OK, for the most part, but that episode scared me so much that I needed and wanted to do everything possible, as soon as possible, to be OK.

She did not answer her phone, which was not unusual before I was diagnosed with cancer but completely not like her since the diagnosis. She even answered my call once while she was in the shower.

It was OK, though, because I didn't have any concrete plans. I had to attend Walter's funeral service, but I wasn't sure when Candice would arrange it.

"Oh, Calvin, I'm so upset," she said. "I read about Walter's suicide on the Internet this morning. How could he do that? I don't know if you know, but he and I talked sort of frequently. He shared with me that he is . . . was . . . bipolar. He talked about strange things sometimes. I could tell when he wasn't feeling quite right. But he never — I don't think — talked about killing himself."

"I had no idea, either, Candice. I was the one who found him in his garage and —"

"What? Oh, my God, Calvin. You found him? That had to be horrible."

"I was stunned and hurt. Can't get the image out of my head of him hanging there in his garage. The reporters were looking to interview me. But I didn't want to have to describe it or how I felt. It was an undignified way for Walter to leave this earth. I can't pretty that up and I don't want to dirty his name. So I'm saying nothing."

Candice and I talked for almost an hour. And if a conversation or experience was enriching, you learn something about *yourself.* I was a little frustrated that so many things had come to light as my life light flickers, but it was better to have learned than to not have learned at all.

Listening to Candice talk about surviving divorce and providing for her two children by working a second job after she left the high school and how it was never an option to *not* do what was necessary for her kids made me realize the strength I had in me, too. I knew I would do all that Candice did to provide for Maya. I just had it easier than Candice.

And because of that, I sometimes looked at myself as privileged and maybe even docile. I taught kids, yes. And I cared about them deeply, yes. But because I never had to struggle, would I have inside of me what it took to grind it out? I listened to Candice talk about her love for her children and it was the same unbending, unconditional love I had for my child. For Maya I would have worked extra jobs, too, if necessary.

And then Candice forced me to look at myself. Doctors told me I was going to die in a few months from cancer. I could have curled up in the bed and whittled. Or I could have let them shoot me up with chemo and rested in the bed and faded away.

But I decided to live. And in that decision I actually lived and did more than I had before the horrible news. I didn't view it as a race against death, but so much was happening that I was occupied with thoughts so vast that I often pushed aside my imminent demise and kept pushing forward. That took special strength.

I hung up the phone with Candice with these words: "I'm glad we got to talk. I understand why he liked you so much and trusted you so much. You should feel good that you were a good friend to a good person."

She said: "It's hard to take credit for doing what you're supposed to do. I do know the kind of world we live in — people are looking out for themselves. So, thank you. But thank you for being a friend to Walter, too. He liked you. It wasn't that he didn't like a lot of people. He just didn't see anything in most people. He saw something in you."

I was glad to hear that, but it made me sad, too. I wished I could have had a notion of the turmoil within this man who was a wonderful teacher and who cared about his students. Before I could completely sadden myself, Maya called me back.

"What's wrong?" she said when I answered.

"You tell me."

"Oh, Daddy. I'm sorry. I was in a meeting when you called. Closing on a house. You know I get scared when I hear from you."

"You should be scared when you *don't* hear from me." I said, and we laughed.

We talked about Atlanta. She had already contacted the holistic "doctor" and sent in the initial payment. I was psyching myself out on getting enemas. Still wasn't ready, but I believed they would help.

"But I can't go anywhere until Walter's funeral. I'm going to make sure it's done soon, though."

"Daddy, that's not your responsibility. I know you want to do right by Mr. Walter. But you've got to do right by you. It's Tuesday. You need to be in Atlanta on Monday. Funeral or no funeral."

Funny how kids grow up and the roles change. They dictate — or try to. She believed she knew more than me, what was best for me and how I should function. I smiled whenever Maya went there with me.

"OK, dear. Let me call Walter's bickering family now. Which leads me to something, actually. I know you don't want to talk about it, but we've go to talk about my funeral and will and other things. And —"

"Daddy, please. You're going to make me upset. I don't want to think about it. Let's just get to Atlanta and see what happens."

"We can delay it, but we have to have this talk. Atlanta is not going to save my life. It could just prolong it so that I'm more comfortable. But the inevitable is the inevitable."

"I'm going to go now. If you need me, just call. Let's have dinner this week. I will cook something for you."

I didn't feel like dealing with the drama of Walter Jr. and Donovan, but I called anyway. Wanted to let them know I had the will and that the probate lawyer was expecting us in his office the next day.

"You have the will?" Donovan asked. "So why did you leave us here searching for it?"

"I wasn't sure what to do. There was more stuff for you to search for and find, anyway. Like bank account info, insurance papers. And have you all decided on a funeral date?"

"We ain't decide on shit. I'm about to let that boy join his father in hell."

"Why would you say something like that?"

"When you kill yourself, it's a sin. You sin, you go to hell."

"So you're going to see your brother one day then, right? What you're doing and what you've done surely are sins. It's got to be a sin to disregard your brother and after he dies travel across country to seek his money."

"You ain't the judge of me."

"And you're not the judge of Walter."

"Man, this is getting us nowhere. What did the will say?"

"It said a lot. I'm not allowed to talk about it. The lawyer will read the entire thing tomorrow. I will be there as well as Candice, who worked in the Main Office. Will you tell Walter Jr. or do I have to call him?"

"I ain't telling him a thing. He can fall off the face of the earth as far as I'm concerned."

"That's your blood, your brother's son. That's the best you can speak on him? Over money?"

Donovan did not say anything so I said, "A shame. I will text you the address."

I called Walter Jr. next and he was equally angry at his uncle.

"We didn't get anything accomplished today because his sucka ass said he was all about the money . . . until I said we were going to get the flat-screen and some other stuff out of there. He lives in California but sweating my dad's TV? So we got to rumblin' in there. I ain't never had no love for him. And that damn sure ain't change."

I could not fathom what I was hearing. My family was small, but tight. Some of them were strange and some I didn't like that much, but there was nothing like the animosity I heard from Walter's people.

In fact, I didn't want to hear more of their bickering, so I gave Walter Jr. the address and told him to meet us at the lawyer's office at eleven in the morning.

The whole thing made me ill. Well, maybe it wasn't the strife between two people who should come together at a time of sorrow. But I surely started to feel bad. So I curled up in bed — hadn't had a bite to eat all day — and hoped I could sleep away the discomfort.

I rested there in silence and cried. So much was going on in my life and around me. It was too much.

I couldn't get the vision of Walter's body dangling in his garage out of my sight. I couldn't dismiss how I feared for my daughter after my death. I couldn't stop thinking about how uncle and nephew disliked each other so much that they got into a fight over Walter's money and belongings. I couldn't get over the fact that I was dying.

I said I was going to do what Kevin wanted to do in his life, but I got nowhere on that list — except for getting a bald head. Strangely enough about the bald head, I did notice more looks. Women stared a little longer. I also felt a little menacing, like Marvin Hagler. But when those distractions subsided, I was scared.

I cried myself to sleep and woke up just as petrified. I didn't know what to do with myself. I had a plan of going to Atlanta to get holistic treatments to make my days, my final days, more tolerable. But what would I do to actually *live,* knowing I'm going to die? That question haunted me.

If I didn't have to go to the bathroom, I would have stayed in bed. But getting up gave me air, and air helped me to think. I thought about what I would do in Atlanta and decided to pull out my laptop and do a search.

Before I could get to Google, I received notification in my e-mail that I had a message from Kathy Drew-Turner. And suddenly my heart rate increased. I was excited and hopeful.

Kathy and I had a love affair that was as romantic and organic as it was brief. I loved her. Never stopped loving her, even after about two decades.

The hyphenated last name meant she was married, and I accepted that because she deserved to have a family. She was smart and kind and gentle and ambitious . . . the hallmarks of a strong mother and wife.

I was uncertain of where I found the discipline, but I sat and smiled as I thought of her before opening the e-mail. I needed to reminisce before getting bad news. That was another thing that happened to me: I subtly became negative. I went to the doctor just to get a checkup and he gave me the worst news possible. I began to expect the worst. Even when I went to Walter's house, I didn't expect him to be dead, but I didn't feel like I was going there to have a few light-hearted moments. I felt something was wrong.

I was opposite that prior to my diagnosis. I had a positive outlook on life, even if I didn't do that much besides work, golf when the weather was good, date some really nice women and read. I watched TV, too, but that was hard to do with all the crappy programming nowadays. Had about two hundred channels and most times couldn't find a thing worth watching. Anyway, that was enough for me. I had more excitement in the last few months than I cared to experience.

Finally, I got up the nerve to open the e-mail from Kathy. I read it once. And then again. And one more time for clarity.

OMG. I can't believe it's you, Calvin. You're so not the person I would expect on Facebook. And you must have just joined because I tried to find you more than once. How are you? Why don't you have a photo on your page?

We have not spoken in more than ten years, and yet I still feel connected to you. We had something special, you know? And I can't seem to figure out how or why it didn't last. That's the question of my life.

How is Maya? She's a young lady now in the world doing things, I'm sure. I have two sons — Robert and Malcolm. I have been married since we last communicated. But it's a challenge right now. More on that when we talk. We will talk, right? Come to think if it, it's been about ten years since I heard your voice. Anyway, I would love to catch up with you. I live in Charlotte, but will be moving to Atlanta soon. Maybe. Please catch me up on what's going on with you. I'm waiting . . .

I could almost hear her voice as I read those words. I wasn't sure if it was because of my state of mind or what. But I felt like I was falling in love with her all over again.

How could that be? I guessed true love was timeless and priceless and unyielding. I loved Kathy and I never stopped. That's the long and short of it. And while I dated women after we parted — including trying to rekindle something with Skylar, Maya's mother — Kathy never left my heart. That's how I knew it was true love.

I placed my fingers on the keyboard intent on pouring my emotions into a missive to her. But I was too scared. She wrote that she was married. It was challenging, as she put it, but she was still committed to someone. Then again, she was so excited to write me and wrote of still being "connected" to me and of trying to find me.

I was confused. Really, I confused myself, just as I did when she and I were together. In my heart, I knew she was ready to marry and spend her life with me. In my head, I was scared. I did not trust who we were to each other and kept talking about waiting and waiting . . . until I was waiting alone. She took a job in San Francisco when I did not tell her to stay, and we drifted apart as time passed.

Kathy, I'm almost shocked to hear from you. So often I think of you and miss you and wonder about you. I'm relieved to know you are well and that you have not forgotten me.

Life is short and I wasted a lot of years not being true to my feelings with you, and that's a regret I have to live with. I'm sorry. But there's something magical about reconnecting with you that's so exciting. I want to hear all about your life, your family, your career (you did become a human resources consultant, right?), everything.

You're married? You deserve someone who loves and honors you. I hope he does. I hope he's all you desire. It's hard for me to write that because I always felt I was that person for you, but I blew that. I never married because I never found anyone like you. I'm sorry for being so dramatic, but I don't like to waste time anymore. We never know how much time we have to waste anyway.

I could write you all night, but I'm not going to do that. I ask that you drop me a line again when you can, or call me. Would love to hear your voice again.

I left my personal e-mail and cell phone number and wrapped it up. I read it a few times before sending. When I did, I had a feeling that was foreign to me. I had just sent a love letter.

It was silly to feel that way because, one, she was married and, two, she was *married*. Still, I felt an adrenaline rush to have communicated with Kathy, married or not.

That's how I knew she was so different to me. The young lady I met right before I went to the doctor, the woman I had developed a serious interest in? Well, I found out that she was married. Found out while I was struggling with the realization that I had cancer and I got a phone call from her husband.

119

I was distraught and confused. When it finally occurred to me what he was calling about, I felt terrible. "Man, listen. I met your wife at Nando's in downtown D.C. We were in line waiting to order and struck up a conversation. She wasn't wearing a ring and didn't say she was married. We talked on the phone once and talked about connecting. But we never did. And if I knew she was married, I would never have communicated with her beyond the restaurant. So, I get why you're calling me. But that's the entire extent of my knowledge of your wife."

The guy wanted to ask me more questions. I cut him off. "My man, I'm sorry. I told you *everything*. I have to go. But I'm telling you, there is no more to it than what I told you. I'm not trying to be rude, but I have to go."

And then I hung up. Didn't know how he got my number and didn't care. But I knew I didn't want Kathy's husband calling me. I'd have more to say to him if he did, though.

I noticed something: My fear and depression went away after hearing from Kathy. That was the power of love. I had a bounce in my step and even grabbed my cell phone and downloaded the Facebook app so I could access it anywhere and anytime.

Hearing from Kathy moved me far away from Walter's family drama and even my own issues. I felt like living.

CHAPTER EIGHT: WILL READING

Kathy did not e-mail me back that night, but I slept far more comfortably than I had in a month — after crying myself to sleep. That was my routine.

That was the first night, though, I went to sleep with some pleasant thoughts, which likely accounted for the dreams I had: playing golf, teaching kids, dancing — fun things.

In the morning, I realized I had gone the entire previous day without eating. I stepped on the bathroom scale and I had lost six pounds since I went to the doctor . . . without trying. How can you eat when you know you're going to die? I had problems eating when my daughter was sick with Bell's palsy, fearing it was something worse. I couldn't eat when Kathy and I started to drift apart. And after my violent stomach pain of a few days ago, I was afraid to eat.

"Daddy, you're not helping yourself by

not eating," Maya said. "At least you should go to Whole Foods and get some juice. Drink the green one with spinach, kale, apples and lemon. It has lots of protein. That will give you something in your system and some nourishment. Please promise me you will get something."

"I will, sweetheart. I'll stop by there on the way to Walter's lawyer's office in Sliver Spring. He's reading his will today."

"Oh, wow. I don't know what to say about that. I will be with clients, but call me when you can."

We hung up and I headed to the lawyer's office. Traffic on the Beltway was notoriously horrible, and even though it was technically after rush hour, the lanes were bogged down. Candice called me and I was glad to break of the stop-and-go monotony.

"I hope I'm not doing too much," she said, after the pleasantries, "but I have pretty much arranged Walter's funeral. I have the funeral home, the church, a program and all I need is the green light to put everything in motion."

"How did you do all this? Why did you?"

"He wanted me to; that's what you said. Walter was very kind to me, Calvin. I never asked him for a thing, but all of a sudden, every week for several weeks he would leave

123

money at my desk. And we began to talk, and the two things I got from talking to him was that he was troubled — he never gave me any details, but it was apparent; and he didn't believe he had any family, even though he had a brother and a son.

"He told me: 'My family exists, just not in my life'. I asked why and he said, 'They just don't love me.' It broke my heart. I know you knew Walter; he was a kind man. What could have made him take his life, Calvin?"

"He wasn't well, Candice. He was bipolar. He suffered from depression. And without the proper medication, which he didn't always take, it apparently made him more erratic. I was at his house the last two days and read a lot of his stuff — he became more depressed this time of year, when school was out. I think the kids, helping the kids, teaching them, interacting with them, kept him straight, for lack of a better word.

"Listen, I know you're struggling with what you could have done to help Walter. Don't do it to yourself. I have done the same thing. In the end, his illness got the best of him."

Eventually, we both made it to Mr. Watson's office. He was a thin man with a serious expression. He was all business. We sat at a conference table in his office: Mr.

Watson at the head, with me and Candice closest to him across from each other with Donovan next to me and his son next to Candice.

Mr. Watson offered us water and got to it: "I will read this uninterrupted. There really are no questions to be asked. It is all laid out. If you agree to the terms, I will give you documents to sign and we can be on our way.

"I knew Walter for nine years. He solicited my services from a recommendation and I have been working with him on addressing his health, his mental health concerns: He was bipolar and acutely depressed. It was remarkable for me to see him one day be lively and attentive, and another day quiet and withdrawn. He had few people in his life — you all amount to it. His students, of course, meant everything to him. He was someone who was in the profession strictly out of passion for the kids. He was wealthy enough to retire nine years ago when I met him. But he wanted to help young people.

"That said, here is his last will and testament . . ."

I knew what was coming and so I waited for the fireworks. When Donovan learned he was getting nothing except money for his child's education — which really was a big deal — he banged the table with both hands. Walter Jr. smiled. He knew the bulk of the money was his. But he was wrong.

Mr. Watson laid out what Walter's only child would get and the conditions he had to adhere to, and Walter Jr. pushed himself back from the table. "That's it? All that money he has, and that's all I get? And I have to do drug tests? This is some bull."

Mr. Watson did not stop. He went to Candice, and she held her breath and put her both hands over her heart. "Oh, my God."

"She gets two hundred thousand dollars and I get some chump change a month for a year and a half?" Walter Jr. complained. "You must have been his little sex toy."

"You're so disrespectful," she said. "I did something you apparently didn't do. I treated your father with respect. That's all he wanted."

Mr. Watson waited until they finished and continued. Donovan said to me: "No wonder you're all in the middle of this — he left you two hundred thousand dollars, too. You manipulated him."

"You can feel whatever you want to feel," I told him. "I had a relationship with your brother. I didn't abandon him. If you want to blame someone, blame yourself. But I said it all yesterday: It's embarrassing that all you both want is money, to where you actually fought over it. And now look at you."

Mr. Watson resumed before either could respond. And after he laid out the money dedicated to bipolar research and the scholarship fund for Ballou High seniors who were going to college, he said, "This is the will of Walter. He was of sound mind and body when he created this document. We went over it several times. It's been signed by a notary. It's iron-clad. Above all, it's his will."

"Well, what if I want to, you know, take it to court, challenge it?" Walter Jr. said.

"You'd be wasting the money he did leave for you on legal fees. There is no wiggle room here for any interpretation other than what is written here," the lawyer said.

"Came all the way here —"

"To do the right thing," I interjected. "Bury your brother."

"Man, I'm not prepared to do that," Donovan said. "I'm headed back home tomorrow."

"We can have the service tomorrow — or more likely the next day," Candice said.

"Who are you again?" Walter Jr. asked.

"I worked with your father at the school," she said. "We were friends. Calvin said neither of you had done anything and that Walter, your father, had asked me to arrange his services. So I started already.

"I don't want to step on either of your toes. He was your family. But I do want to honor his wishes."

"Go ahead, do it," Donovan said.

Mr. Watson stepped back in with the legal matters to wrap things up. I signed some papers and received a check for two hundred thousand dollars. I felt so guilty about it that I couldn't feel excited about it. And Mr. Watson could tell.

"Calvin — and you, too, Candice — Walter cared about you and you should feel good that you were people he felt good about," he said. "There were not many of them."

I looked at Walter Jr. and Donovan and for the first time, a look a shame came over them.

"What did Walter mean when he said in the will that he wishes he could give you more life?" Donovan said.

I didn't expect that. I had pledged to tell almost no one of my situation. I didn't want anyone looking at me with pity and sorrow. So I lied.

"I don't know. Maybe he wanted me to be more lively and the life of the party. Or maybe he's talking about my age and wishing I were younger. I don't know."

Because I didn't look sick, they bought that bull crap I told them. But when I glanced at Candice, I saw something different in her expression. She knew. Walter had told her.

I diverted my eyes from her and went back to the business at hand. "So you need us to do anything for Walter's service?" I asked.

Candice said: "Not really. I just have to make the calls. He's already at the funeral home. I have the chapel there held for the day after tomorrow. If that works for you all, then I will invite a handful of people from work and some students to the home-going service."

"So neither of you have anything you want to add to this?" I asked. I still was amazed at how cavalier they were about things.

"Sounds like you got it under control," Walter Jr. said. "Just let me know the time and place and I will try to get off from work."

"You got off to be here this morning," I said.

"Yeah, well, I had to be here to see about this money."

"Wow," Candice said.

"Hey, man, listen: My dad and me ain't

get along. He helped out a lot at first. Then, after I came out of rehab and got myself together, he said he wasn't gonna support me no more with money. Said I was dependent on him. Some shit about having to fail to succeed. I ain't got time for that. He coulda just set me straight financially, know what I'm saying — and everything woulda been cool."

"What about you being responsible for yourself and your family?" Donovan asked. "I had my problems with my brother, but he was right about you: Do for yourself before you start asking people for stuff."

"Look who's talking — the man who came all the way from California for my father's money and going back empty-handed."

Donovan stood up and pointed across the table. "Don't make me come over there and kick your ass."

"Come on. You couldn't kick my ass yesterday so I don't know why you trippin' and thinkin' you will today."

"Nobody's fighting anyone — not in here," Mr. Watson said. "Listen, I'm going to say this and then you can leave: Donovan, Walter didn't leave you any money because you didn't trust him. He was insulted that you believed he would try to seduce your wife, even after she said he had not. He was more than insulted. He was hurt. You knew of his bipolar condition and yet you never supported him in any way around that. He was bipolar; he wasn't brain dead. He knew exactly what you *weren't* doing. He decided to not let your child — his nephew — suffer because of your behavior.

"Don't go so fast, Walter Jr. Your father blamed himself for your drug addiction. He said something about giving you so much that you became someone you never had been. Spoiled, to the point where you expected him to take care of all your needs — as a grown man of twenty-seven. He found that to be a problem, and the fact that you dressed like a twenty-year-old and acted like one, too. He was trying to help you grow up. But because it didn't involve receiving money, you didn't see a need to be a good son."

"Hey, look. This is getting too heavy for me," Donovan said. "I'm not going to sit here and be judged by a dead man. So . . ."

And he got up and left, with Walter Jr. following behind. I looked at Candice and she shook her head. Mr. Watson gathered the paperwork and placed it in a file.

"Thank you for being here," he said. "Listen, I see this all the time; family fighting over money instead of grieving over the loss of a life. It's a sad reality."

We thanked him and left. Candice and I walked in silence to the underground parking lot. When we got to her car, she looked up at me. "I'm so sorry about . . . about the cancer," she said. "Yes, Walter told me. I can't even believe it, Calvin. You look great. I was scared when I saw you with this new bald head. I'm assuming this is from chemo."

"Nope," I said. "I shaved it off, in honor of my friend, Kevin, who died not that long ago. He always wanted to get a bald head because he thought he'd look cool. But he never got the chance. So I did it in honor of him. When my daughter saw me like this, she started crying. Said it scared her."

"Can I do anything, Calvin? I . . . I don't know what to say. I don't know how you're here right now. I would be going crazy."

"I *am* going crazy. The funny thing is, dealing with Walter's death and his family — his sick family — is a distraction from my own problems. I wish this wasn't the distraction I had to deal with, though — especially with his brother and son acting like that. Amazing."

"Donovan is just jealous of his brother, even in death. You would think that wouldn't be an issue with family, but it is. Walter did more with his life and Donovan never got over it. And when his wife made a pass at Walter, Donovan just lost it. They haven't been the same since, even though Walter told the wife he would not do that to his brother — and she corroborated his story. Donovan was jealous. You know how you men are. Your cars and your women — those are the untouchables."

"That's funny, Candice. I guess that's true in this case. But to just flagrantly come after the money . . . And the son, he's nothing like I would have expected with Walter as his father. He's a tattoo away from being a hood rat."

We laughed, which felt good because I hadn't done much laughing. "Well, you obviously was a big part of Walter's life," I said.

"One part of me can't even believe he left me two hundred thousand dollars. Another part of me can because that was him. A giver. And that's what I'm going to let people know at the funeral."

"You're right. And if you need me to do anything, let me know. I can be a pallbearer. I can get the other pallbearers."

"That would be great. Please do. I will e-mail you the program and all details this evening," Candice said. "We can start contacting people tonight. Walter didn't want a big production. But I want it to be worthy of the man."

I hugged Candice and we departed. Spending that little time with her felt good. She was a *good* person. Never had a cross word with anyone. Never spoke badly about anyone. Always managed a smile and encouraging words, even as her world was unraveling. Believed in God and His power. Her faith was a force and it showed in how she handled herself.

Those were the kind of people I enjoyed being around, the kind of people that uplifted you without trying. Some people were subtle with their influence over you. Others were in-your-face brash. I would take either over the negative, always-complaining, woe-is-me folks I encountered too often. Those people were draining.

I hadn't given it much thought until I needed people for uplifting — I didn't have a lot of those people in my life. My daughter could lift my spirits with a mere smile. Candice was a joy, but I only saw her when school was in session and not that much then. My boys that I connected with on occasion for golf or carousing were cool — good guys with good intentions. But they didn't inspire me. The memory of my parents gave me a mix of sadness and love at the same time.

Kathy was like Candice in this sense: She gave off positive energy. And with that spirit and my love for her, she was ideal for me. I became determined to reconnect with her.

On the way home, I stopped by Whole Foods and purchased a variety of fresh juices and some Alkaline water. I observed the people there and wondered if anything of them had cancer. I couldn't tell, just as they were right there with me and did not know of my condition.

My friend, Petey, called the all-natural fanatics the "nuts and berries" crew. If they ate everything from this place, they were bound to be healthier than most. But they looked malnourished to me, unhealthy, like they were thin and hungry.

"Everything in moderation," my mother used to say. "You can't eat too much or drink too much or anything too much. Find a balance."

I needed a balance. I needed something or someone to level off my fear of dying and disappointment in my friend's suicide and frustration of dealing with Walter's son and brother. I needed Kathy.

Just saying that, though, was scary. I had

told myself all my adult life that I didn't need a woman. I dealt with women and enjoyed women . . . but I didn't *need* a woman to round out my life. Well, this was a different time in my life and the only woman I knew who had the right mix of fun, spiritual strength, calm and intellect to give me balance was Kathy.

And she was married.

I felt funny about being in contact with her, even though I did not have intentions on anything but being uplifted by her voice and spirit. When I got home, I ate some oatmeal with the juice (kale, spinach, lemons, pineapples, apples) and I felt OK. I believed what I had eaten triggered that major stomach issue I had the previous week — spicy pasta with garlic and scallops. So I toned down my food choices.

No more spicy anything. Everything would be mild and easy to digest. I was scared into this eating profile. It was mid-July, and I had not told the school my condition. I was afraid to face the fact that I likely would not be able to return to school in September — if the doctors were right. I'd be too weak or . . . dead.

Those sad thoughts were about to consume me when my phone made a chime I had not heard before. I checked it and realized it was an indication I had a message in my Facebook inbox.

It had to be Kathy. And suddenly had a spring in my step, as if I was injected with a dose of adrenaline. I clicked on the message and my smile got wider as I read:

Calvin, you ought to know without me saying that you could never leave my mind. I'm almost mad at you (smile). Really, we were young and not the people we are now. But that doesn't mean I don't care about you. Honestly, I still care for you. Of course, my life is different from yours. I have a family.

We can talk about it soon. I'd love to catch up with you and see what the world has in store for you. Thanks for sharing your number. I will use it.

Between now and then, I will be smiling and looking forward to talking to you.

And in those words, I was in flight — my spirits, my energy, my outlook. A man who truly loves a woman, truly *loves* that woman . . . forever. With Kathy, she was the one love that I had in my life, despite several relationships. I dated women and saw the potential of true love, but, inevitably, something happened that turned me the other way.

I was not silly enough to believe that it was all on them. Maybe it was me. I never was good at faking anything, especially my feelings. My feelings for them reached a point and leveled off or faded. I never felt like that with Kathy, even after we went our separate ways.

I actually, unintentionally, measured other women to her. Not in how they looked or even acted, but in how they made me feel. That was where they failed. I didn't feel totally connected or in tune with them. I tried. But it just wasn't there. Funny thing was that I couldn't see or feel it until I was out of the relationship. When I was in it, I was in, trying to make it happen. But I was able to look back on it and realize the women, good women, just didn't move me like Kathy had.

So now here she was, back in my life . . . sort of. It made me smile to myself. It made me feel good. I hadn't had a lot of moments like that.

Chapter Nine:
The Funeral

It rained the morning of Walter's funeral, and I thought that was appropriate. The sky was crying.

I recruited Coach Mosby, Coach Wilkerson and four students that really appreciated Walter to be pallbearers. I decided I'd rather just observe.

I pulled out as a pallbearer because I went to bed with so much on my mind. I wondered whether it was morbid for me to think so much about death. I was going to a funeral knowing my funeral was coming soon. It was too much.

Maya asked to accompany me to the service. My daughter was connected to me. She knew it would be a tough day, in more ways than one. So she picked me up and we made our way early. I wanted a quiet moment with Walter.

The funeral director was the only one outside the chapel when we arrived. Candice had not even gotten there. I asked if I could go in and see Walter, and he said, "Have your time with your friend."

I walked into the small chapel with some apprehension. An illuminated cross hung on the off-white wall at the front of the room. Below it was a cream-colored coffin where Walter's body rested. I walked between the two sections of pews toward him, confidently at first, but more and more feebly the closer I got.

My eyes never left Walter. More and more, his dead body started to look like me. By the time I got to the side of the coffin, I was almost breathless. I was looking at myself.

I had to shake my head to clear my vision and see Walter, which helped me catch my breath. He looked calm. He looked at peace, as if he was where he wanted to be. But all dead people look like that in their coffins.

"Walter, man, I'm so sorry I did not see this coming. I wish you had said something to me. The world is not better without you. I will always remember you. You told me once on the golf course, 'From the errors of others, a wise man corrects his own.' That never left me.

"Learn from other people's mistakes. I am trying to live by that now, with whatever time I have left. I met your son and your brother. That's all I'll say about that. I will say I'm a little mad at you. A lot mad. You didn't have to do this. You could have told me what you were thinking. We could have worked it out . . .

"You were a good man and your students loved you. That's what I will always remember. And thank you for your generosity to me. Thank you very much. Rest in peace, my friend."

I patted Walter on his shoulder, which was paying homage to him. That's how he always said "goodbye" to me when we were ready to leave the golf course. I turned around, and Maya was standing there, quivering.

"What's wrong, baby?" I said. It was surprising she was so upset about Walter's death.

I walked her to the third pew and sat her down, my arm around her. A funeral home employee approached with a box of tissues. I grabbed some and wiped her face.

"It's OK, Maya. It's OK." I held my daughter tight and firm. Finally, she jolted me.

"Daddy, I feel so bad. All I could think about was you being in that coffin."

My heart sank. I didn't know what to do except hold her and cry with her. At some point soon, it *would* be me in that coffin, and that would be a painful day for her. Seeing Walter there only reminded her of my plight.

"Sweetheart, it's OK," I said, even though I didn't even know what I meant. I felt silly trying to offer comforting words because I didn't have any. So I just held her as people started to come in and take seats around us. Surely, they thought she was upset about Walter.

After several minutes, we both composed ourselves, wiped our faces dry and sat up. We held hands.

"I love you so much, Daddy."

"I know. And I love you so much, too, Maya."

Somehow, those words steadied us even more, and soon the services began. It was mostly a blur. I could not keep my mind from wondering to what it would be like when my funeral came in the coming months. It was such a unique and awkward and terrible position to sit. It struck me that I could arrange my own funeral — a morbid, strange reality.

As the preacher preached and someone read a scripture and someone else performed a song, I orchestrated in my head what would happen at my services. I couldn't turn it off. I tried to concentrate but I couldn't control my thoughts. And it gave me anxieties.

I pictured my daughter in the front row, broken. I pictured my father totally devastated. My heart ached. It ached for Walter and it ached for my own funeral that was to come . . . the pain it would cause.

Tears flowed. It was not until the preacher asked for volunteers to speak about Walter that I regrouped. I waited for someone to step up, waited for his son or his brother to share something, *anything,* that would shed a light on him that was favorable. I looked around and found Candice, and she nodded her head for me to go first. And so I did.

Maya patted me on my leg as I gathered myself and headed to the front of the church. The thirty or so people were hushed, making what I said in my mind that much more important.

"That man, Walter, was my friend. We shared two common passions: golf and students. We played golf together a lot, and on the golf course he was at peace. He loved the game, the competition, the camaraderie that came with it. We did most of our talking on the golf course, and a lot of laughing. It wasn't until the last few days when I realized that I hardly ever saw Walter smile as much or talk as much than when he was on the golf course.

"The only other place where he seemed to feel like he belonged was in school in general and in the classroom in particular. It was there, among the students, that he felt accomplished and excited and appreciated. He was frustrated and disappointed when he felt he did not get enough out of a student and he was delighted to see the growth in the young people he taught and mentored.

"You probably didn't know this: Walter Williamson was a rich man. He invested early in life and made significant money. Millions. Instead of retiring and moving to an island and playing golf all day, he stayed here, in Southeast D.C., at Ballou High, to teach students and help them get their life on the right track.

"That says everything about who he was, about his heart. I was at the reading of his will yesterday. He donated hundreds of thousands of dollars to Ballou High School to set up a college scholarship fund for seniors."

Those gathered clapped loudly as I looked at Walter's son and brother.

"That's commitment. That's caring. And

that's who Walter was. Remember that about him. Remember that he cared."

And I was done. Wasn't quite sure what I wanted to say, but the thoughts just came to me. I did want to send a message to Donovan and Walter Jr. Candice and students, one-by-one, came up and gave moving accounts of how Walter impacted their lives.

I glanced over at Donovan and Walter Jr. and they wore expressions that seemed like shame. That made me feel good.

Maya and I let go of the horrifying thoughts of my funeral. Well, at least we weren't crying all over each other anymore. My mind did fade though: What would people say about me at my funeral?

That thought dogged me for days beyond Walter's funeral. What had I done with my life? Before all this, I had not contemplated my legacy. I made sure I was a good father to my daughter and a loyal son to my mom and dad. Otherwise, I just kind of went about my day-to-day. I had a purpose, but not an overall ambition. That changed. I had only a few months to live . . . but they were going to be worthwhile.

CHAPTER TEN:
FAMILY

The repast was supposed to bring relief. You're sad, but the dearly departed had been buried and you could finally begin the process of healing. It didn't begin until then, when we celebrated life informally with food and light conversation and fond remembrances.

Wasn't that way for Maya and me. Seemed like at the same time we started thinking about what the repast would be like after *my* death, and she started crying again and I was overcome with emotions that were hard to articulate.

Part of me was so scared that I was virtually numb. It was inconceivable that something was growing inside me that would kill me. The only thing that kept me from collapsing and rolling up into a corner was that Maya was there. I didn't want her to see me that way.

Part of me was angry; I was only forty-five

and I had plans. They weren't big, grandiose plans, but they were my plans nonetheless. And I wanted to live them out. See my daughter marry. Play with my grandkids. See the Redskins win another Super Bowl. Observe President Obama years later, after all the mess he endured from racist whites and overly demanding blacks. I wanted to play more golf at Pebble Beach and TPC Sawgrass.

What's up with God that he would allow me to be taken in the prime of my life, with a daughter who loves me and who I have loved and helped to raise? I never had any problems with God before, not even when he allowed my mother to die so suddenly, without warning.

Part of me was sad. I wasn't ready to die and I certainly was pained by how broken my daughter was. It . . . it killed me — to use a poor expression — to see her like that. Alzheimer's wrecked my grandmother's life early, and it was devastating to see her lose who she was. I was concerned about how my daughter would live in my absence. I never really knew, but they said my grandmother lost her mind when my young cousin who was in her care died. It crippled me to think that Maya would be similarly affected.

So while others smiled and told stories about Walter, I walked my weeping daughter outside under the mean D.C. sun and comforted her at a time when I needed comforting.

"Baby, I remember a prayer Pastor Henson told me to recite when I was feeling like I do now," I told her.

She wiped her face and pulled her head up. "You do? What is it?"

I hugged my daughter with both arms and pressed her up against my chest.

"Father God, I know you have called me home. My time is coming. Give me strength and courage to walk in Your path in these final days. Thank you for the blessing of life. And thank you for the blessing of death, for I know the greatest gift is coming home to You."

I was leery of reciting it because I thought Maya would break down. But Pastor Henson was right. The prayer placed the burden of death off of me and placed my faith in the Lord. I never had been a particularly religious man, but my mom embedded into us to pray before bed and to say grace before meals and to understand that God governs all things. And that He makes no mistakes.

"We've got to place it in God's hands and

have faith in Him," I said to Maya. "He doesn't make mistakes. We're going to be OK, both of us. We're going to pull ourselves together, right now, and walk in His path for us. And I'm sure His path does not include us being this upset."

"I will try, Daddy." She blew her nose. "But it's not easy. I mean, you're my dad. I never thought about life without you. All I've ever thought about was you walking me down the aisle when I got married and playing with my children and us going to the Redskins games . . . forever. It was never going to end. I just can't believe that's not going to happen. It's hard for me to accept it."

I shook my head as much to distract myself from crying as to express my frustration with it all.

"Let's go back in, Maya. Let's have some food. Let's talk to some people and even laugh. Let's go live our lives."

Maya looked at me and, after a few seconds, she smiled. And in that moment — amid all the pain and drama — I saw strength in my daughter. She gathered herself and was willing to push forward. I was proud of her.

"Calvin, I was looking for you," Candice said as Maya and I reentered the room.

Most people had gone. Not Candice. She was in charge and did a strong job.

"I was trying to get your attention," Candice said. "Those two got into it."

"Who?" I asked, but I already knew.

I was embarrassed for them. Chairs were strewn about. A table had all its contents knocked onto the floor. Candice looked on with confusion and disappointment.

After some persuading, I got Donovan and Walter Jr. to come over and listen to me.

"You guys," I started, "if we weren't in a chapel right now, I'd bust you upside your heads. This is stupid."

"You ain't busting me upside my head," Walter Jr. said.

"Can you just be quiet for a minute?" I asked. I looked at Maya and Candice and they took my cue for them to leave us alone. When they exited the door, I turned back to the men, who were sitting across from each other.

"I want you both to do me a favor. Look at each other. Don't say anything. Just look at each other."

They both frowned, but did as I asked. After a few seconds I asked, "Now, what do you see? Take your anger out of it. What do you see? Who do you see?"

Neither of them said anything.

"What do you see?"

"I see my dad," Walter Jr. said, finally.

"Ah, huh," I said. "Donovan?"

"I see my brother," he answered.

"Exactly. Family," I said. "You look like you could be Donovan's son and he looks like he could be your father. My point is . . . you all are blood. *Family.* And I tell you this: There should be nothing more important than family."

The men glanced at each other again.

"Family gets on your nerves," I went on. "Family takes advantage of your niceness. Family disappoints you. But, in the end, no matter what, it's still your family. You two are connected by Walter and by blood. Nothing should come between that."

I could tell I had gotten to them but they didn't know what to say or do. So I took it to another level.

"It's not too late for you," I said. "You have to take advantage of today. Not tomorrow, because we know tomorrow might not come. Look at me. I'm dying right here in front of you."

"What? What do you mean?" Donovan asked.

"I have terminal cancer. Probably have a few more months on this earth. I found out about a month ago and I've been struggling with it, as you might imagine. Walter knew. I told him. He told me to live my life. That's about all he said: Live my life. I think he might have known then he was going to take his life.

"But my point is, you're still here. You have your health. You have each other and there's no reason — no reasonable reason — to be at odds. You're family. I know you wanted Walter's money. But I also know that you feel bad that he's gone, that he's gone and you didn't do anything to stop him. That's a guilt you will carry with you the rest of your life.

"At the same time, you can lessen it by coming together. Walter wanted you to be family. You're his blood, both of you. You want to feel better about letting him down? Don't let him down now."

I felt like I had just given a short sermon. But it just flowed out of me. I had a responsibility to Walter. Bringing his son and brother together would be a nice tribute, I figured.

Donovan stood up and extended his hand to his nephew, who looked at it for several seconds before standing up, too. He ignored his uncle's hand. He moved around the table and went in for an embrace. They hugged each other and cried together, as much for their loss as the feelings they shared about their bond.

I left them there, hugging and crying . . . and coming together.

CHAPTER ELEVEN:
PICKING UP THE PIECES

I had another episode that knocked me to my knees. My stomach was so knotted up and throbbing that I buckled to the ground as I went for my walk at Anacostia Park. No one was around, and so I lay there scared that the pain would never let up.

I didn't pass out this time, which was worse because I had no break from the excruciating pain. I knew then I had to get to Atlanta to get the holistic treatments started. I needed something to fend off these attacks.

It took about thirty minutes of laying on the grass and dirt in the fetal position, praying while looking up at the blue sky painted with picturesque white clouds before the pain subsided. Like the last time, I was scared to stand up for fear it would cause more pain.

Also like the last time, the pain exhausted me. I went home and virtually collapsed on the couch. This time, though, I was even more scared. I was dying. It wasn't normal pain. It was death pain.

I called Maya.

"I think I'm going to Atlanta this weekend. Catching the bus tomorrow."

"Dad, what's wrong? I thought we were going next week."

"After Walter's funeral, I'm just ready to get it started, the treatments."

"OK, well, don't catch the bus, Daddy. Let me buy you a plane ticket. If it's really expensive, we can split the cost."

"Cost isn't the problem, remember? But no, I'm good; not doing planes, Maya. Maybe I will catch one back."

She was not happy with me, but she wouldn't dare push it. Not then. So I wrapped my head around going to Atlanta and e-mailed Kathy, who had dropped me another note that said she wanted to see me.

I will be in Atlanta, which is only about three hours from Charlotte, so maybe we can somehow connect while I'm down south. Here is my contact number. Call when you can.

I was excited about the chance to see her after so long, but also sad. Another part of me thought seeing her would soothe me. Not heal me, but certainly make me feel better. Yeah, I was confused.

I called Uber to get a ride to the bus station on Friday morning, and arrived at Greyhound looking forward to reading and resting and making the best of the twelve-hour trip. I read that it was mental how you handle long plane or bus trips, and I went into it as a necessary thing as opposed to dreading it. So, I was OK that it would take half a day when I could be there in less than two hours on a plane.

The bus experience was something I hadn't had since college, so it was weird to me that the process seemed exactly the same. Other than being able to purchase my ticket and print it out on the computer, it was the same procedure: Stand in line for a bus that would leave at least thirty minutes late, sit on the bus another ten minutes before it takes off and hope and pray no one sits next to you.

Probably fifteen people were in line before me, but that meant I could get a window seat and place my bag on the aisle seat to discourage someone from picking it.

I pulled out my laptop and looked up the weather in Atlanta and for our entire route. But I was disappointed when I realized the battery was not fully charged. I had only about a half-hour of computer life before it went dark. And I didn't know what the heck they were waiting on, but our eight o'clock departure didn't pull out until almost nine. My battery was already dead before we left D.C.

Worse than that, this guy decided to sit by me on the second row from the front.

"Is anyone sitting here?" he asked. I looked around at the rest of the bus. There were plenty of available seats. There was not an empty row, but I couldn't help but wonder why he chose to crowd me.

When you *know* you're going to die, you become less politically correct.

"All these seats on this bus, why you want to sit here?" I asked. I did not try to hide my disappointment.

The man, who looked to be in his late fifties or early sixties, was taken aback.

"What's your problem? I like to be near the front, so I can watch the bus driver and see the road in front of me, see where we're going. So if you have a problem, blame yourself. You picked the seat in the front."

"Well, I didn't mean any disrespect," I said. "I was just curious. I like to stretch out if I can."

"I don't care who I sit by. I just need to be in the front."

"OK. I'll be sleeping and reading most of

the time anyway."

I really wanted to look at the sights in comfort and think. And pray. But I could tell this guy was a talker. Worse, a talker about stuff I had no interest in.

By the time we crossed the bridge and rolled past the Pentagon, I had learned about the man's children, grandchildren, two ex-wives, his retirement from the Army . . . more than enough — especially since I didn't ask him about anything.

We rolled along and I just nodded my head and said, "OK" or "uh huh" or "right" as he cleared seemingly every thought out of his head. I was almost totally checked out. I responded just enough to him to give the impression I was engaged.

When we hit the inevitable bumper-to-bumper traffic just beyond Potomac Mills outlet mall on Interstate 95 South, he caught my attention. He said he was a cancer survivor.

My ears perked up then. I looked at him for the first time, *really* looked at him. He was older that I first thought, but carried himself younger than he was. His hair was cut really low and neat. It was all gray. He had sideburns and a thin mustache, sort of a Clark Gable look. He wore a plaid shirt that was more hip than lumberjack.

And I noticed the YSL emblem on the stylish eyeglasses he wore.

"What kind of cancer?" I asked.

"Throat."

"How did you do it?"

"Wasn't me. It was God. I always believed in Him. After what I went through, I believe in Him even more."

I didn't want to pry, but I wanted to know.

"How did God get you through it?"

"Well, science, you know, medicine, doctors . . . had a part in it, too. They caught it early and were able to shrink the tumor with chemo and go in and take it out with surgery. But something could have gone wrong and I'm giving God the credit that it didn't. Know what I mean?"

I knew what he meant, but I also wondered what he meant. Did he mean God wanted me to die? Chemo and surgery couldn't cure my cancer. So if God saved him, is He forsaking me?

For a minute or two, he was quiet, which gave me the time to ponder that.

"Ever know anyone with cancer?" he asked.

No way was I going to tell him my story.

"Who doesn't?" I said. "Not everyone has been to New York or been on television. But everyone knows someone who has or has had cancer."

"Well, it's an ugly, ugly thing. It can make you feel like you can touch death, like you can feel death. Don't know anything else like it. Don't want to know anything like it."

I knew what he meant.

"What's your name?"

"Eugene. You can call me Gene."

"I'm Calvin. Calvin Jones."

We shook hands.

"It takes a lot of strength to overcome what you did," I said.

"No one can know what it's like . . . unless you've been through it. They gave me two months of chemo, eight rounds, but they didn't know it was going to work. It was about fifty-fifty. That's some scary — excuse my language — but that's some scary shit. To think: If this doesn't work, I'm going to die. That's not easy to live with.

"I mean it's different from war. I was in Desert Storm. I knew being out there meant we could roll over a land mine and that could be it. Or take some fire. But that came with the territory of being in the Army, fighting for your country.

"I saw some ugly, awful stuff over there — guys I knew, standing next to me one minute fighting, laying dead next to me with a bullet to the head the next. I saw stuff you would never want to see. My dreams are still filled with them. I can't watch movies about war. Brings back too many terrible thoughts.

"But, still, when I survived that without losing a leg or an eye and with my life, I was more relieved than anything else. On the flight home, I went to the bathroom and cried. I had seen too many people die. Death is not pleasant, no matter how you experience it. But to actually be there . . . well, that's a burden no man should have to see.

"Anyway, though, I felt like God spared me because I was two feet from guys who were just blown up. And getting on that plane home meant more than that I had survived. It meant I had been spared. Nothing could challenge me the way living with the fear I had during my Iraq tour. That's what I *thought*.

"Then six years ago happened. Had pain in my neck. Wasn't sure what was going on, but it lasted too long. Felt like a sore throat. I gargled and took medicine and nothing worked. It takes a lot to get me to go to the doctor, but something about this just didn't feel right.

"An hour after being there, they said I

needed to speak to a specialist. An oncologist. I don't pretend to be the smartest guy in the world, but when I heard 'oncologist,' I knew my ass was in trouble."

He said it with a comic tone, but the same thing happened to me, so I could relate.

"Immediately, I started praying. I asked, 'God, why would you let me survive all that death in Iraq to come home and die of cancer? It doesn't add up, so I'm going to believe You spared me over there so I can make a difference over here. If I wasn't doing enough, I got your message. Get me through this and I will be a faithful servant.' "

"How did you live thinking you could die?" I asked. "That has to be terrifying."

"I started thinking about all I didn't do, all I could do if I didn't die," Gene said. "I thought about my kids and grandkids and my ex-wives. I thought about it being not fair to have to live with thinking I was going to die. It crippled me.

"I was scared in Iraq. But I was petrified with cancer. It's hard to have a clear thought thinking you're going to die. Everything becomes magnified, more serious. And some things become less important. It wasn't until after the surgery and the doctor said things went well and all was good . . . it wasn't until then that I truly breathed. For months, I was just existing, hardly living. It's been some time now, and I'm doing OK. But that was the scariest time in my life. And you know what? It was the most confusing time of my life. I had to actually think about dying. It was just tough."

I believed God moved Gene to sit next to me. He talked too much, yeah. But he got to a point that resonated with me, making it a good thing he was there.

"Let me know if I'm getting too deep into your business," I said, "but did you think about natural treatment options that didn't require chemo?"

"Yes," Gene answered. "I thought about it. But because it hadn't metastasized to the lymph nodes, they didn't want to waste time. They said it was fifty-fifty, but the sooner they shot me up, the better chances they had of getting it."

He was a stranger, but suddenly I wanted to open up to him. *Wanted* to; I couldn't.

"You look good, so I guess the prognosis is good for you, huh?"

"You can never tell," Gene said. "I know at my next checkup they can say it has returned. I almost don't even want to know now. I just want to keep living. And that's what I do: I keep living because I could be dying."

I looked off to my right, outside the bus, and places passed by. Gene stopped talking for an extended period for the first time since he sat down. It was as if he knew I needed time to digest all that.

"I live in Baltimore," he said. "And I saw the bravest thing I've ever seen on television the other night, on the news. One of the anchors, a man who had been there for nine years, announced on the air that his brain tumor returned and it was too big to operate. He said doctors gave him four to six months to live.

"He did it with such grace and poise. I would have been a wreck. He said he's a Christian and he has faith in God. I was so impressed with him. I could barely handle *thinking* I *might* get that diagnosis. And there he was talking about his fate on TV. It made me feel like I was weak."

I didn't say a word. I couldn't say anything. I could only grunt — and turn to the window. Gene received a phone call and turned his body away from mine and lowered his voice so I couldn't hear.

I propped my elbow on the armrest and placed my head in my hand and tried to get comfortable to sleep. Or give the appearance of sleep. I closed my eyes and thought about what Gene said about the TV anchor. He was strong, telling millions of people about his condition. Did it make me weak that I told hardly anyone?

It was a personal choice; I knew that. But was my silence born of fear or not wanting to talk about it or not wanting people to feel sorry for me? Those were the reasons I told myself. And I believed them. But was it more? Was it because I wouldn't be strong enough to talk about it effectively enough to help someone? What I came to understand was that I had to be about two things: living my life and helping others. Simple as that.

Coming to that realization startled me, but also ignited me. I still was not going to blurt it out to just anyone. But I wasn't going to hide it anymore. And I had to figure out how I could help others through my crisis . . . if possible.

"Where are you going?" I asked.

"Headed to Jacksonville, Florida. My grandson is turning twenty-one. Need to be there for that. And you?"

"Atlanta."

It was the perfect time to tell him why I was going there. And he was waiting for a reason.

"Oh, just to get away. I'm a schoolteacher and one of my colleagues killed himself last week. After getting through that, it was the perfect time for me to get away."

"Man, I'm sorry to hear that. I experienced the same thing after Iraq. I guy in my unit saw more than I did. He came back to the base once with someone's arm in his backpack. Said he and his team took heavy fire one day and three of five guys were killed, right there beside him. I could tell that he was damaged by all he saw . . . How could he not be damaged?

"We got back here, to the States and I heard he got treatment. But it didn't take. Took a gun to the head and bang. Sad. He was a good man. A good soldier.

"Worst part was that I could see it coming. I could see how bad off he was. He talked strange, about staying over there to rescue guys that were confirmed dead and stuff like fighting a war in America. He said he would kill himself if he failed to kill the Taliban. He would seem fine, but then talk crazy. He wasn't that way before we got over there. Being in that war killed him. And I didn't — or couldn't — do anything to help him."

"My friend was bipolar. Didn't learn it until after everything happened. He set it up for me to find him. Hung himself."

"I know that had to be tough. I've seen that scene."

"So I need to get away."

"You ain't running from something, are you?"

"Why would you ask me that?"

"Just asking. I travel a lot on the bus. And many times, I find out people are running from something — or someone . . . Trying to find a new life or at least leave the old one behind."

"Isn't that the same thing — leaving an old life behind and finding a new life?"

"You'd think so, but a lot of people don't know what starting over is or how to. They just know how to leave a life behind."

Once again, Gene made me think. I wasn't leaving a life behind, but I did have a new life to live. Did I know how to do it? Did I know the life I wanted to live? And then I asked myself a question I never considered before:

What haven't I done that I would like to do?

Figuring that out would be a start to living. I still had to figure it out and then *do it*.

"I'm going to take a nap," I told Gene. "I stayed up pretty much all night so I would sleep on the trip. Sleep is coming down on me now."

I got myself as comfortable as I could get and pondered what I wanted for the rest of my life until I drifted off. It was one of the first times I did not cry myself to sleep.

Chapter Twelve:
Speed

When I woke up, I was disoriented. The sun was about an hour from setting as we cruised along somewhere in North Carolina. We were on Interstate 85 South. I saw a sign for the Charlotte airport.

We were about an hour from North Carolina when I dozed off. To be in Charlotte meant I got in about three hours of sleep. I needed it. I was exhausted. But not so tired that I didn't realize the irony of waking up in Charlotte; that's where Kathy lived.

Knowing that made me feel closer to her. I woke up Gene so I could get by him to head to the bathroom. I smiled about that as I worked my way down the narrow aisle. Most people were either sleeping or listening to music. A few gazed out the window while others read books.

I had to psyche myself out about using the bathroom on the bus. I made sure to get off in Richmond to pee. But there was no option on this occasion. I had to go. The bus bathroom was one of the downfalls about taking the bus. It stunk.

I held my breath and turned my head away from the toilet as I relieved myself. But I could not avoid the stench. It was intense and made me immediately think about taking a flight back to D.C. when it was time.

Halfway back to my seat up front, I noticed the bus wobbling. The ride was unsteady and forced me to almost fall into someone's lap. I made my way to my row and Gene stood up so I could get to my seat. Something, however, told me to take a look at the driver, and the man who had to be in his early sixties, seemed shaky.

I backed out of the row and walked the six feet or so to the front. I noticed sweat pouring down his neck.

"Hey, you OK?"

The driver grunted, and the bus started to veer to the right. My instincts kicked in. I hurried to him, grabbed the wheel and prevented the vehicle from careening off the highway.

"Gene," I yelled.

I looked down at the driver and he was struggling to keep his eyes open.

"Can you stop the bus? Stop the bus," I

said. He did not respond.

I could hear rumblings behind me from passengers who could sense something bad was happening.

"Gene, he's passing out," I said, panic in my voice. "Pull him out."

I moved aside with my head on the road and hand on the steering wheel, keeping us from crashing. Gene and a woman who was sitting up front carefully pulled the driver out of the seat and laid him on the floor.

"Call nine-one-one," I said as I slid into the driver's seat. He was a taller man, and I couldn't find the seat adjustment. Immediately I called on my skills from when I drove for D.C. Metrobus for a year. My route was in Southeast, and after a period where it became dangerous for drivers, I quit. Kids were robbing passengers, commandeering busses at gunpoint. I didn't need that.

I managed to get the bus under control, but I was scared. What happened to the driver? Was he OK? I felt like Sandra Bullock in the movie *Speed.*

"What's wrong? He OK?"

"Take the next exit," a woman yelled. "He's having a heart attack. There's a hospital over here, near the airport. Carolinas Medical Center."

I kept looking back to see what they were doing to the driver. The woman had opened his shirt to get him air. Gene checked his pulse.

"Can you feel anything?" I asked.

"Faint pulse," Gene said. "He's in trouble."

It got loud, with almost everyone aware of what was happening. A woman slid past the lady and Gene who were helping the driver.

"I used to live here," she said to me. She was standing on the steps of the front entrance. "Take this exit right now and turn left down there."

"Hello. We are on a Greyhound bus. The driver had a heart attack and we will be at Carolinas Medical Center in about three minutes," she said into her cell phone. "He's alive, but not doing well. Have doctors waiting on us. We're coming straight to emergency."

"Come on, Calvin. Go, go," Gene said.

The pressure was on. I was scared and excited and desperate to save this man's life. Or have some role in saving his life. But it was one thing to drive on the highway. Now I had to stop the bus and get it going again — and maneuver through traffic. In a hurry.

"Go, go," the woman on the steps said. She was telling me to run the red light at the bottom of the ramp. I eased my way out, and was surprised how shifting the gears came back to me in an instant.

A car that had the right of way stopped and I glanced down to see the driver look at me with a confused expression. I turned left and shifted the gears and picked up speed.

"Go about a mile down this road to the light and turn right. The hospital will be down on the right," the woman instructed.

"How's he doing?" I asked.

"Anyone have an aspirin?" Gene yelled.

"What?"

"Anyone have an aspirin?" he repeated as he rose from the floor. He walked the aisle. "The driver is having a heart attack. We need an aspirin. Anyone have an aspirin?"

"Wait," a woman said. I glanced into the rearview window. She scrambled through her purse.

"Here," she said, handing the bottle of Bayer to Gene.

He opened the bottle as he hurried back to the man. He was so frantic that pills spilled all over the bus' floor as he ripped open the top. One stopped near his foot. He picked it up and the woman raised the driver's head and opened his mouth and Gene forced in the pill.

"You've got to swallow this," he said.

"Hold his nose."

The women did. "OK, I think he swallowed it."

Meanwhile, I flew down the street with no concern for the speed limit. I blew the horn at a car in front of me that did not get the message that I was in a hurry.

"Get out of the way," the woman up front and other passengers yelled.

I felt like I was driving an oversized ambulance. I also felt like I was in a movie or a dream. A man's life depended on me. That's how I felt about it.

"Turn here," the woman said.

I turned, but did not press the brakes enough, so the passengers swayed all the way left into the wall of the bus or into each other. I heard women scream and people groan.

But I straightened it out. The woman was on the phone. "Are they there? We need immediate help now."

Gene's experience as a medic came into play. He gave the man CPR, holding his nose while breathing into his mouth. When he paused for a second, he lifted his head and said to the woman: "Tell them I think he took an aspirin, but he's had ventricular fibrillation. They need to have a defibrillator ready to go."

I almost rammed into the back of a FedEx truck that did not realize I was rolling in the world's largest ambulance.

"Right here, right here!" the woman yelled — I was going so fast I was almost passed the entrance to Emergency. But no way was I going to miss it, though, so I shifted down while I depressed the brakes and whipped that oversized steering wheel as if *my* life depended on it. And, really, it was that important to me.

Maybe it was me, but it felt like we were almost tilted over as I made that dramatic turn up the road to Emergency. For sure I heard the passengers scream.

I did not break speed as I straightened out the bus and barreled ahead to the Emergency entrance, where I could see what looked like a team a people — doctors, nurses, aides — waiting. It was exhilarating. My heart pounded. I came to a sliding, screeching stop in front and had a few seconds where I could not find the button to open the door.

So I got up and told the lady to look out. She moved aside as I kicked the door open — with one effort. My adrenaline was that high.

The team of medical people rushed on board. In seconds the driver was on a

175

stretcher with an oxygen mask on his face and hurriedly wheeled into the hospital.

My heart continued to pound like an African drum beat. I was breathless. I looked at Gene and we just shook our heads. The two ladies who helped out hugged each other and then hugged Gene and then me. They were crying.

The four of us stood there, and all of a sudden I burst into tears. I was so overwhelmed by what I did, by what we all did, to save a man's life . . . it was the ultimate show of humanity — strangers bonding together for one cause.

Gene put his arm around me. "I understand your emotions," he said. "I cried the first time I saved someone's life. It's a powerful thing."

The passengers came off the bus and congratulated us. I was overwhelmed.

"I was so scared," a woman said to me. "I felt like I was in the movie, *Speed.*"

"I said the same thing to myself as I was driving," I told her. "It was more fun watching it in the movies."

We milled around the front of Emergency for a few minutes. I heard people talking but my mind began to wander. "What if we were too late? What if he dies, after all that?"

A nurse came out to the front. It's like we

all knew she had the news we needed to hear. We gathered around her as if she were a quarterback on the field about to call a play in the huddle.

"You all saved his life," she said. "He's going to be all right. But if you didn't tend to him — get him an aspirin, administer CPR, get him to us as quickly as you did — it very well could have been a different story."

And a near bus full of people celebrated as if their favorite football team won the Super Bowl on a last-second field goal. We exalted and looked up to the heavens, hugged each other and breathed a collective sigh of relief that was wonderful to share.

It was not for another five minutes that we even thought about continuing our trip.

"I guess we have to figure out how we're going to get where we're going now," Gene said.

I didn't care about getting to Atlanta at that moment. Then it hit me again: Kathy was in Charlotte. I went on my phone to my Facebook account to e-mail her in the hopes that she would receive it. Wasn't sure what I expected to come of it, but I had to try. I was close to her.

To my surprise and delight, she had e-mailed me from our last correspondence. And she left her cell number. A hospital administrator came out and asked me to move the bus to an open area and that Greyhound had been alerted and would send a new bus and driver for us. Should be to our destination in less than an hour.

I moved the bus from the Emergency entrance and then dialed Kathy's number. I was expecting to leave a message. She answered.

"Hi, Kathy?"

"Oh my, God. I know that voice anywhere. Calvin. Calvin how are you?"

"Hi Kathy. So good to hear *your* voice. Thanks for leaving your number."

"Sure. I was hoping you'd call."

I did not respond because a hospital official came over and addressed me.

"Hello?" Kathy said.

"I'm sorry, Kathy. Can you hold a second?"

The official had a reporter with her from the local CBS station. She wanted an interview. Someone had alerted the station about our adventure. They wanted a live interview in that moment.

"How did they get here so fast?"

"They had just left here after doing another story and turned around. They were just up the road," the hospital employee said.

"Kathy, are you at home?"

"Yes."

"Can you turn on the news, your CBS channel? And then I will call you back."

"Really? What's going on?" she asked.

"Watch the news about the man on a bus having a heart attack and I will call you in a few."

I hung up and tried to ready myself for the interview. They placed me in front of the side of the bus, so it would serve as the backdrop. The reporter came up, a fine young lady named Karen Turner.

"Really nice to meet you," she said. "We're going to roll tape in about thirty seconds. I'm just going to ask you about your role in what happened. Maybe five questions. Forget about the camera. Just talk to me. You good?"

"I think so."

I ran my head over my baldhead. I said a quick prayer that I would articulate like I had some sense and then she started.

"We are here live at Carolinas Medical Center in Charlotte with Calvin Jones, who started out as a passenger on a Greyhound bus headed for Atlanta and ended up as the driver when the original driver suffered a heart attack behind the wheel. His and other passengers' actions saved the driver's life, according to hospital officials. Calvin, tell us what happened as you remember it."

I looked into the camera, the very thing she told me to not do. Quickly, I turned to her.

"I was returning to my seat near the front when I noticed we were swerving. I looked at the driver and he basically looked in distress — sweating and losing consciousness. He was too out of it to stop the bus, so Gene and another passenger, a woman, pulled him from the seat as I steadied the wheel so we wouldn't crash. I jumped in the driver's seat and started guiding the bus. But it was apparent he was in bad shape. So, Gene and the woman tended to the driver.

"Another passenger, a woman, came up front and directed me to the hospital and called nine-one-one. I was a bus driver in Washington, D.C. for a short time years ago, so I wasn't unfamiliar with controlling a bus. But it was a desperate situation, and we all just let our instincts take over to help someone."

"Wow. It sounds like it was chaotic."

"You would think so, but it wasn't. It was really almost a spiritual experience. We didn't know each other but we came together with no hesitation to save a man's life. Last week, a friend of mine committed suicide and there was nothing I could do about it. Being able to help this man meant the world to me — and everyone on that bus."

"The hospital says you all saved his life. Did you realize how dire the situation was when it was happening?"

"Definitely. Gene, who is a Desert Storm veteran, and the woman — I didn't get her name — attended to him the entire time. He was fading. I could see that as I looked back as I was driving. We were racing against . . . against death, really. Gene gave him mouth-to-mouth. When I saw that, I knew for sure it was dire."

"I understand also there was somewhat of a celebration among all the passengers when the doctors announced the driver, sixty-three-year-old David Osbourne, was in stable condition."

"It was a celebration of life. When the passengers in the back realized what was happening, they were shouting, "Go, go." Their encouragement made me feel like there was nothing that would prevent me from getting that bus to this place. This experience should show us all that life is valued. We'll never forget this. You should talk to others because it definitely was not just me. We were a group of people going to various parts of the country, strangers, and we bonded for one person who needed us. That's powerful . . . and worth celebrating. We cried together when it was over."

"Amazing, Calvin Jones. Just amazing. Thank you and everyone on the bus that contributed to saving David Osbourne's life."

CHAPTER THIRTEEN: RECONNECTING

I had not been on television before and didn't give how I came off much thought. I was more concerned with calling back Kathy.

I looked on as the TV crew moved to another passenger to interview. I called back Kathy.

"Calvin," she said loudly into the phone. "Oh, my God. I . . . that was amazing. I almost didn't recognize you. When did you get a bald head?"

"Oh, a while ago now. In honor of my boy, Kevin Hill. He passed."

"Oh, no. I remember Kevin. So sorry to hear that. I had heard that he was sick. But what in the world happened on the bus? I watched that interview with my mouth open. I recorded it."

"It's a lot to share. Wish we could really talk about it."

"We can," she said. "My kids are with

their dad. His brother's son is having a birthday party and he took them. So I'm available. But are you getting back on the bus?"

"No. I mean, I don't have to. I have an appointment in Atlanta on Monday. But that's a few days away. So, I can get there whenever I need to. I can stay if you're available."

I thought I was dreaming. This day was shaping up to be one of the more memorable of my life. So much happened. To have this drama of the heart attack happen in Charlotte, in Kathy's town, and for her to have sent me her cell number and for her to be available to see me . . . well, I had to take it as fate.

Kathy said she would be at the hospital in about forty-five minutes. That gave me enough time to get a few minutes with Gene before the replacement bus arrived.

"I've got to tell you something," I said. "What we just went through together, well, I . . . uh, I just think it's only right that I tell you this."

Gene nodded his head. I was surprised. He talked so much that I knew he'd have something to say. I was wrong.

"I have cancer. Some kind of stomach cancer. Rare. Nothing they can do. I've been

184

given about six months. Maybe. They don't know for sure, but they know it's spreading and they can't control it.

"So that's the real reason I'm going to Atlanta: To see this holistic expert to cleanse the toxins out of my body. It won't save my life. But it could extend it and allow me to not be beaten down as chemo would."

Gene shook his head and looked away. "I'm sorry to hear that. I appreciate you sharing that with me. I almost wish you hadn't. I see you as a guy full of life."

"Well, you should because I'm alive. And until that changes, I'm going to be full of life. I don't really know what that means or how that will play out. But I'm open to whatever is out here.

"I don't know about you, but what we did today, that makes me want to live even more. I told the TV reporter: We were strangers who bonded to save another stranger's life. That's the biggest thing I've ever done, along with helping create my daughter. I have helped give life and I have now helped save a life. Those are extremes that motivate me to live."

"I'm glad to hear that," Gene said. "Life is an adventure and —"

"And my life has been more of an adventure since I learned I'm going to die," I said.

"I hadn't really thought about it, but that's the truth. I feel like anything can happen now. The crazy part is I never felt that way before now."

"All I can say is live your life, man. Do things that make you happy."

"That's why I'm not getting back on the bus. I have a friend, a woman I was in love with, who lives here and is coming to pick me up. Haven't seen her in more than ten years. But I'm still in love with her . . . even though she's married."

"What are the odds that this would happen here?"

"That's what I said to myself."

We exchanged numbers and vowed to keep in touch. And I believed we would. Many times, I met people and exchanged business cards and never had another conversation. This was different. We experienced something that I believed would keep us connected.

I chatted with the other passengers until the replacement bus and driver arrived. I retrieved my bag and watched as the bus pulled off I said a quick prayer that they make it safely to their destinations.

I rolled my bag inside the hospital to make sure I looked presentable for Kathy. I ran a small comb through my facial hair and pulled out my toothbrush and toothpaste and cleaned my mouth. I splashed on a little Vera Wang for Men cologne, but only a little. I remember how good a nose Kathy had. A lot would be overpowering to her.

A smile came to me as I thought about that little trait about her. It reinforced that I was connected to her. I went back outside and spent the remaining ten minutes waiting on her by thinking of things about her that made her unique to me.

Like, she wore a watch on her right arm. She used to say, "Who came up with the rule that you have to wear it on your left? You *have* to wear it on your left? I don't think so."

She'd also pinch you when you said something that was borderline mean or inappropriate. One time, I said about her girlfriend: "She needs to do something with her hair. How can she come out in public like that?" Kathy smiled, came over to me and pinched me on my shoulder. Not too hard, but just enough to be right on the line of playful but still punishing.

And when she laughed a good laugh, it was so loud you'd be shocked that it came out of such a small woman. She was only about five feet four inches, but she seemed taller because of the four- or five-inch heels she insisted on wearing. In fact, I made a bet with myself that she would be wearing tall heels when she arrived.

Interesting: When I met her, she wore flats. We were standing outside at the Washington Harbour, near the water, and I noticed her not far from me. "How are you today?" I asked, and she said, "Better than that guy right there."

She pointed to a man who was sitting with one woman having a drink when another woman approached. We could not hear the words, but the body language told that he was busted.

I said to her: "Is a guy gonna come up to me for talking to you right now?"

And she said, "Well, if he does, it will be a case of mistaken identity."

We laughed and chatted and set up a date for the next day. We met back at Washington Harbour to eat at Sequoia, and she pulled up at valet right behind me. I noticed her, so I waited as she got out of the car. What I saw astounded me.

This woman in flats and a loose skirt of Friday wore fitted jeans that revealed a curvy body I had no idea was hidden under her clothes. Her breasts were pushed together and sitting upright. I was like, "Wow."

"You look nice," I said. "Different, but nice."

After a few Crown Royals with a splash of Coke, she shared: "I look totally different today, don't I? I thought I'd let you know what I was working with."

"A lot, I see. It's nice, but I had no idea. I enjoyed our conversation."

"And that's why I was so interested in seeing you again. You had no idea how I really looked. I was just out to enjoy the weather and we met. But you were interested in me, and not because I was all glammed up. I don't think I'm all that or anything like that. But I've dealt with men who showed right away that their interest in me was about what they saw, not what they saw in me."

That was the last flashback to our beginning that I had before noticing her pulling up in a black Maxima at the hospital. I could see her smile seemingly lighting up the interior of her car. Her smile always made me smile.

I pulled my bag toward the rear of her vehicle. She popped the trunk, but also exited the car. Seeing her again after so long almost gave me chills. And it warmed my heart at the same time. It was as if she was moving in slow motion and I was transfixed on the pavement, unable to do more than

189

stare at her.

She walked right into my arms, smiling the entire time. "Oh, Calvin," she said as we hugged. "Where have you been? I can't believe I'm seeing you now."

My eyes were closed. I had a couple of serious relationships after Kathy, but nothing that was worth me even maintaining the friendship after it was over. Maya's mom, Skylar, was the longest relationship I had, and it lasted with me in the wrong way for the wrong reasons. The sweet essence of Kathy lasted with me like a virus for which there was no cure.

We finally, after about a minute, ended the embrace, took a step back and looked into each other's eyes. I won the bet with myself. She had on heels.

"You look like I remember. And I feel like I used to when I looked at you," I said.

"Really? How do you feel?"

"Alive," I said. What irony.

"I *like* the bald head on you," she said. "It threw me off when I saw it on television, but you have the right peanut-shaped head for it."

"Nothing changed, huh? Still think you're funny."

"*You* think you're funny? I am hilarious. Maybe I'm not funny to you or anyone else, but sure enough to me. I crack myself up."

I smiled and hugged her again. She hugged me back tightly. I didn't know if there was a message in her hug, but I took it as one.

"Good to see you — and feel you."

"Put your bag in the trunk. What are we going to do?"

"This is your town. I've been here for a Panthers game once, and that's about it."

"OK, well, are you hungry? Let me take you to dinner and tell you about my life."

And so we went to a place called Harper's, across the street from SouthPark Mall, which, amazingly enough, was the one restaurant in Charlotte I had been to. I did not say anything to Kathy about it, though. Didn't see the point.

"I think we have aged well," she said as we walked into the restaurant.

"And you have two children, so you really have taken care of yourself." There was no indication that she had given birth. I didn't care if there was, but she happened to have managed to keep her weight down.

We were seated after about ten minutes of chatting.

"How have you been able to keep your weight under control?"

"When I am upset, I don't each much,"

she said — her first words she uttered without smiling. "And I've been upset a lot."

I was hardly psychic, but I knew where this was going: the marriage.

"Upset about what?" I had to make myself ask it. I didn't like giving in to people's whims. Want to tell me something, just tell me. Don't drag it out.

"My life in general, my marriage in particular."

I tried to look surprised.

"Well, marriage can be challenging, I'm told. You can work it out. You just have to be committed to it."

That was my weak advice for the day. Felt guilty saying words that indicated I supported her marriage when I really did not. But I had no reason to *not* support it.

"I'm tired of working on it," she said. "I always could be honest with you. I work on the job, work raising the kids, work on my relationship with my mother. And I have to work with the person who's supposed to be my soul mate, too? Where is my break, my relief?"

"You're having it right now; no kids, no husband. Just two old, dear friends catching up over a meal. Priceless."

She laughed and we ordered our dinner, talked, had dessert and talked some more.

"You sure enough ate well tonight," I said. "You wolfed down that roasted chicken as if you used a straw."

"Being with you, I'm not upset. I can be myself."

Our server came over to check on us and removed the plates. "And now I want a coffee," Kathy said. "Not that I need it to stay up. This one right here (pointing to me) will keep me up."

The server smiled, and Kathy realized what it sounded like. "No. Wait. I'm sorry. I didn't mean for it to sound like it did. What I meant is that we haven't seen each other in a long time and I'll be thinking about this conversation before I can go to sleep."

"None of my business," the server said, and then winked.

"This guy thinks he's a comedian, with his eavesdropping ass," she cracked.

Kathy was the easiest person for me to let loose. Part of it was that I trusted her. She was not judgmental with me. She listened and had responses that indicated she wanted to know more. And she trusted me. Kathy was direct by nature, but the things she shared with me were intimate details of her life that were not details someone would entrust to the masses. I respected her for trusting me.

"So, if you're tired of working on your marriage, what are you going to do?"

"My kids are twelve and ten. It sounds like a cliché to me, but I'd hate for my kids to learn that I hate their father, that he's boring and a liar. More than that, I don't want them to not have the family environment."

That was the first thing she ever said that disappointed me.

"Kathy, if you feel as you say you do about your husband, how can your children benefit from being in a home that has no love? It's dysfunctional, if I may say so, and I hear it all the time. Makes me crazy."

"Well, don't go crazy on me. Not yet anyway. I know what you mean. It's very awkward. We basically have had separate lives for the last two years. We sleep in separate rooms. They don't see us showing affection toward each other. I wonder how it's making them look at relationships."

"You can believe they notice. They may not say anything, but they notice . . . But you know and love your kids and will do the best for them. I know that."

"I can't even act like I know what I'm doing. I'm hoping they will be fine. The truth is that neither of us can afford to live on our own. Together we can maintain a home.

Separate, it gets tough. So, that's probably the main reason we stay in the same house. But that's all we share — the house and the kids."

The look on her face was unfamiliar to me. It made me feel sorry for her.

"In the end, you have to do what you have to do. You look and sound great. So, you're handling it."

She got teary-eyed. She used the back of her hand to wipe the corner of her eye. "I'm a little emotional because I did not see this life for myself. When I look at you, well, you remind me of a different time, when my life was carefree and all in front of me. I remember thinking about being happy and in love.

"It shows you that life doesn't always work out as you planned it to."

She was telling me? At least she had a chance to still make her plans a reality.

"Your life isn't over, Kathy. You're young — what? — forty-two? You can turn your life into what you want it to be."

"I was a housewife for the first nine or ten years we were married. When it went bad, it went truly bad — first he started acting distant, then disappearing on weekends, and finally he wasn't even trying to hide it. It was devastating. I loved him, but it wasn't that. I loved him because he filled a void and he was good to me. But he wasn't the one that took my breath away.

"But he was my husband and I was faithful. I was so faithful that I made sure to lose contact with you for all these years. I knew if I were in contact with you it would threaten or challenge my marriage. I gave up you for him. I gambled on him and lost."

I wasn't sure how to take that. We had a wonderful relationship when she could not pass on an awesome career opportunity. I understood mostly because I believed what we had could stretch across the miles and we'd be able to sustain the relationship. But I was wrong. Not because I didn't try. I didn't want to admit at the time, but I was able to look back and confirm that Kathy eased her way out of my life. I wasn't sure why at the time. I thought it was all about the distance. That's what I *thought.*

For a few silent moments, I was insulted and mad. But I looked at her from across the table and I saw regret in her face. And I checked my ego. Ultimately, I knew it did not matter.

"In the grand scheme of things, what happened that long ago doesn't really matter. I'm just glad to be here with you now."

"Wow, you have mellowed out some, I see. I would have figured you'd go off on me.

We had something good and I blew it."

"Long time ago. Life is too short — trust me — to dwell on something that cannot be changed. Here we are . . . right now . . . in this moment. That's what it has to be about."

"See, this is what I need — someone to be positive. I have plenty of girlfriends, and all they say is, 'Girl, leave that fool.' Or 'He's ruined your life.' Or 'It's hard being single out here. Better keep him. At least you have somebody.' I'm not depressed enough to believe any of that helps me.

"And then you come along. It's crazy we're sitting here. I mean, what happened on that bus? I saw the report on TV. But this whole thing is crazy that it happened not even two hours ago and now we're having dinner together."

"An act of God, on a couple of levels." And I was so serious. Hardly did I invoke God into my conversations, but I believed in Him, despite not understanding how He could allow terminal cancer to be the last part of my life story.

I didn't understand that, but I did trust in Him.

"I don't remember you being particularly religious," Kathy said.

"Not openly, no. But I pray, occasionally

go to church and believe He is the Man, the Almighty. All this had to be the act of a higher power.

"Think about it: We were going to ride right through Charlotte on the way to Atlanta. But not only did the driver have a heart attack on the highway right here in Charlotte, but I saw him in distress and came to his aid to help him out. God put me on that bus, in that position, in that scenario to ultimately put us together.

"I definitely had planned to contact you over the weekend from Atlanta. But this . . . just like the drama on the bus. It was like a movie."

"You're a hero. Anyone who sees that segment on the news would think so. I'm sure that driver thinks so."

A hero? Never even considered that. Hadn't done anything heroic in my life. I raised my daughter, but I never sought credit for doing something I was supposed to do. Maybe facing life knowing I was going to die was heroic. Maybe.

"You don't think you're a hero?"

"I just did what I was supposed to do — help someone who needed help."

"See, this is good, talking to you. It's helping me remember everything about you. You were always humble and practical. You're just being yourself. But I will put that news report on Facebook. Watch all the responses you get."

"I have to tell Maya first. I can't let her find out about it on Facebook."

"How is she?"

"Worried about her dad."

"Worried about her dad? Why?"

This was my opportunity to tell Kathy about my cancer. Couldn't do it. Didn't want to do it. And I wasn't sure why.

"You know how kids are. The older you get, the more the roles change, the more they start caring for you and thinking they're in charge. You have that to look forward to."

"It's better than the alternative."

"It is. But there are times when I'd rather she was a little girl, around ten or eleven. That's when she was the most mature while still being sweet and innocent."

I was expecting a response from Kathy, but she was quiet. Her body language changed. She looked down, at the table.

"What's wrong?"

She didn't answer.

"What's going on, Kathy?" came a voice over my shoulder. It was a man's voice, and it was not a pleasant tone. Right away I realized the mistake I made by sitting with my back to the door. This guy could have blasted me and I never would have known what happened.

I slid to my left in the booth to get an angle. I turned and looked up to see the face of a guy who was not happy. I looked back at Kathy and she finally looked up. She didn't speak. She just looked at the man.

"What's going on, Kathy?" he repeated. This time, though, he was looking at me as he spoke.

My instincts kicked in and I went on the defensive.

"Eric, hi. This is my friend . . . Calvin," Kathy finally said. It was like she didn't want to say my name.

"What's going on, Kathy?" he said for a third time.

"What's going on with *you*?" I interjected to Eric.

"I'm not talking to you." He moved toward Kathy's side of the table.

I'd never been considered a punk, and I wasn't a bully, either. But I damn sure was not going to look like one in front of Kathy. I didn't care who he was.

"Well, I'm talking to *you*," I said with a serious edge.

"Calvin . . . Eric is my husband's friend,"

Kathy said. "Eric, why are you doing this?"

"What am I doing? I just said hello."

"So it seems to me you should be moving on," I said. I didn't want to fight and hadn't been in one in decades. But I had enough of this guy posturing as if he was Kathy's guardian.

"This is none of your business," he responded.

"And it's none of yours," Kathy said. Her stock in my eyes elevated immediately. She was not going to play the meek role.

"Yeah, OK. Right," Eric said. "I'm sure this will be interesting to Thomas."

Thomas was her husband, I figured. When Eric finally left, Kathy turned to me.

"I'm sorry. What are the odds that my husband's best friend would be here, too?"

"Why is he acting like your bodyguard or something? Doesn't he know what's going on with your marriage?"

"I'm sure he does."

"So what's with all the posturing?"

"Because he's a man and men think they own you, even when they aren't your man. Eric is an egomaniac. That's why he and Thomas are friends — they both think they own the world."

"So what are you going to do, Kathy?"

"About what?"

"About your life. You're not happy. You're just going to stay there because of money? For the kids?"

"Those are real reasons, Calvin."

"Real, but not enough to sacrifice your life."

"Sacrifice my life? I'm not sure it's that deep."

"Kathy . . ."

I was about to get really raw with her and tell her she's been silly or, at least naïve. But I toned it down.

"Kathy, you've heard the expression that life is short? Well, believe it. There has to be a way to get out of this. And let me say now that I'm not saying this for me. I'm saying this for you. If you really want a divorce, then you should do all you can to make it happen because you deserve to have a good life. You can't be enjoying life if you're living with a man you detest, as you said."

"It's easier said than done. I do want a divorce. I've been dishonored and disregarded and . . . it's just been awful, especially the last two years. I'm over it. But I worry about my kids and being able to provide for them."

I had $200,000 in the bank from Walter. I planned to leave some of it to Ballou High and to my dad and my daughter and donate

202

to suicide prevention. But I had life insurance that my daughter would receive — $400,000 — so I was in a position to really help Kathy. I wanted to help her.

"What if money wasn't a problem? Then what?"

"Well, money isn't everything or the only thing. It's important, though. I have to be able to provide."

"I hear you. But what if you had the financial resources? What if a bag of money fell into your lap? What would you do then?"

"I don't know. I don't want to be one of those women who uses the kids to punish the father. You're really just punishing the kids because I believe they need both parents in their lives if they can have them."

"Does that mean you'll stay just for the kids?"

"Why are you asking me this?" she said. She sounded irritated.

"I'm not trying to press you or anything, Kathy. I'm not. I just want you to be happy."

"You want me to be happy? Then sweep me away from here."

We laughed, but it was an awkward laugh for me because I knew as soon as I saw her I felt I would love to sweep her away. It was my first thought, actually. But sweep her to where? My funeral?

"You deserve the life you want. You deserve a man who loves and appreciates you. I might as well tell you that I regret not fighting for our relationship. It was ours and it was great. And I let it fade away when you moved, thinking it was the right thing to do. I supported you growing your career. But I should have made more of an effort for us to stay together. I . . ."

"Me, too. It wasn't just you. I let my career dictate my life and ended up quitting my job when I got married because Thomas insisted. I gave up the career that I left you for. Stupid."

"Don't call it stupid. You made the decision based on what you felt at that time in your life. It is what it is. I just don't want you to be unhappy the rest of your life."

Her expression said, "Kiss me." That's the way I took it, anyway, and I was mesmerized, so much so that she had to snap me out of it.

"Calvin?"

"There's so much I want to tell you," I said.

"So tell me."

I wanted to tell her that I never stopped loving her, that I wanted to take her with me to Atlanta . . . but the fact that I was dying kept me from saying any of that.

"I will . . . in time. This won't be the last time I see you, will it?"

"I hope not. It's really good to see you. You look great. I like the bald head. Sexy. Oops. I guess as a married woman I shouldn't say that. But to hell with it; it's true."

I didn't know how to take that. I mean, for a while, I was so immersed in the conversation and just being around Kathy that I didn't think about cancer. That didn't happen often. But her compliment made me think about how sick I was and how crazy this whole thing was.

There was no physical evidence of my situation. But I knew I had an expiration date on my life, and that was sobering beyond words.

CHAPTER FOURTEEN: WHAT A DOGGONE DAY

We walked to her car from the restaurant. I looked up at the sky. It was filled with stars.

"Been a hell of a day," I said.

"And a beautiful night," Kathy said.

"Can I kiss you?" It just came out.

"Please."

I leaned in and kissed my old girlfriend, the only woman I ever loved. It felt like the sun came out.

When our lips finally parted, I looked into her eyes — and then turned away. I thought she would be able to see the truth through my eyes.

"Where are you staying?"

"There's a Crowne Plaza down Tyvola Road, on Westpark, about five minutes away, according to the website. It looks decent. I'll get up in the morning and head to Atlanta. But I'll think about you before I go to sleep."

We hugged and I felt love through her

embrace.

"Let's go," she said.

On the drive to the hotel, I felt sorry for myself. I had reconnected with the woman I wanted . . . and I could not have her. The reality of it made me sad. And it made me mad that I went from feeling so good to feeling awful in a moment's time. I was angry for allowing the negative to creep into my psyche.

As we wove our way to the hotel, happiness and sadness alternately covered my mood. I hid it from Kathy, smiling at her when she glanced at me. It was hard to fake it, though.

We finally pulled up at the hotel. It apparently was busy, based on the nearly full parking lot. I began envisioning myself in the bed; fatigue was coming down. I didn't sleep on the bus as I expected. I got my bag out of the trunk and hugged Kathy one more time.

"Text me your address when you get home. Your work address."

"Why? You sending me something?" she asked, smiling.

"Yep. It's a surprise. But I'm sure you'll like it."

She shook her head — not in dismay, but happiness, which made me feel good. I watched her drive away and took another look at the sky. I appreciated God and his magnificence more and tried to take it in whenever I could.

Just as I was about to turn and walk into the hotel, I saw an image out of my peripheral vision. When I turned to see a dog approaching me, I was startled and stepped back.

I didn't like dogs; I was afraid of them and I didn't like the idea of them as pets. Didn't make sense that a human would get attached to an animal. I looked around to see where I could run if the dog attacked.

But it was not a big dog. Looked like a Labrador retriever. I guessed that because it looked like my cousin's dog from my childhood. I hated that dog.

For all those cars in the lot, there was no one outside. The dog and I stared at each other from about ten feet away. I figured he was sizing me up; I surely was doing the same to him.

My fear eased, though. First of all, he was too little to do any damage. I also I assessed what I was looking at — a dog looking for comfort. I noticed he was bleeding behind an ear and along his back. It looked like he had been in a fight — and lost.

I quickly looked around for the dog that

delivered the beating to this little mutt, who had to be no more than a few months old. I did not see one.

"You OK, doggie?" I said, trying to sound comforting.

The dog murmured, as if he understood me. Then he lowered his head and slowly walked toward me. Somehow, I felt sorry for him.

"You OK? You been in a fight?"

The dog crept closer, to where I could bend down and touch it. I had no interest in touching dogs and certainly not a stray dog. But something in me forced me to bend over and rub the dog's fur. So I did, tentatively and softly.

The dog flinched. I looked at my hand and there was blood on it. I looked into the dog's eyes and he looked to have tears welling up. My heart sunk. I had to help the dog, somehow.

"Come on. Come with me," I said, as I walked into the hotel lobby. This dog understood. Well, maybe he didn't. But he followed me.

"Hi, sir," the front desk clerk said. "Is that your dog?"

I looked down at him and he looked up at me. I couldn't leave him hanging.

"Yeah, he is."

"I'm sorry, but we don't allow pets."

"Oh. OK, well. Thank you."

"Did you have a reservation?"

"No, I called and was told you had rooms available. But I have to find someplace else. Can't leave my dog."

"Try the Hampton Inn, across the street."

And so I did. With the dog in tow, I walked across Tyvola and went down a block to the Hampton Inn. I got us a room with no problem. As I walked, I wondered what the hell I was doing. *I don't like dogs. I can't take care of a dog.* And yet I was making accommodations for a dog?

"What's your name?" I asked stupidly. As if he was going to respond.

"OK, I'm going to give you one since you don't have a tag or collar," I said, sitting on the bed. "Moses. That's your name, OK. Moses."

The dog looked at me and was probably saying, *What's up with this dude?*

"First thing I'm going to do is clean you up. You don't smell too fresh. Then I will find you some food . . . somehow."

So I ran a warm bath for this dog and talked to it as I did. It seemed as if he was intently listening.

"I don't usually like dogs. And the only reason I can think of that I'm looking out for you is because I have a new appreciation for life. I'm going to die. I know — that's sad. But this . . . uh, diagnosis by the doctors has made me look at life differently, you know? I've been a good person, for the most part. But have I done enough? So you're a part of this whole thing I'm feeling. I can't let you wander around and get hit by a car or beat up by some big dog."

This dog, I mean, Moses, eased his way over to me and rubbed his face against my pants leg. I was shocked and a bit scared. *Did Moses understand me?* Nah. No way. But he tried to comfort me — or so it seemed. Maybe he could tell through my inflection. Dogs have instincts, I had been told.

Anyway, I found myself, in less than an hour, going from feeling sorry for the dog to liking him. I didn't know, though, how he would react to a bath. All I ever saw were dogs resisting the water and making a mess.

I wasn't sure if regular body wash was OK for a dog, but I used it anyway. The tub was half-filled and here came the hard part. Getting him in it.

"OK, Moses, this is a test for us right here. I need you to get into this water without getting me soaked. It's going to be nice and warm. It will clean your wounds and you'll smell good. Then I'd feel like I can pet you. 'Cause nobody likes a stinky dog. OK?"

Moses just looked at me in those sorrowful eyes. He probably was saying, *Dude, you don't smell so good yourself.* And he probably thought: *Are you OK? You know you're talking to a dog, right?*

But I didn't care. It felt strangely appropriate to me. So I tested the water. It was warm.

"Come on, Moses."

The dog just sat there, looking at me. I took his look to mean, *If you want me in that water, you'd better put me in it.*

And so, I smiled at him as I picked him up and eased his paws into the water, which I had doused with my body wash. He needed something with a scent. I think the bubbles in the tub distracted him enough for him to not understand what was happening.

But when his feet hit water, he squirmed, and I almost dropped him. But it was important for me to protect this dog, so I tightened my grip to keep him safe.

"Hey, you have to get into this bathtub. No joke."

His expression changed, and I took it to mean, *OK, let's do it.*

And I lowered Moses into that warm

water and he stood almost neck high in it, never uttering a sound. I bathed that dog thoroughly but delicately, and he seemed to appreciate it.

I smiled at the strangeness of what was happening: I never had a dog as a kid, never wanted one, never liked dogs. And here I was, about an hour after finding a stray dog, had it in my hotel room, giving it a bath. *What was going on with me?*

I looked at Moses as a possession I coveted. I needed to save his life. Was it because I was losing mine? Was it because I had helped saved the bus driver? There was, as Gene said, an exhilaration that came with that.

Whatever it was, I had a new best friend. I dried Moses off, wrapped him in a towel and placed him on the small chair in the room. "Stay here and relax for a while." I chuckled to myself. I was sure this dog did not understand me but I felt compelled to speak to him as if he did. Crazy.

I called the front desk. "I need to get some dog food; is there a Walmart or grocery store nearby?"

The front desk clerk told me about a not-too-far Walmart. I wasn't sure if I should take the Moses with me, if the dog would be allowed in the store, so I called Uber and had a man-to-dog conversation with my pet.

"I'm going to get you some food and a leash and some water and vitamins and all the stuff you need to get healthy. OK? But I need you to stay here and relax. I'm going to turn the TV on. You probably want a cartoon or something, huh? Here, look: Here's the Cartoon Network. Don't tear up this place. Just relax. I will be back soon with goodies for you. OK?"

Moses' eyes were transfixed on me as I spoke, like he was trying to understand. I rubbed along his small back and backed my way to the door. "Be right back."

I laughed at myself after I closed the door. I found it necessary to talk to a dog, as if he understood me. That was amusing. I waited for a minute before the Uber car arrived. On the way to Walmart, which was about ten minutes away, I received a call from Kathy.

"I've been thinking about you," she said. "When I got home, I found out my husband and sons are not coming home tonight. So, I was thinking . . ."

"Thinking what?"

"I was thinking I could come and get you and we could do something. Or I could just come over there and spend some time with you."

That put me in a dilemma. I wanted to see Kathy, but I had started looking forward to spending time with Moses. It was the weirdest thing. I felt a stronger sense to be with the dog than the woman.

"Kathy, after you dropped me off, this little dog came along. A stray dog. He looked lost and helpless. There aren't any homes over in that area, so I have no idea where he came from. But I ended up taking him with me."

"What? You picked up a stray dog? And took him where?"

"Well, I had to change hotels because the one where you dropped me didn't allow pets."

"So what are you telling me? You have a dog in your hotel room with you? Wait a minute . . . you hate dogs. I remember that."

"That's why this is so weird. For some reason, this dog struck a nerve with me. I call him 'Moses.' He's in my room now. I'm in an Uber headed to Walmart to get him food and a leash and other stuff."

"You're going to keep this dog?"

"Yes. He's mine now."

There was silence on the other end of the phone for several seconds.

"Hello?"

"I'm here. I'm just shocked."

"I'm more shocked than you, trust me. But for some reason I need to take care of this dog. I couldn't leave him on the streets. He looked a little battered, like a bigger dog had beaten him up. I gave him a bath. And —"

"You gave the dog a bath?"

"Yes. He smelled like a dog, so I shampooed him good and dried him off and he was great. He didn't squirm or fight. He enjoyed it. When I talk to this dog, he looks at me like he understands."

"Oh my goodness. Did you walk him, too?"

"Oh, damn. I forgot about that. He probably has to go by now. I forgot. I hope he doesn't go in that room."

"You can bet that he will."

"That's the one thing I have no interest in doing — cleaning up after a dog. I barely like washing the dishes."

"So I guess you're telling me you plan to spend the evening with a dog over me." I knew it was coming. And I couldn't lie.

"That's what I'm going to do. Not because I prefer that. The dog needs me. He was stranded and had a look in his eyes that was fear. He's depending on me. I can't explain it."

"I've heard it all now. I'm being rejected over a dog."

"That's not true, Kathy. But this is something I have to do. I need to do this. Tonight, when I get settled, I will call and explain."

"What possible explanation can you have, but OK."

We arrived at Walmart and I made a beeline to the pet section after a worker told me where it was. I had a cart and I filled it up with Pedigree Complete Nutrition Dog Food, water (I had Googled the importance of water to a dog's diet), a black leash that was made of soft leather, a cushioned black-and-white ball and roped bone toy, a chrome dual bowl to put his water and snacks side-by-side, dog vitamins, two plush blankets for Moses to relax on and a pooper scooper.

I didn't even note how much it cost because I didn't care. I just wanted to have all I needed to make Moses comfortable. My Uber driver waited for me. I didn't care about the cost.

I called my daughter on the way back to the hotel and told her about my new friend.

"Dad, you hate dogs. What's going on? You feel a need to save someone, anyone or anything after today with the bus? Is that it?"

"You're smart; I thought the same thing. I don't know. He looked so pitiful, so scared — but he came right to me. It was like he was communicating with me that if I didn't take him, he was going to die. I just couldn't leave him."

"I will be in Atlanta on Monday. So I guess you're renting a car because I don't think you can take your dog on a bus."

"Moses."

"Huh?"

"His name is Moses."

"Could you take a photo of Moses and text it to me, please? I don't think I will actually believe this until I see it."

"Will do."

We arrived at the hotel just as I finished my talk with my Maya. I tipped the driver twenty dollars. He was grateful. With my bags full of goodies for Moses, I slowly entered the room, not sure if it would be ravaged or stinky or both.

I couldn't believe what I saw. Moses was sitting right where I left him. He stood up in the chair when I entered, jumped down and scampered over to me as if he knew me and as if he had missed me. My heart sank.

"Hey, buddy. Told you I was coming back."

I rubbed him as I spoke and his tail wagged. "Hey, let me get this leash on you so we can take a walk. I'm sure you have to go by now."

It took a minute or so to get the leash around his neck and off we went to the side of the hotel, with pooper scooper and small plastic waste bag, where there was a small field. Moses walked around for a few minutes, sniffing the grass until he found a spot to claim his own. And he peed.

I turned my head. I wanted him to have some privacy. When he finished, I felt a tug on the leash. By then, it was after eleven o'clock. There was no place in the field for him to run off to, so I let him off the leash so he could bounce around.

Moses could not have been but maybe three or four months old. He had a beautiful brown coat. He was smaller than he should have been, I figured, but the way he ran around that space told me he liked to enjoy life. When he ventured about twenty-five feet from me, I squatted and called for him.

"Moses, come here, Moses."

And right on cue, that little dog bounced over to me. "Good boy."

I wasn't sure what Moses understood and what he didn't. But just in case he did understand, I talked to him. At the very least he'd understand that my tone was pleasant.

"I have the best all-natural food for you," I said when we got back to the room. "We're going to get you all the healthy. I hope you like it."

I poured the dog food into his bowl and some alkaline water into the other bowl. And I sat back and delighted in Moses enjoying his meal. It was as if I had saved two lives in one day: the bus driver and Moses. Eugene was right: There was power in saving someone.

Chapter Fifteen: The Pleasure Principle

As Moses enjoyed his meal, I pulled out my laptop and made a rental car reservation for the drive to Atlanta in the morning. Then I called Kathy. As I shopped for Moses and on the ride back, I struggled with the idea of telling her about my situation.

"How's your dog?" I sensed sarcasm, which didn't make me feel good.

"Are you really trying to be jealous about a dog?"

"Not jealous. But I don't understand."

I learned something about myself in the weeks after learning I was going to die: I minimized the filter that sanitized my thoughts. I was sort of like the really old grandparent who just said whatever was on his/her mind. "What comes up, comes out," my dad used to say about his mother.

"You don't have to understand, Kathy." It came out before I could temper it. "You have a husband and a family. Before I reached out to you, found you on Facebook, I hadn't heard from you in years. So, I'm not cool with you thinking I owe you an explanation."

"Oh, really? Well, I didn't mean anything by it. And still, you don't have to be so sensitive about it. I'm just asking to find out what's going on. Am I wrong for that?"

I felt bad. "No, you're not. I apologize. There's a lot going on that you don't know about."

Kathy did not respond, and I quickly recalled that was a mechanism she used all her life. To avoid saying something she would regret, she would not say anything. So I knew I just had to continue.

"Kathy, I have cancer. I —"

"What? Why didn't you tell me?" The concern in her voice was obvious. But I also noticed that Moses stopped eating and looked up at me, as if he understood, even though I had already told the dog. It freaked me out.

Can this damned dog understand what I'm saying? What the hell?

I was going to tell Kathy what I saw, but she wouldn't have believed me. But Moses looked at me with those sad eyes for several seconds. Finally, I said to him, "It's OK. Finish eating."

"Who are you talking to? Never mind. Calvin! I'm so sorry."

"I'm sorry for not telling you earlier. But I haven't been exactly spreading the word."

I gave her the details of what I had, when it was discovered, etc. And then I gave her the bombshell news.

"It's terminal."

Again, Moses raised his head from the bowl and looked at me. Kathy didn't say anything for several seconds.

"Calvin, can you hold on a second?"

I waited about a minute before she came back. "Calvin, I had to have a good cry in private. I'm so scared for you. I'm so sorry."

Tears began to flow down my face. I had become good at talking while crying, without the person on the other end of the phone knowing. They'd say stuff like, "I'm so proud of how you're handling this" and "You're so strong." And I'd be thinking, *If only you knew.*

"Thank you for caring so much, Kathy. But it's going to be OK."

OK? How is it going to be OK? I was lying to myself and to Kathy.

"I don't know how you can say that. I mean, I'm not trying to be selfish, but we just reconnected and now you're telling me you have terminal cancer. That's not OK for me or you."

She was right but I had to tell myself that to move on. Or try to move on. I hadn't exactly accepted my fate. I had gotten off the floor and sought to live a semblance of a life. But how can you, when you know you're going to die? The conflict was ongoing.

Kathy wanted to know all the details, what the doctors said, how long they projected I had . . .

"Wish I could say it's a long time, but it's not. A few months. I feel fine right now. But every few days I get these pains that literally knock me out."

She got quiet again when I told her I was not taking chemo.

"I can't do that to myself. I know it has worked for millions of people and saved lives. But they told me it would not save my life. They're certain about that. It would just have me laid up. I wouldn't even be here right now. I wouldn't have gotten to help save that man's life today. I wouldn't have seen you tonight. I wouldn't have found Moses. All that happened because I decided to live.

"I know chemo works for a lot of people. For me, it wouldn't work."

I went on to tell her about the holistic

treatment I was going to receive in Atlanta.

"It's not going to save my life, either. But it will — if it really works — help cleanse some of what's bad in my body and help me to feel better and have less pain. If it can do that, then I'll be all right."

Finally, she spoke. It was surprising to me that, after all those years, what Kathy had to say meant so much to me.

"All of this is just too much. I can't right now. What can I do, Calvin? How can I help you? This is so crazy to me.

"I mean, we talk after all these years. I see you on TV. We go out to dinner and I feel like whatever we had was still there. I'm not even going to talk about my situation, my marriage. And now you tell me that the doctors say you're dying? This . . . this is too much."

And I'm thinking, *No shit?*

"You telling me?"

"Well, can I come over there and see you now?"

"I need to get some rest, read a little —"

"Just say you don't want to see me, Calvin. You don't have to make excuses with me."

"Don't want to see you? That's a joke, right. Really, I'm just tired I gave you my room number in a text. Can you come in the morning, before we leave?"

"We're both up now, but OK." I could tell she wasn't happy. But I couldn't tell if it was because I rejected her or because she really wanted to see me.

"Do you understand the day I have had?" I asked. I felt compelled — another word for guilty, in this case — to make it clear to Kathy. "Got up early after no sleep to catch a bus. You know all the stuff that has happened since then. That might not be a full day for you, but for me, it's more than enough."

"OK, Calvin, I get it. I'm not trying to pressure you or add drama to your day. I just wanted to hug you. That's all."

I didn't say anything because a hug from Kathy always led to sex, something I actually had not even thought about for weeks. I didn't have a lot going on, but I always had someone to fulfill that part of my life, whether she was serious to me or not. Learning I was going to die took away my sex drive, something I actually thought could never happen.

"OK, well, get some rest, Calvin. I will call you," she said.

CHAPTER SIXTEEN:
THE KNOCK AT THE DOOR

I put a little food out for Moses, set up a comfortable place for him to sleep and took a hot shower and got into bed. I closed my eyes and took a deep breath. The dog lay in his place, looking at me. I went over to him and rubbed along his back.

"Crazy day, Moses. Crazy day. But I'm glad it all happened. All that had to happen for me to be at that hotel at the time you came up. So, it was meant to be that we meet, buddy. You're a good dog. I'm sorry what happened to you but I'm glad we met. Now, you get some rest. But let me know if you need to go outside."

I rubbed his head and made my way into the bed. I wanted to read, but needed to say my prayers first. I had gotten back into the routine of praying after the funeral. I had my problems with God, I was not ashamed to say. But that was my pain taking over. I grew up understanding God made no mistakes, and that there was no place better than heaven. I wasn't ready to see it, but it was out of my hands.

Just as I was about to begin, there was a faint knock at the door. It was not loud, but I knew what I heard. Plus, Moses rose, too, from his pile. He heard it. Immediately, I thought someone had followed me and was there to get Moses. In the time it took to conjure that thought, I got sad. I had grown attached to the dog that quickly and was not ready to let him go.

I started not to answer, to act as if we were not there, but Moses barked. So, I yelled in a deep, I'm-not-taking-any-bull voice: "Who is it?"

"Calvin, it's Kathy."

I had a mix of relief and frustration at once: It was not someone looking to claim Moses; but it was someone who violated my wishes.

"What? Kathy?"

"Please, let me see you for five minutes, Calvin."

If it were anyone else, she would have remained outside that door. But it was Kathy. I was weak to her. And I was, even though sort of angry, excited that she was there.

"I can't believe this."

Kathy had changed her clothes. She was now in shorts, a button-up white blouse with wedge heels. And she smelled like love.

"Can I please just hug you?" she asked as she walked into the room. Her eyes were filled with tears. She walked into my arms and held me tightly as she cried on my shoulder.

"I'm so scared. Aren't you scared?"

"Petrified."

After a minute or so, we let go of each other. But holding her in my arms felt so right, the best feeling I had since the diagnosis. I told her that.

"You don't even look sick, Calvin. You look wonderful. Did you get a second opinion?"

"And third and fourth. It is what it is."

"Can I stay for a while? I'm struggling with this."

"I was about to say my prayers and read. I don't sleep that much anymore. Can't sleep."

"I can't even imagine. And here you are . . . brave, living your life. I'm really proud of how brave you are. I . . . I think I'd just be sitting in the dark crying."

"No, you wouldn't. And you know why? Because you love life. I feel like I've had a good life, but there was so much more I could do. Could have done."

"Then do it. Why not? You can do whatever you want."

"I'd like someone to do some of it with."

"I wish I could spend some time with you, experience some things with you. Right now, I have to get my finances together before I can do anything."

"Well, I was going to just send it to you as a surprise," I said.

"Send me what?"

"A check."

"What are you talking about?"

"I have some money. One of my co-workers, my friend Walter, died recently. Actually, he committed suicide. Hanged himself in his garage. Before he did, he asked me to come over. I got there and found him hanging by his neck in his garage."

"Calvin, get the *frick* outta here."

"Seriously. A good man, too. He wanted me to find him. Anyway, I said I have money because Walter left me some. I had no idea he had money like that. He was a teacher at my school, but he invested well and had a small fortune. So, I have some money. Some money to help you."

"Calvin, I can't let you do that."

"What? You can't let a friend help you?

That doesn't sound right."

"I just mean that there are more people out there worse-off than me. They need it more."

"Well, obviously I don't have enough to help everybody. But I will definitely try to help as many people as I can — starting with you."

"I don't know what I did to deserve this from you."

"You've always been special to me. Even when we were apart, doing our own thing, you always stayed special. Still are. So, I'm excited about helping someone who means so much to me. It gives me pleasure, and I need to do that as much as possible now."

"Can I give you some pleasure?"

She said it in a way that made it clear she was talking about sex, something that had meant little to me. The doctors' news made me flaccid. The only times I thought about it was when I dreamed about it, which was not that often.

When I did, though, I would awake with an erection. Once or twice I handled it myself — jacked off — and my mind went somewhere else. But I did think about how lovely Kathy looked when she picked me up at the hospital. Looking at her across the table at dinner, I saw the sexiness in her that I loved when we were together. And there she was sitting on the bed beside me, looking and smelling enticing.

It wasn't just about her facial features or body. It was her smile, the way she used the back of her index finger to move her hair from covering her eyes, the way she pursed her lips when she intently listened — subtle things that drew me in. I did begin to think about sex with her, just about the time her husband's friend rolled up on us. The erection that was developing in my mind flatlined.

Now, there she was in my hotel room asking if she could give me pleasure. *Damn right, you could give me pleasure.* But she was married. But I was dying. That was no excuse; it would be wrong. But it wouldn't matter because I'd be gone. I played that back-and-forth game in my head long enough for Kathy to wonder.

"What's wrong? You don't . . ."

"It's not that." For some reason, I thought she was taking pity on me because I was dying. I also thought she felt obligated because I said I was going to give her some money.

"It's not that . . . Kathy. I don't want you to do anything that compromises you morally. You're a good girl. And you're married."

232

"In name only. That's it. There's nothing there. Hasn't been for a long time."

"And you don't have to do something to make me feel good because you know I'm sick. You don't have to do that."

"I wouldn't do that, Calvin. How could you think that? I know it's been a while, but act like you know me."

"And the money, it's yours — I don't want you to feel like you owe me something." Mistake.

"If I didn't know better, you just called me a whore," she said, standing up from the foot of the bed.

"You know I would never do that."

"You just said, basically, that I would sleep with you because you said you were going to give me some money."

"Yeah, but I didn't mean it as crazy as it sounds. I don't know, Kathy. I didn't mean to insult you. You know how I feel about you. I hope. But I'm not thinking right. My confidence, my . . . it's just always a lot going on in my mind.

"I'm overwhelmed with thoughts and fears and I just can't balance them all the right way sometimes. I'm sorry."

She sat back on the bed, only this time thigh-to-thigh close to me. I looked over at Moses, who was looking at me like, *What you gonna do?*

"Do you know, when I saw you when you picked me up and at dinner, it's the first time first time since the doctors told me I had cancer that I really thought about sex?"

"I'm glad to hear that. Calvin, I don't want you to do anything you don't want to do. I just feel like right now, at this moment, we need each other."

She ain't never lied. I could feel an erection growing in my pants just from her words and the thought of sex with her. And her scent. I wasn't sure what I was going to do, but it did make me feel manly. Most men tie manhood to sex, and how well and how often we get it. Yes, it was caveman thinking, but it was what it was. My manhood did not seem to be slipping from me, but sex slid way down the priority meter for me, to the point where it did not matter. I had more important things to think about.

Before I could say anything, Kathy jumped on me as if I were a horse — straddled me like a jockey would a mare. I held her by her waist and she leaned in for the most extended sensual kiss. It brought me right back to our time together — and out of my indifference.

So I started working off memory. I knew all her arousal points and I targeted them in a fit of desperate passion that was electric. I kissed her neck and down her shoulders. I pulled her tee over her head, exposing her breasts sitting up in a lace bra. Without hesitation, I grabbed them both firmly, but gently, too.

She threw her head back just as I recalled, and I pulled the straps down each arm, which allowed me to remove her breast out of the cups. I kissed them delicately, alternating between the two. She loved it when I took them in my mouth, squeezing them as I sucked on the nipples. Kathy began to make sounds, the kind that tell a story of passion.

"I have missed you, Mr. Jones," she said breathlessly.

I could not respond with a mouthful of titties. I figured she would rather I do that than speak. After a few more minutes, the foreplay achieved its purpose — I was hard as a jackhammer and Kathy was dripping-through-her-clothes moist.

She maneuvered off my lap and around the bed to the nightstand, where she turned out the light. "Your dog doesn't need to see this," she said, smiling.

I laughed. "You're right — don't want to traumatize him."

From either side of the bed, we watched

the silhouette of each other as we undressed. We were deliberate, sensual in how we moved, building the anticipation of what was to come.

We pulled back the covers together and, totally naked, entered the bed. My erection was so hard Kathy noticed when we embraced. "Damn. You got a log down there."

"Ain't nothing changed."

"I see — or rather, I feel."

"But, listen," I said, "don't we need a condom?"

"Yes. I have one in my purse."

I was going to ask why, but at that point, I didn't care. Pussy makes a man mind get tunnel vision. All I could see was her tunnel.

"This might not last that long," I warned Kathy. "I haven't had any in going on three months."

"Sometimes, it's better to have none at all than to have something that does nothing for you. And that's been my situation for a long time."

"We're talking too much about stuff that has nothing to do with the beauty of this moment," I said. I had no idea where that sentence came from. I guess it was from the heart. Whatever the case, it worked because we stopped talking and began kissing, kissing like teenage kids in love for the first time in the backseat of their parents' Buick.

It was all so romantic. She was not another man's wife in that moment. She was *my* woman. I felt her love in the passion. I just hoped she felt mine, too.

I had enough foreplay — I was about to explode before anything really happened. I would not be able to take that embarrassment, so I stalled.

"Kathy, this is very special to me," I said. I was buying time to regroup, but I was serious. "Being here with you like this, it feels like when we were together a long time ago. I wish the circumstances were different. But it still feels right."

"I'm a married single woman, if that makes any sense," Kathy said, falling back on a pillow. Looking at the ceiling, she added: "If I was here with someone else, maybe I'd feel guilty. With you, I feel absolutely no guilt."

I had calmed down by then, and leaned in to kiss her again. We frolicked around for several seconds and somehow, amid all the groping and squeezing and kissing, we almost effortlessly rolled on that condom. I guess two horny and determined people working together accomplished a lot.

She lay on her back, her legs invitingly

open, and I slid between them like that was where I was supposed to be. As I kissed her shoulder, she reached down and inserted my hardness, and I felt the warmth of her insides just as she squirmed and moaned.

I hadn't had sex in the close-to-three months since learning I had cancer — the longest stint of my life without it since I was twenty-one. I hadn't forgotten how to make love in general and to Kathy in particular. Our sex life was so dynamic that I would fly to San Francisco for a day and a half just to so we could satisfy our urges a few times and fly all the way back across country to D.C. We were animalistic . . . but still romantic.

All this time later, I knew how physical she liked it, and I gave it to her just like she wanted. She used to say, "Don't be delicate with me," which was code for *bring it.*

And so I brought it hard and deep. I held her legs in the air as I pumped manically. I turned her on her knees, grabbed her by her waist and pumped furiously. Neither the smacking sound nor her moans gave me pause. I kept on thrusting . . . until the pleasure point was reached and the sensation of passion burst out into the condom — and I collapsed on her back, breathlessly exhausted but totally fulfilled.

I kissed her back and shoulders and neck. When my weight seemed too much, I moved off of her and she snuggled onto my chest.

"You have a good dog," she said. "Didn't hear a word out of Moses."

"Moses knew I needed that," I joked. "But, seriously, he seems to know how to behave himself, as if he understands."

"That's what all dog lovers say," Kathy said.

"You know I'm not a dog-lover," I said. "But I do . . . I really like this dog. But it's only been a few hours."

"You're only going to love the dog more as days go by," Kathy said.

"I can tell," I said. "What a day? The bus thing, finding Moses and now this . . . you. That's a good day."

"How do you feel?" she asked.

I pondered the simple question for a minute.

"I feel like I'm dreaming. As much as I wanted this, I never would have expected it to become a reality."

Kathy held me as I held her. I felt wetness on my chest. She cried. I was not sure if they were tears of joy or tears of sadness about my plight. And I didn't ask.

CHAPTER SEVENTEEN: CAPTAIN SAVE-A-HO

It wasn't that I didn't care enough to ask Kathy why she shed tears. It was that I didn't want the moment to be lost. Moments meant more to me because I was not sure how many more I had.

Denzel was in this movie with Gene Hackman. *Crimson Tide.* They were on a submarine, floating on top of the water before submerging deep into the sea on a mission. Gene Hackman admired the beautiful sunset with Denzel, who was seeing it for the first time. Denzel admired it, too — without saying a word.

Hackman's character praised him for not ruining the moment by talking through it. I remembered that as Kathy lay on my chest. I was not going to ruin a moment I had imagined for nearly twenty years with a question that would be answered at some point anyway.

So, I closed my eyes with the one woman

I loved on my chest and soaked up that feeling. And that feeling lasted long enough for me to doze off into a deep sleep.

I could feel myself snoring, but could not do anything about it. I hadn't gotten as much sleep on the bus as I had planned and so much had happened along the ride. I dreamed dreams that were not about cancer or death.

I could only remember two of the dreams. One, I was playing golf with Walter. We were on some lavish course that was in the mountains and was crowded. It was my turn to tee off on No. 1 and I didn't have my golf clubs. I had left them at the clubhouse — something that could only happen in a dream.

I ran to find them, but they were not where I had left them. Then it was getting dark, meaning we would not get the round in. I finally found my clubs in the same place I had already looked. I jumped in a cart and caught up with Walter, who had already hit a nice drive down the middle.

It was my turn to swing when the marshal came over and started giving us the rules of the course. Even in my sleep, I could feel myself getting antsy and frustrated. I wanted to hit the ball. But I never did.

It started raining and we had to leave the

course. There was frustration all over me as I woke up, moving Kathy slightly from me chest to my left side.

"What's wrong?"

I didn't answer. I just hugged her, and she relaxed and we lay there in silence. Before I fell asleep, I tried to figure what the dream meant. It was a feeble, desperate act of a man desperate to learn something about himself, through any means.

I thought about it and in all the dreams I had about golf, I seldom actually hit the ball. I wondered if that meant I had not taken my swings at life like I should have, that I had not done enough when I *thought* I had life under control.

I couldn't be sure, but my mindset was to ponder everything. Before I knew it, though, I was asleep again, this time dreaming about being able to fly.

It was so weird at first because my borderline fear of heights was apparent in my dream. But somehow, I was on the side of a mountain in D.C. (where there are no mountains, by the way) and I jumped off. Don't know why, but I believed I could fly.

Still, I felt so free and alive. It was so real. I could feel the breeze and my heart raced as I floated above Anacostia Park, across the river and over the Nationals' baseball stadium, over toward the Capitol. I woke up before I could get to the Washington Monument, and I was irritated that it was a dream.

But Moses needed to go out for a walk, and he let me know it by making some sort of sound that was a cross between a whine and howling. Instinctively, I knew what it meant.

So I made my way out of the bed, made a quick bathroom run and took Moses on his leash outside. I watched him run around as my mind wandered to what I had experienced over the course of that day. It was wild, to say the least, and it ended with the love of my life lying in bed waiting for me to return to her.

That thought brought a smile to my face. I rubbed Moses' back and talked to him. "Hey, man, it's been a good day. I feel bad you lost whoever you were with. But I got you. Gonna take great care of you."

He just looked at me and wagged his tail. As we headed back to our room, which was about two hundred yards from the little grassy area where we walked, Moses began barking. I hadn't heard him so animated. So I knew something was wrong. And sure enough, I looked up and ten feet away was a woman, a white woman, bleeding from her lip, with her blouse ripped.

I looked around before approaching her. Before I could ask if I could help her, she said, "Please. Please help me. Can you take me away from here? Please. He's going to come out here soon."

"What's going on?"

"Do you have a room? Can I go into your room and make a phone call? Please?"

Last thing I needed was this white woman in my room, bloodied, when the police came. But I never had the heart to not help. Especially then.

"Come on," I said. We walked hurriedly and I repeatedly looked over my shoulder. I didn't know whom she was running from and I didn't want to know.

I looked down at Moses and it looked like he was telling me, *Don't do it.* But it was too late. I was committed.

When I opened the door, Kathy was startled to see the woman. She pulled the bed sheets up to her neck. "What . . . what's going on? Who's this?"

I hadn't asked the woman her name.

"She's in trouble and needs some help," I said.

"Help? What's going on?"

"I . . . my friend, we had a fight and —"

Before she could finish, there were several

loud bangs on the door, the way cops do when you don't need them.

"Oh, god, it's him," the woman said.

"Kathy, go in the bathroom and lock the door. Call nine-one-one," I said. I was remarkably calm considering I had no idea who was on the other side of the door and what trouble awaited us.

"Open the fucking door," the man yelled. "I saw you take her in there. Tracy, get your ass out here."

I walked toward the door. "No," Kathy said. "Calvin, I'm calling the police. Don't open that door."

"It's OK," I said and flung open the door.

The man tried to push his way in. He was white, too, with dirty blond hair strewn all over his head. And he was obviously drunk. I blocked him from entering.

"Hey, man, that's my girlfriend. This has nothing to do with you. Now get out of my way."

Then he stepped back and pulled out a gun. Pointed it right at my face. I moved aside.

"Fucking nigger," he said as he stormed in.

And that word enraged me. I had been called that twice before: Once in Boston by a cab driver who was upset that I would not tip him after he damn near killed me and my daughter, driving in and out of traffic like a lunatic. He was smart enough to wait until I got out of the car to yell it at me. I was so angry I began to sweat.

The other time was when I ordered a pizza when staying at a hotel in New Jersey. The guy came late and had an attitude. I told him to "slow down" when he rushed me. He said, "Man, just give me the money."

Later that night, the phone in my room rang. I answered and heard someone laughing. I asked who it was and he said, "This is the white boy calling you a nigger."

Again, I fumed. I could tell from the noise in the background that it was the pizza shop. Plus, no one had the number at the hotel to call me. I got dressed and found the store, but it had already closed. But that moment stuck with me.

Now here was this guy, with a gun, calling me that word. I had no fear, only anger. The word, used with venom, meant the ultimate insult, coming from a white man. I wanted to strangle him.

"Nigger? Is that what you said to me?"

The man turned around.

"Timmy," the woman called out.

"Shut up," he said to her then turned back to me with the gun pointed at me. "You got a problem with that?"

"Yeah, I have a problem with that. You're a woman-beater and a racist. What if I called you cracker or poor white trash?"

"What if I shot you in the face?"

"You'd still be a woman-beating cracker, poor-white-trash racist."

Moses started barking and he pointed the gun at my dog.

"Hey, what are you doing? You're that much of a punk to shoot my dog?"

"Punk?"

"Timmy," the woman tried to intervene. "Let's just go."

"The police are on the way," Kathy chimed in.

The man reached into his back pocket and pulled out a badge. "I *am* the police."

"And you're calling citizens 'nigger'? And threatening to shoot me in the face? That's exactly why we had all these unarmed black men shot by cops. *You're* the reason why. Racist bastard."

"I can arrest you anytime I want." The gun was still pointed at my face.

"I should make a citizen's arrest of your racist ass. How many black men have you killed and lied that your life felt threatened? Look, if you're going to shoot me, do it. Otherwise, get that gun outta my face."

"Come on, Timmy, let's go. Please," the woman said. She turned to me. "I'm sorry you got caught up into this. Thanks for trying to help."

This guy, Timmy, and I stared at each other, the gun still pointed at me.

"Timmy — Tiny Tim — you'd better use this moment to change your life. You're an officer of the law and you're pointing a gun at me, calling me 'nigger' because I was trying to help a woman who needed help, a woman you beat up? Really? Am I threatening your life? This is where the system has gone wrong. You guys —"

"Calvin, just let them go," Kathy interjected.

"He can go whenever he likes. But since he's still here, pointing a gun at me, I should be able to speak as I'd like. Think about all the cases, Kathy — and you, too, Timmy — of black men being killed by police for no reason: choked, shot in the back, shot in front of Walmart, shot in a park with a toy gun. Near Atlanta, a man who served his country, Anthony Hill, suffered from post-war stress in Iraq, was naked and obviously disturbed. Instead of getting help, a cop shot him.

"You guys pull out your gun and start shooting as the first response instead of valuing human life. Do you understand how precious it is to live? I know how precious life is. You know what you do to families when you just shoot and kill someone? You've got to stop this. *You.* Get that gun outta my face and figure out a better way to police, because pointing a gun at someone isn't it."

I was as clear and calm in my thoughts as I have ever been. I was not afraid of that man shooting me.

"Tim, baby, let's go," the woman said, slowly pulling down his arm and the gun away from my face.

"And you can't let him beat on you like it's a sport," Kathy said to the woman as they headed out. "He's not going to stop if you don't leave."

The woman looked back at Kathy for a second and they continued out of the door. Kathy rushed over and shut the door and locked it. She turned to run into my arms, but I was already down on the floor, holding Moses. I could tell she was taken aback.

"Are you crazy? Do you want to die? That man could have killed you. You put your life in the hands of some drunk lunatic."

"I didn't. My life is in God's hands."

Her shoulders slumped. She didn't know what to think. I put down Moses and hugged her. "We're protected by God," I said softly into her ear. "You know I'm not the most religious guy in the world. But my life has changed knowing it's ending."

"What am I going to do with you?" she said. "What am I going to do without you?"

"You're going to do what you told that woman to do just now. You told her she had to leave or the abuse will continue. Well, that same thing applies to you."

She didn't say anything, but she nodded her head. I led her to a chair alongside the bed. She wiped her face as I provided Moses with a little water and food. It was almost five thirty in the morning. I called the police and told them about the racist cop name Timmy and his girlfriend Tracy. That would be enough for them to find him. I was not going to let him get away with pointing a gun at me and, as an officer, calling me a racial slur.

Kathy agreed he had to be dealt with. And then she moved onto more pressing matters. "So, when will I see you again? How are we going to do this, Calvin? What are we going to do?"

"I'm going to be in Atlanta for several weeks for these treatments. I'm hoping they will minimize the pain that I get every so often and at least clear out some of the bad shit in me. So, I don't know what your situation is, but you can definitely come visit me whenever you like."

"I will have some freedom because the kids are out of school soon and then actually go to a few camps. One is in Birmingham, Alabama, and I would drive right through Atlanta to get them there. I can see you on the way to dropping them off and the way back. Instead of coming back here, I can just stay there with you, if that's OK."

"OK, sounds good." That was being optimistic. I wasn't sure how I'd feel like after the treatments or if I just wanted to explore Atlanta on my own. But I knew how much I cared about Kathy, so I was far more for her coming than against. Still, she was married. There was no way around that.

CHAPTER EIGHTEEN: ROAD TRIP

On the way to the airport to pick up the rental car, Kathy and I did not talk much. I reflected on that gun being pointed at me. I knew I would not have handled that the same if I did not know I was going to die. I surely would have been scared to death.

Growing up in Southeast D.C. exposed me to a lot of stuff. But I never had a gun pointed at me. The way I dealt with that cop made me want to seek therapy. He could have shot me right where I stood. Was I on some kind of a death wish? Was I in some twisted state of daring death?

It made me pause because staring into the barrel of a gun directed at your face and feeling no fear was not normal.

"Kathy, let me ask you something. Did you think I wanted that guy to shoot me this morning?"

"What? Wanted him to shoot you?"

"Yeah. I mean, I didn't flinch or try to

move from the gun. He pointed it at me and I just stood there."

"Why, because of your condition, you think you're not afraid of death anymore?"

"I don't know because I really have been afraid of death. You're seeing me now, months later. When I learned there was nothing they could do for me, I was a total wreck. Couldn't eat, couldn't think. Just scared. I realized after about two weeks of barely eating, sleeping much of the day and crying that I was still alive. I was going to die, but I hadn't yet. *Pull yourself together, man.* And I did.

"But now, I'm feeling like I'm at a different place, where, if I die, it doesn't matter how it happens. So if it happens while trying to save a woman from getting beaten, so be it. I wouldn't want you or Moses to see me get shot, but at that time I was doing more than trying to help that woman — I was challenging my fear of death."

"Damn, Calvin. I'm so afraid for you. If that's true, I'm afraid for what could happen. You shouldn't challenge death. You're still here. You look great. You're feeling OK, I guess. So let's make the most of it. Let's live. That should be your goal. Not challenging death because you know you're dying."

"Is that why you were crying in bed last night?"

She paused. "I was crying because, as much as my marriage is messed up and over, I broke a vow. I was crying because I should have never let us grow apart a long time ago. I was crying because I loved how wonderful it felt to again be in your arms. And, I cried because I don't want you to die."

"Yeah, well, I've cried enough for both of us. Now I've got to live."

"But living isn't challenging death, you know? I need you to be around . . . as long as you can."

"We want the same thing, Kathy. No doubt."

The rest of the ride was in silence. When we arrived at the Hertz, I gathered my and Moses' things and held Kathy in my arms.

"It has been great seeing you again, being around you. I missed you more than I realized."

"Same here. But I will see you again . . . soon. I'll come to Atlanta."

"Before you do, take this. You can't open it until you get home. Promise me that."

It was a card I had purchased at Walmart — with a check made out to her for $50,000. That's not life-changing money on the surface, but for what Kathy faced, it was a way to get from under some bills and find a better life, if she so chose.

I smiled to myself thinking about her expression once she opened the envelope. Moses and I jumped on Interstate 85 South, a straight shot into Atlanta. My first appointment was two days away, and I was actually more frightened than I was excited about it.

Having to take the treatments only reminded me of death, more than of making life better. That was part of the extreme mental struggle that came with knowing there was nothing that could save your life.

After making love to Kathy, I had the best sleep I had since I learned my fate. Most nights, sleeping was something that happened because it was supposed to happen, meaning it came after I was exhausted. It seemed I didn't sleep for a week in the beginning. I just couldn't. Fear ruled.

Love is a powerful force, though. I only experienced it once, with Kathy, and it consumed me. Now that I'm forty-five and dying, it made me sad to know that the other relationships I had with women were something less. Actually, it was less about them than it was about me. To receive love you have to be open to love.

I was so in love with Kathy that twenty years of relationships with other women was just about holding a place until she and I got back together. I didn't know that then. But after one day together, it was all so clear to me.

Knowing my time is coming has given me more clarity about most everything. Things I thought I understood about others and me or never understood all came into focus.

For instance, my daughter's mother, Skylar. I always thought her animosity toward me was about wanting a relationship with me after our child was born. I know now that it was my ego. She just wanted a family for her child.

I realize that as Moses and I took the drive to Atlanta. Skylar texted me, saying "I hope you're hanging in there." That forced me to think about her and my first thoughts went to her upbringing.

She was raised by her mother after her father left home one day when she was four, and became the victim of a drunk driver. In our good, close times, she talked about how hard it was on her to not have her father, how not having the family structure impacted who she became as a young lady in the dating world.

She told me once, "I was jealous when I'd

see my cousins playing with their daddy or my classmates' mothers and fathers at school events. It was just my mom, who sometimes had to work, and me, and it'd be just me and a neighbor who would pick me up. I'd feel so empty. So, when I got older and started developing, men would notice me and I embraced it."

Skylar then told me something that stunned me. "I was involved in a big scandal. I was dating the assistant basketball coach. He was my history teacher, and he gave me attention and was kind to me and patient with me in class. One day, he said, 'What do you do for fun? There's a play at a small theater downtown that you should see. I have a ticket that I could leave for you. You can call it extra credit for the class.'

"I was young and dumb. Seventeen. I wanted the extra credit and went to the theater. I got to my seat and then, a minute later, Mr. Randon came in and sat beside me. I was surprised; I didn't know he would be there. I told him that. And he said, 'What kind of a date would it be if you were to sit here alone?'

"I was shocked, but flattered. He was a handsome man, and there were many girls in my class who used to say how much they liked him or would date him. And there I

257

was sitting there on a date with him. It only led to so much trouble.

"We messed around for about two months. That night after the play, he took me to a restaurant, some place that was beautiful and romantic. We ate dinner. I asked if I could have some wine and he told me I was too young to drink — at a restaurant — but that he had some pretty good wine at his house.

"I know it was stupid, but I loved the attention from a man and I went with him to his house. He got the wine out and, to his credit, said, 'I don't know if you should have this. Alcohol makes people do things they don't want to do.' And my dumb behind said, 'Anything I do, I will want to do it.' So, we drank and I got more loose and free and he started complimenting me and the next thing I know, we were in his bed.

"So, every week for about two months I would go see him. Having a man care about me made me feel wanted and loved. But it all blew up because I had a boyfriend. We took Mr. Randon's class together. And me being a silly girl, I wrote a note to him saying I couldn't make it to his house that night we had planned, but the next night would be good.

"Well, my boyfriend, Lee, saw the note. It

was in my backpack and he went in there to get a book of his that I had and he found it. He was mad and he took the note to the principal. And all hell broke loose. It was all in the papers and on TV. Mr. Randon was fired. Even though they didn't release my name, people knew it was me. It was totally embarrassing. I had to transfer schools. It was a rough time. And I trace that back to not having a man in my life as I was growing up."

When she told me that so many years ago, I dismissed it as making an excuse for being a too fast. I couldn't see beyond my disappointment. Now, because I'm forced to look at myself, who I *really* am, what my life really has been, I can see Skylar's view or at least accept that she needed a father in her life — and that her anger with me was not about me not wanting her but more about not wanting Maya to have the same feelings she had.

Believe it or not, I shared much of this with my new dog, Moses, as we drove along. Instead of questioning my sanity, I instead reasoned that Moses was a good listener and I needed to share it with someone who would listen and not interrupt.

In my honest moments, though, I did wonder if I were cracking up. I mean, I detested dogs, but there I was with a stray one who I had grown to need in a day. I glanced over at Moses, sitting upright in the passenger seat, and he seemed so content and at peace. He looked out the window and looked at me and it was just a happy place for both of us.

Moses distracted me from my life. He gave me a purpose, which I definitely felt I had lost once I was told I was going to die. My daughter was doing great and didn't really need me anymore. Well, not that she didn't need me, but she could function without me. It wasn't like she was six or seven and needed me to show or teach her things. She had already reached that point where she had flipped the script and began telling me things I didn't know and teaching me things. I was proud of that. But it also took on a bigger meaning when I got my diagnosis. She didn't need me to survive.

As I was dying, I needed someone to need me. And then along came Moses, as if sent by God. It was strange for a dog to be at that hotel parking lot, looking battered, no one looking for it. A strong feeling came over me to care for him, and that responsibility gave me life, even as my life was slipping away.

I needed the responsibility of something.

School was out, so there was no teaching to be done. Plus, I wasn't sure I could concentrate on a curriculum anyway. Caring for Moses did not require deep thought, but it did give me responsibility and something to live for, crazy as that might sound. The dog needed me. I needed the dog.

When we got deep into South Carolina, I asked Moses, "You need to take a leak?" He stood up and wagged his tail. I didn't know what that meant — how could he understand me? — but I took it to mean he did. So, we pulled over at a rest area.

I put him on his leash and we found an open area for him to stretch his legs and roam free. I got so much joy out of seeing that puppy bounce around in the grass without a care in the world. Making sure he was happy took my mind off of my troubles.

I decided we'd stop for about ten minutes and then continue our trek. I sat on the hood of the car and responded to text messages and e-mails as Moses ran around the small field. After a few minutes, I looked up and the people who got out of a car that had pulled up several spaces to our left had a dog, too. A dog bigger than Moses, and the woman immediately let her dog off its leash.

And the dog immediately took off for

Moses. My heart practically burst out of my chest. *This big dog was about to eat my dog.* That's all I could think. I hated and really was afraid of dogs, but I bounded off that car hood with no hesitation and charged toward Moses as I yelled for the other dog to stop and the owner to stop it.

"Hey, hey, get back! Get your dog!"

The woman screamed for him to stop, but the dog plowed on. He got to Moses before I did, and went for him with his mouth open. Moses acted like a running back, and eluded him with a swift sidestep, and the big dog went sliding by.

That gave me enough time to scoop up Moses with my left hand and slash that dog across his face with Moses' leash as he came back toward us. "Get back," I yelled again. He whimpered away.

The woman was irate. "You have no right to hit my dog."

"Did you see what was happening? He was going to hurt *my* dog. You think I was going to allow that? You should control your dog."

The woman's husband came over. He was slightly bigger than me but he didn't know I had nothing to lose. Before he could say something, I said, "Man, don't come over here like you're going to do something. You need to control your dog."

"You need to control *yourself.* What if I hit your dog?"

"If my dog was attacking your dog, then you'd have every right to protect your dog. But that wasn't the case. You have a much bigger dog — damn near a pony — who was not coming over to play with mine. So, I'm not sure what you wanted me to do. What if I didn't get there in time? What do you think would have happened?"

The man was stumped, I think — I didn't wait around for his response. I took Moses to the car and we left. But my heart was pounding. I was so scared that something was going to happen to him. And I could feel the fear in Moses' little body as I held him against mine. He'd already been in a fight, from the look of things, the day I found him.

I drove with my left hand and rubbed his back with my right. "It's OK, Moses. You're safe. I'm not going to let anything happen to you."

He seemed to calm down before I did. I turned on some soothing jazz and rubbed my dog for the next several miles. It scared me to think how I would have felt if Moses had been hurt.

CHAPTER NINETEEN:
YOU CAN FIND ME IN THE A

We pulled into Atlanta around one o'clock Saturday afternoon — and hit traffic as if it were a weekday. I had heard that Atlanta's traffic was as bad as D.C.'s, and it was no exaggeration. It was bumper-to-bumper from Jimmy Carter Boulevard in Gwinnett County all the way to the Lenox Road exit. I changed my reservation from the W in Buckhead to the Residence Inn on Piedmont Avenue to accommodate Moses.

My GPS got us to the hotel with no problem. I had not traveled much in my life and even with all I had heard about Atlanta, I had not visited. So, there was a level of excitement about finally arriving.

I left Moses in the car as I checked into the hotel. Our room was open, which I liked because it gave Moses some room to roam. I noticed that he seemed so happy and free. The change in just a day was significant. The way he looked at me told me I had taken on a real responsibility.

I found an area that would be Moses' to enjoy. I figured he was hungry, so I put out some food and water and placed his toys nearby. We would be there at least three weeks, so I wanted to establish boundaries. I wasn't even sure if that was possible with a dog. But I knew I didn't want him thinking he could get into the bed with me or climb up on the table.

But the strangest thing happened: I wasn't sure what to do after I finally got to Atlanta. It was Saturday afternoon; my treatment was on Monday. I unpacked, got Moses settled and sat on the bed uncertain of my next move.

Finally, I realized I had not eaten all day. My appetite had all but evaporated, especially after I started having those excruciating moments when my stomach felt like it was going to explode. But I actually had a bit of an appetite, so I took a shower to freshen up. Then I got on the computer and searched for some place I could have a nice meal and kinda feel the city.

I found a place called Negril Village. I checked out the menu and decided on the Ginger Lime Brick Chicken. I had to return Kathy's call first. She had called me three times and texted twice, too.

"Why didn't you answer your phone?"

"I was driving, listening to music, talking to Moses . . . didn't hear it."

"Well, are you in Atlanta?"

"Yes, we made it fine. No problems. Took our time and enjoyed the ride. Hit a little traffic when we got close to the city, but we're settled in the room. I apologize. Just wanted to concentrate and make it a peaceful ride."

"Well, you know why I have been trying to reach you."

"You miss me?"

"Very funny. I do miss you, but, Calvin. You gave me a check for fifty thousand dollars. I can't take this."

"Why not? I want you to have it. You need it. It's a gift."

"But Calvin . . . My mouth just flew open when I looked at that check."

"Listen, Kathy, you deserve to be happy. That's what that check says. That's what it represents — an opportunity to be happy."

"I don't know what to do."

"If you really want to be free of your marriage, take your time. Make an exit plan. Pay off your bills. Find some place to live. Find the peace that you deserve. You know that I know better than most people: Life is short."

"I don't even know how to thank you."

"Find your peace. That's the thanks I need."

"I will do just that. I promise, Calvin."

"OK, well, I'm about to get something to eat."

"Do you know that Jerry Lantham lives in Atlanta?"

"Jerry from D.C., from back in the day?"

"Yes. He's my friend on Facebook. I have his number. You should call him."

I took Jerry's number and called him immediately. He was a former teacher who I liked a lot. He quit teaching out of frustration and went into pharmaceutical sales. I lost his number when I lost my cell phone at a Wizards game.

"Yo, what's up?" Jerry said when I identified myself. "Where the hell you been, man?"

"Nowhere, really," I said. "Still teaching at Ballou. You know how it is. Same ole, same ole."

"We've got to connect. Where you staying? How long you here? What you doing now?"

He was excited.

"I'm staying in Buckhead. About to head out to get something to eat."

"You should come to this spot, Suite

Lounge. It's a day party going on. It's a good look. Plenty of honeys."

"Suite Lounge? OK, I'll look it up and head down there."

We coordinated to meet at the front door. I put on some nice linen. Moses watched as I got dressed. He knew I was leaving him.

"Buddy, I'm going to hang out a little, see Atlanta. Live life. I will walk you first and then you can just relax until I get back. I won't be long. OK?"

I could not help but shake my head after I finished talking to the dog. We walked, he relieved himself and when we got back to the room, I turned on the TV to the Animal Channel, I rubbed his little body and told him, "You're my dog. See you soon."

I took a pain pill with some water. My stomach had not acted up in a few days, and I was scared to have an episode at all, but especially while out in public. I put the "Do Not Disturb" sign on the door and left.

I allowed the GPS to guide me to Suite Lounge, which was downtown. I admired the Atlanta skyline on the way. I was impressed. It felt like a big city, just as I had been told.

When I got to my destination, I let the valet park my car. There were women approaching the place from all directions, women elegant and sleazy, underdressed and overdressed. I loved the variety.

I noticed Jerry immediately. He was trying to stop a pair of attractive women who were entering the building. That's what I always liked about Jerry — he was audacious, confident and lively. He was not deterred by rejection. And he had no ambition to settle down.

He didn't notice me at first — the bald-head threw him off. But when he did, he greeted me the only way he knew how. Loudly.

"Oh, shit. Calvin! What's up, boy?" he said as we embraced. "Good to see you. Come on, let's go in and get some drinks."

I would not dare drink alcohol. Maybe I could handle it. But I felt like my stomach would catch fire.

"Man, I'm going to have water to start. Had a long night last night. Plus, I haven't eaten anything."

"I hear you."

He got a drink and I had sparkling water and we walked through the place, which was laden with people in a great mood. I looked at each of them and wondered what their life was like. They glanced at me and had no idea I was the walking dead.

"So, you just down for vacation?"

Before I could answer, he ran into some friends. They chatted for a few. He introduced me and we all moved on.

"Those guys are actually from up the way — Alexandria. We play golf sometimes. You play golf, don't you?"

"Yeah. I brought my clubs with me, too."

"That's what's up. How long you here? Maybe we can get a round in."

"I'm here for about three weeks."

"Oh, you're on a serious vacation. Cool. I'm a member of Canongate/Club Corp. Plenty of great courses to play here. I'll let you know when I can play. You used to play with Walter, right?"

"Yes. You heard?"

"Heard what?"

"About Walter. He killed himself."

"What? You're bullshitting me. Why?"

"Turns out, he was troubled. Bipolar. I found him hanging in his garage."

"Oh, shit. Man, that's crazy. You found him? Damn. I'd be having nightmares about that shit forever."

If only he knew. As awful and haunting as that was, that was not the biggest worry in my life. I did not consider sharing that with Jerry. We were cool, but I hadn't seen him in a few years and I was not telling most people, anyway.

"Yeah, an ugly scene. I'm just sad I couldn't do anything to help my boy. That's what haunts me."

"Man, life is short. You never know what's going on in someone's life," Jerry said.

He did not realize how on point he was.

I left Jerry to go to the bathroom. I passed one attractive woman after the other on the way, and they all seemed to make eye contact. I loved women in D.C., but these women seemed more relaxed, more open to conversation, just by their body language alone.

When I returned from the bathroom, Jerry was talking to two women, both of whom looked younger, in their thirties. But super-attractive and friendly.

"This is my boy, Calvin. He's visiting from D.C."

I shook the hands of Venus, who was dark and radiant, and Natalie, who was tall and poised. If I had a choice, I would have taken both of them. They were equally beautiful and engaging. But I got "chose," as we said back at home. Venus started a conversation with me.

"After I left Louisville, I moved to D.C. for three years," she said, moving over to me and away from Natalie and Jerry. "I liked it up there, but it's expensive. And I'm from Atlanta, so this is home for me."

"I'm almost ashamed to say this is my first visit to Atlanta; just got here about two hours ago," I said. "But I'm feeling it so far."

"What are you going to do while you're here?"

"Whatever you'd like."

That would never come out of my mouth in the past. But the nothing-to-lose me just let it fly.

"Really? How do you know you want to do something with me? We just met."

"That's true. Well, I'll rescind the statement if you turn out to be crazy."

She laughed. "Oh, it's like that? OK, well, I have the right to decide if I want to do anything with you after we talk."

We both laughed. "What's there fun to do here? And don't ask me what I like to do. What's fun to you?"

"If you want to hang out and be around people, there's Magnum Mondays at STK, late night at the Red Martini on Tuesdays, Wednesdays at Boogalou's, Thursdays Do, Fridays the Gold Room. Is that enough for you?"

"I see who the party animal is," I cracked.

"No, don't think that. I'm just in-the-know."

272

We laughed again and talked about so much over the next thirty minutes. I even found myself sipping on a rum and Coke. Venus was beautiful, smart, charming and she drank bourbon. Total turn on that a woman could be totally feminine but still sip on what's considered a man's drink — and maintain her softness.

Jerry and Natalie had disappeared by the time Venus and I stopped talking. We went upstairs to the deck that provided an stunning view of the skyline. My drink went down smoothly, without complications. We had some appetizers. There I was with a pretty woman feeling like the world was mine to be had.

It was just then that I came back to my sad reality. Venus was so lovely and funny and likeable that she took me away from my troubles. And then all that good feeling I had blew away like the Atlanta pollen in a breeze.

She noticed.

"What's wrong?"

"I almost wish I hadn't met you."

She was taken aback. "Why? What is it? You're married?"

"Married? No, never been married. I wish that were it. That would be easier to deal with."

"Wait. Are you telling me you're gay?"

"No, I'm not *gay*. I have heard you all have a large gay community here. Not me . . . No, I'm sick. Really sick."

"What's wrong?"

I could barely believe I was going to tell this stranger my most intimate secret.

"Cancer," I said, looking into her eyes. "Terminal."

"What? Oh, my God. Calvin, are you serious?"

"Too serious."

"I don't know what to say. I don't want to get too personal. I'm just shocked. You look healthy."

"You know, for the most part, I feel healthy. It's some kind of cancer in my stomach. It's rare. Nothing they can do to stop it from spreading. So, I'm just trying to live, you know? Do some things that I probably wouldn't have ordinarily done."

"I am so sorry. I hope it's OK to ask, but how do you do it? How do you not let it keep you down?"

"Well, this is one of the good days. Not every day is like this. I spend most days trying to, as they say, get my affairs in order. Some days I'm too confused to do much of anything. Some days I'm productive. But lately I've been kind of just going with the flow. I was diagnosed around two months ago. I'm getting better at handling it."

"I admire you. I don't think most people would be at day party, looking good and acting like nothing is wrong."

"That may be true, but I've learned that you never can tell. I've also learned that if you decide to live your life, all kinds of things start to happen. I had a good life, just not that exciting. I was content doing very little. Once my attitude changed, it's been a different world for me."

"You mean in a good way?"

"In a way that's more exciting and more interesting. Crazy stuff has happened. I found a friend who had committed suicide. I helped save a man's life. I found a stray dog and took him in. I saved my new dog from being devoured by a big German Shepherd. Oh, and I met this lovely young lady named Venus."

She smiled. "All that really happened?"

"In the last week or so. It's been *that* crazy. And now I'm here to get some holistic treatments. Probably three weeks of treatments. Maybe they can stop the attacks of pain I get every so often. After that, I have no idea."

"You said you found a dog?"

"Yeah, Moses. He's at the hotel. Found

him yesterday. But here's the thing, Venus — I don't like dogs. At all. And now, in a day, I love this dog. He just popped up out of nowhere. I was in a hotel parking lot in Charlotte. He was just standing there, looking scared and beaten. It's like God placed him there. It was an industrial area. There were no homes around. No reason for a little dog to be there. No leash. No nametag. He was there for me. I felt that. I never felt that way about a dog before. So I took him in. And in one day I have grown close to this little puppy — a dark brown Labrador Retriever."

Then I did something a parent would. I pull out my cell phone to show photos of Moses to Venus.

"He's so cute. And it's cute that you're showing him off."

"I guess this is part of the new me."

"Well, I didn't know the old you, but I'm glad to know this version of you," Venus said.

"You know, I haven't told many people about my situation. I didn't even tell Jerry. It's not something you tell everybody, I don't think. But I don't know . . . I felt comfortable with sharing it with you. I think my senses have gotten keener since I learned about . . . about this. And I'm feeling good vibes from you."

"I'm glad you said that. I was enjoying our conversation before you told me about what you're dealing with."

"But sense then?"

"Sense you told me, it's been probably the most interesting conversation I've had in a long time, maybe ever. You really amaze me that you could be here, talking to me and acting like you have no cares in the world. I just couldn't do it."

"Yes, you could. I think we just do what we have to do. That's what it comes down to. The first two weeks after I learned that there was nothing they could do, I could hardly move. I was so scared — I'm still scared. I just don't think about it as much as I used to. Things are happening — like meeting you — that help me take my mind off of it. That's what I need."

Just then, Jerry and Natalie came over. "So y'all up here enjoying the view. That's what's up," Jerry said. "Man, you're gonna love Atlanta. Dude just got here and already met a dime."

"Two dimes I said," acknowledging Natalie. "I'm glad I came out."

"Me, too," Venus said. "I'm really glad we met."

"I'm going to head out," I said.

"What? You only been here an hour," Jerry said.

"I have my dog at the hotel. It's like a kid — can't leave him but for so long."

Jerry and I shared a manly handshake. I extended my hand to Natalie, and she placed hers in mind and we shook. Then I turned to Venus. Without hesitation, she hugged me. Tightly.

"Damn, dog," Jerry chimed in. "What were y'all talking about up here?"

Neither of us said anything. "Put my number in your phone," Venus said. She recited it and I programmed it. "Now call me, so I can have your number."

I did. "I will see you later. Soon," she said. The way she looked at me, I couldn't tell if she liked me or if she felt sorry for me — or some mixture of both.

And I did not feel the need to tell her to keep my situation to herself. I took from her character that she would not share it with Natalie or anyone else. She had a sincere spirit.

I smiled and walked away, feeling revived having met Venus but sad that the meeting, in the long run, did not mean much because there *was* no long run.

Chapter Twenty: Black Lives Matter

On my way back to the hotel, I listened to talk radio about the protests around the country over young black men being killed by police. It was a disturbing conversation because here I was trying to build a life before a disease ended it, and consistently there were black men shot and killed by the people designated to protect them.

On the program, they brought up Anthony Hill, the former Army veteran who was naked and obviously disturbed — and unarmed — and yet was shot and killed about twenty minutes from where I was driving, in Decatur. He suffered from a post-war trauma syndrome that apparently made him hallucinate. He fought for his country in the Middle East and died ignobly in Georgia because a cop decided to kill him instead of apprehending him and getting him help.

I thought about Trayvon Martin and Michael Brown, Eric Garner and Tamir Rice, Akai Gurley and Kajieme Powell, Ezell Ford and Tyree Wilson and Freddie Gray and on and on. They had their lives taken from them unnecessarily, violently, by white men. I was never big on pulling the race card or conspiracy theories. But for so many black people to die so violently by whites who are supposed to protect during President Obama's terms didn't seem like a coincidence anymore.

I didn't believe that theory, but hadn't thought that way until I listened to talk radio. My eyes and mind were open to new possibilities, and some of that was not comforting. The police, by and large, were the enemy, and there was a bullet with my name on it if I was in the wrong place at the wrong time or said the wrong thing or dressed the wrong way.

It could have happened in Charlotte. That cop could have shot me, planted evidence, said he felt I was a threat to his life and likely never see a day in prison.

It was a place I didn't want to be. I had so much life to live, and I felt that way even more after taking the attitude that I needed to actually live life instead of riding the wave of life. That passive approach did not serve me well. It was safe but uninspiring. Unfulfilled.

It made me sad that I had to learn I was losing my life to begin *living* my life. With that I knew that I had to do as Pastor Henson said: Help others.

I was not going to try to save the world, but I had a responsibility to be a positive influence when I could, and in different ways. That approach opened me up to an entirely new life.

Here I was leaving a party and Venus, a woman of substance, because I had a dog cooped up in a hotel room. It very well could have been a luxury resort to Moses. What did he know? But my affection for him could not allow me to have fun believing he was tortured. I got that from my momma.

When I finally made it through Atlanta's traffic downtown, I hurried to the room. I was excited to see my dog. And there was Moses, sitting in the area I had laid out for him. He either understood what I conveyed to him or he was the best dog ever. Either way, I was so happy with him, partly because he seemed happy to see me and partly because he was comforting company. He represented life to me.

So I rubbed him as he wiggled in my

arms, tail wagging. I had to calm him down. I grabbed his leash and we went for a walk and stayed outside on the property almost until sunset. I wanted to tire him out a little because I was tired.

The lack of rest the night before, the ride to Atlanta and then hanging out had gotten to me. And it was like Moses knew it.

When we got back into the room, he went right to his area and looked over at me, as if to say, *I'm good. You get your rest.* At least, that's how I took it.

So, I got dressed for bed, although it was just a little before nine at night. I pulled out my laptop and tried to catch up on what was going on in the world, knowing reading would make me sleepy.

But I ran across a story that almost gave me chills. It was about a kid in Virginia who had told his parents when he was six that he had been on earth before as a man. More than that, he gave his profession (a Hollywood agent) and the year — in the 1940s. The parents, scared and curious, did the research and found the man their son described. His life story fit every description their son had told them, from his name, age, profession, where he lived and how he died.

The child said the man was seventy-one

when he died. The newspaper from that time published that he was sixty-nine. But further research found that he had given an inaccurate year of birth — by two years, making him seventy-one as the child had said.

Experts said there were thousands of cases where reincarnation was a viable explanation for someone — usually a child — being able to give details about events long before they were born. There was no other explanation.

I looked at Moses and wondered if he was so smart and well-mannered because he had been here before. *Did he really understand me?* My mind ran amok. I wondered if I were to come back, to be reincarnated, would I remember all this. The newspaper story said the boy's memory began to fade as he got older.

I believed the article wholeheartedly. Something changes in you when you know you're going to die. This kind of knowing is different from knowing that we all *eventually* will die. When your ticket has been stamped, you become the keenest person on earth. You notice everything and everyone.

Funny thing was, that was just called living. The people who get the most out of life are the keenest and the ones who decide to live it. You do that, and you will notice more than the next person and experience more than the average person. You'll consume everything and retain a lot of it — and become stronger, smarter and more well-rounded because of it.

I loved being a teacher because I love knowing things and sharing them with kids. But it became my world when *the world* should have been my world. I finally got that.

My friend Kevin got it. And he got that I was not doing enough, that I needed to do more than teach and golf. That's why he wrote me that letter. That's why he gave me his kidney. I didn't have that much time to live — I reluctantly accepted that. But I believed my past few weeks have made Kevin proud.

I got out my own way. I still was not sure what that exactly looked like, but I knew what it *didn't* look like. It didn't look like me staying in D.C., reading and waiting for school to start again. That was a slightly exaggerated portrait of my unfulfilled, uninteresting life. But the point was I could have and should have done more.

I was different from the black men who were slain by cops. They did not get the chance to realize that life could be better and to do something about it. Their lives were abruptly taken from them. That was the other part that was sad about cops killing unarmed black men: They were young and the world was in front of them.

I wanted to go to one of those cities — Ferguson or New York or Cleveland or Baltimore — and march with the protesters. As much as they understood the value of life and as angry as they were about the killings, I was probably more understanding of the value of life while also angry. We should all get to live out our lives, make our mistakes, correct them, grow from them and take a place in the world that was ours to mold and shape.

Having it stripped from you — by a bullet or by a disease — just wasn't right.

CHAPTER TWENTY-ONE: THE MAN ON THE STREET

Those were my last thoughts before I dozed off, which likely accounted for the dream I had of being hunted by Atlanta police. They wanted me for driving in an HOV lane with no passengers in the car. I pulled over and the cops immediately had their guns drawn.

In the dream, I pulled out my gun and pointed it at them.

"You don't get it; I'm dying. You think I'm worried about you shooting me? So pull the trigger. You can't kill a man who's already dead — not even with a bullet."

And so the officer pointed the gun right at me and said, "Have it your way." And pulled the trigger. I stuck out my chest and took the bullet. It was so vivid that I could feel the pain — or at least I thought I could. I didn't go down. I laughed at the officers and they riddled me with shots. I had taken away their power because I wasn't scared.

Without a gun, many police officers had

all the power of a limp noodle. In the dream, I shouted, "Black Lives Matter," and they stopped firing. And I felt so empowered.

Of course, I was disappointed when I woke up and I saw a dog sitting there watching TV. I was in bed with my laptop having fallen off to the side.

It was an intense dream, but I had gotten used to intense dreams. There was a time when I didn't even want to go to sleep — every dream I had was about death. And not just my death, but just about anyone I knew.

When I dreamed I was at my daughter's funeral, that's when I was afraid to go to sleep. *That* scared me. That *shook* me. For all I felt about my own eventual demise, it was Maya who I worried about. I woke up from that dream so frightened that I was unable to go back to sleep. It was about two in the morning and I lay in bed, my heart pounding, for at least a half-hour before I could calm down.

Finally, I was able to gather myself, but only after I had texted Maya. I wasn't sure if she was up at that early-morning hour or if my text awoke her, but she texted me right back. "Daddy, I'm great. Just a couple more days and I will be there. Now go to sleep.

Can't believe you're up at this hour."

Those words eased my mind. My life had been committed to protecting her. We had come to rely on each other. Wherever I was going in death, I could not imagine it would be better without my Maya.

Thinking about her could make me cry. I cried at the thought of being without her; and I thought of how hurt she would be without me. That hurt me.

She loved her mother, looked like her and, at times I couldn't stand, even acted like her. But she was a daddy's girl. We connected from the moment she was born. I took her to her doctor's appointments when she was a newborn. I took her to the park, to school, to school with me.

I taught her how to play golf and basketball and how to drive. We went to the park together, to the movies, to restaurants. When she was ten, she ordered filet mignon — and sent it back because she said it was not cooked enough.

She grew up to be everything I would have expected: smart, funny, caring, kind. That attitude she could have sometimes when she did not get her way, well, I could have done without that. She was spoiled and it was my fault. But she was as much a part of any happiness I had as anything.

My only concern was that she was like me in that she was not as social or adventurous as she needed to be. How would a good man find her if she didn't make herself available?

Of course, when I brought it up to her, she didn't want to talk about it. "Daddy, I'm fine. I have more going on in my social life than you."

I did not believe her, but I never pushed Maya, either. I just shared my views and hoped that they stuck with her and she applied whatever I said that made sense.

It spooked me a little when she called me on my cell just as I was thinking of her. That happened a lot and not just to me, but it still freaked me out a little each time it happened.

"Hi, Baby Maya."

"Really, Daddy?"

"That's my nickname for you that you used to like. You think you're too grown for your daddy to call you that?"

"I am too old for that, but I know you're going to call me that anyway. What I'd like to know is how things are going; how you're feeling."

"I'm fine. I ended up calling my friend from home, Jerry, and meeting him at a day party."

"You went to a day party?"

"I did. And I met a woman, too, thank you very much."

"Well, that's good to hear. I hope you're not doing too much, though."

"I can't do enough, Maya."

"I figured you say something like that. And I agree with you."

I knew there would be a "but" coming. "You do?" I asked.

"Yes," she said, "but there is such a thing as too much — for all of us."

"You'd rather I sit in my room with a sweater and socks on and watch old movies?"

"Once in a while, that's OK. All the stuff that has happened — Mr. Walter dying, the bus thing, finding a dog, driving to Atlanta —"

I jumped in.

"You don't even know about the battered woman I tried to protect whose boyfriend pulled a gun on us."

"What? When? And who's us? I know you're not including the dog."

"Last night — or, actually early this morning. I walked Moses and out of the blue this woman looks beaten and pops up out of nowhere — kinda like Moses did, actually — and pleaded for us to protect her. So I took her to my room and —"

"You what? You took a stranger to your room?"

"I know I taught you a long time ago to never talk to strangers, but this was different."

"That's not funny, Dad."

"You would not be proud of me if I told you I just abandoned the woman. I thought of you, actually. That, God forbid, you were in that situation and no one helped you."

"So what happened?"

"We get to the room and Kathy —"

"Wait, Kathy?"

"Yes, my old friend Kathy."

"How did she get there?"

"She lives in Charlotte and we connected after the bus thing."

"And she was in your room early this morning."

"Not that I have to explain anything to you, but yes, she spent the night. Now can I finish the story?"

Maya did not respond, so I went on.

"So her boyfriend comes banging on the door — some blonde dude who was obviously drunk."

"I'm sorry — this was a white woman?"

"Yes, Maya. Now don't interrupt me again, please . . . Kathy says she's calling the police and to not open the door. But I did anyway. So he storms in and has his gun in his hand. We go back and forth and he points the gun at my head."

"Daddy!"

"I wasn't even scared. I was calm. He pulled out his badge — he was a cop. Can you believe that? I dared him to shoot me. He finally just left. And Kathy screamed at the woman on their way out. It was crazy."

"Oh, my God. And then you drove to Atlanta with your dog and then went out to a day party and met another woman? And you don't think that's doing too much."

"Well, I'm in the bed now, so all is good and I'm going to rest tonight and tomorrow. Well, maybe tomorrow."

"Dad, I fly in tomorrow night. I land around seven."

"OK, I'll pick you up from the airport. Just text me the flight details. But I've got to go. I'm tired."

I was tired, and my stomach had begun to hurt and I didn't want Maya to know.

"I was going to tell you something."

"Tell me in person tomorrow. That's better," I said.

"OK, I guess it can wait. But Daddy, please get some rest. I love you. I love you so much."

"Yes and I love you even more, baby. Good night."

I made sure to end the call before I dropped the phone on the bed and grabbed my stomach. The pain was increasing by the second, and I had no idea how to stop it. I grabbed a pain pill from the bottle on the nightstand and in my rush to take it, fumbled it onto the floor. I grabbed another and took it — no water. Just swallowed the damned thing. Then I fell to my knees to pick up the one on the floor — I didn't want Moses to get it.

How I could think of him as the pain tore through my stomach, I had no idea. But I did not want anything to happen to him.

Meanwhile, I dropped the pill into the trashcan and tried to get back into the bed. I couldn't. My stomach was so knotted up and the pain so intense that I was powerless. I just rolled onto the floor and curled up, praying that the pain would go away.

It was so intense that my vision was blurry. It was torture. I opened my eyes to see Moses standing over me. He looked panicked. He walked away from me and then toward me, as if he were pacing. He barked at me.

The pain continued and I finally felt myself losing consciousness and that scared me. I didn't want to slip into a coma. I knew I was dying but I wasn't ready to die. I had reasons to live.

But the pain was winning, and I couldn't do anything about it. I apparently passed out, like before, only this time I woke up to Moses licking my face and bouncing his little body on me, as if he were trying to shove me to wake up. And he barked non-stop. He was trying to save me.

I still could not move much, from the pain, but I was awake.

"It's OK, buddy," I managed to get out, trying to calm him. "It's OK."

But for another few minutes, I was in too much pain to say anything beyond a moan or grunt. Moses' barking distracted me a little. And when the pain finally began to ease, Moses stopped. He could see my body uncoil and the agony on my face diminish. All that expressed relief. But I was too spent to get up.

"Moses," I said in a low, exhausted voice, "I'm good. It's OK. It's OK." He wagged his tail.

I relaxed there for another five minutes looking into the eyes of my dog. He stared back. Was he studying me? Was he gauging how bad I was feeling? Did he know how scared I was, how close to death I felt?

The other episodes scared me, but this one terrified me because I began thinking I was somehow getting better. Well, maybe not getting better, but that I would make it to my first session with the holistic lady and her enemas would get out all the bad stuff that was causing so much pain.

It also scared me because if an attack happened while I was in public, it would not be pretty. I knew then I was not leaving the room on Sunday until I went to pick up Maya from the airport. The attacks lasted several minutes, but the mental damage lasted a few days. I was suffocating in fear that it would happen again. That's why I ate so little. It wasn't because I didn't have an appetite — well, I *did* lose my appetite in the beginning, when I first learned of cancer. But after I pulled myself up and began dealing with it, I was afraid to eat more than enough to prevent drastic weight loss.

As I pulled myself off the floor and onto the bed, still holding my stomach, I wished I could see the holistic woman at that moment. The aftermath of the pain was bad, too, and I held my stomach for probably an hour. Moses looked at me with sorrowful eyes, as if he wanted to help but was helpless.

"Thank you, buddy. I know you care. I'm glad you're here. It's going to be OK."

I wanted to wash my face from him licking me, but I decided to just stay still until my stomach stopped constricting and the pain had totally gone.

I was exhausted and was easy for me to drift off into a deep sleep.

When I woke up, it was almost three in the morning. If I dreamed, I didn't remember. I was in a coma-like sleep, and it felt so good, the kind of sleep that makes you wish you didn't wake up when you did. I was stunned to see Moses staring at me.

"Have you been just sitting here all this time, man? Were you watching over me? You're such a good dog. Let's go out for a walk."

I felt significantly better. But I was still paranoid about another attack. Moses and I took a walk so he could relieve himself and then we took a trek along Piedmont Avenue. It was the end of a party night for many; people were leaving the Havana Club when we passed it. Several cute women gave Moses lots of attention.

"Oh, he's so cute. He's adorable. What's his name?"

"Moses. He's going to be a leader."

I had no idea women loved dogs so much.

Had I been thinking, I would have gotten one long ago if it was going to attract attention like that. I was not above using Moses if I had to. Just saying . . .

At that point, there was no need to attract women, although it felt great to talk to Venus and feel at least the early part of a connection to her. She was lovely — in spirit and appearance. That's what always worked for me.

Over the years teaching, I had fellow teachers from Ballou and other schools show interest and a lot of parents. And even a student once. But I would never do the unethical thing and date a parent of a student I taught, but also would never date someone just because people considered her physically attractive. That would be shallow. And maybe I was shallow about some things — where I lived, what clothes I wore, what car I drove — I was not shallow when it came to women. I needed depth. Maybe that was a reason I didn't have one that meant so much to me.

That's part of the reason Kathy stayed with me over all the years. We had a connection that was unique for me. She kept telling me, "Live your life. You're still here, aren't you? Well, that's reason to live. You have more reasons than most people to live your life without regret."

I thought about Kathy and Venus on our walk back down Piedmont to the hotel. And a smile creased my face, something I was doing more and more as I began to accept my circumstances.

My thoughts of women were interrupted when we came across a homeless man, who was walking aimlessly. Moses caught his attention, too.

"That's a Labrador Retriever," he said.

"How do you know that?"

"I had one once," he said.

"What happened to it?"

"Lost it. He was there one minute. I turned my head and he was gone. Never saw him again."

"Ah, man. That's rough. Where you going?"

"Not sure. Just walking. When I walk, I can think. Ever try it?"

"Yes, right now, in fact. But I usually don't walk this late at night. I just needed to stretch my legs as I walked Moses. Why do you walk so late?"

"Why not? I have no place to be. So I walk. When I get tired or sleepy, I find someplace to sleep."

"How do you do that? I don't mean any harm. I don't. But since we're talking, I just had to ask."

"You don't have enough time for me to tell you my story."

"I don't have anywhere to be." I had *always* wanted to get into the head of a homeless person, to find out what happened that would force him to the streets.

"I can't tell you the whole story. How old do you think I am?"

"I'm not good at that." I looked him over. He was a little taller than me, but his ragged clothes and deep wrinkles around his eyes, which seemed to be set back into his head, told of a troubled life. His shoulders were hunched and his head angled down. "You're young. Maybe fifty-five."

"You're right — you're not good at guessing. I'm forty-five."

"Oh, wow. We're the same age."

"You look a little younger than me. It's the bald head."

"So, tell me your story."

"I can't tell you the whole story. You haven't earned the whole story."

"Trust me, I'm going to help you out as much as I can."

"What do you want to know?"

"Whatever you want to tell me."

"I've been out here for four years and three months. Tried to get off the streets a year ago, but it didn't feel right. I didn't deserve it."

"Why? What happened?"

"I killed someone. A little boy."

I took a step back. I thought: *Did he just say he murdered a child?*

"You what?"

"I was driving. I wasn't drinking that time. The one time I wasn't drinking. It was raining. I was tired. And I didn't take my meds. The boy just appeared in front of me. I thought I was dreaming. I heard the noise. But when I didn't take my meds, I sometimes would see things, hear things, you know?"

"What kind of meds?"

"Aripiarazole. Paliperidone. Reisperidone. Duloxetine."

I shook my head. After Walter killed himself, I was so curious that I felt compelled to learn as much as I could about being bipolar, including treatment and medication. I read about all those meds. They were antipsychotic drugs.

"What happened?"

"About five minutes later, the cops pulled me over. I had no idea what they were talking about. I saw a boy, I think, but couldn't tell. I saw birds, too. Saw my mother, who was dead.

"They took me back to the scene. The boy was dead. Blood was everywhere. And I haven't been the same since then. I haven't felt right."

"Man, I'm sorry."

His voice was lower and sad.

"I don't feel like I deserve to live but I don't want to die. So I just live like I'm dead on the streets."

"Won't the medication make you feel better?"

"Maybe. But I don't want to take it. I don't want to feel better. If I feel better, I remember what happened too much. If I don't remember or focus on it, I'm OK . . . right here on the streets."

"I hear you. Have you ever gotten therapy?"

"I had to get some — they found me not guilty because of insanity and the boy was not at a crosswalk. They gave me meds. And I had to speak to a therapist for two years."

"It didn't help?"

"For a while. I didn't like the way the meds made me feel. And then I lost my dog. Padre was the only thing that seemed right for me. I had him for two years and then he was gone. That set me back, you know?"

Because he was bipolar, I didn't know what to believe. He talked like he had sense, but he looked like a homeless person.

"To be honest with you, I'm walking tonight just to find a place to die — like every day."

Before learning I had cancer, I probably would never have a conversation with a homeless person. I probably would have continued to act like they don't exist. But I felt we were meant to connect.

"Dying is overrated."

"How do you know?"

"Because I have terminal cancer."

I didn't mean to say, but I was glad that I did. I wanted to somehow touch him, to inspire him to change his life.

"I have a few months to live. Some kind of rare, complicated cancer in the stomach. My days are numbered. But I know there is a lot to live for.

"I'm not going to preach to you. But you've got to understand that life is a blessing. You have an illness, but it's treatable. Listen, before I learned my situation, I lived an ordinary life. Since then, I changed my attitude, and life has been so interesting and exciting for me. There's a message in this: Live your life. Seize the day. There is something wrong with someone who is dying wanting to live more than someone who is not dying. I know you're hurt by what happened to the boy in that accident. But it was an accident. You've got to live, man. Live."

"What's your name?"

"Calvin. Calvin Jones."

"I'm Todd. Todd Jones."

"See, we could be related." He laughed.

And then I did something I never thought I would do with a homeless person: I extended my hand to shake his.

He looked down at it, confused. "I haven't shaken someone's hand in more than four years. And I won't shake yours. Not because I don't want to, but because my hands are far from clean. But the gesture means the world to me. You're one of the few people who has actually talked to me and shared with me. Most people . . . well, you know how people are."

"I can't blame anyone for how they act. People see the homeless and are saddened and also afraid. My whole world has opened up in the last few months. I see the world differently than most now."

"I bet you do. I wish you the best, Calvin. See, I remembered your name . . . Thank you for the conversation. Haven't had a real conversation with a sane person in a long time. A long time."

"What can I do to help you?"

"Help me what?"

"Get some food. Get off the street. Get some meds."

"Now you want to save the world?"

"Just you."

Todd just looked at me. "Why?"

"Why not? You have every opportunity to live a good life. You just need to take your meds, get some counseling and get to work. Todd, it's too much out here — too many programs and job counseling centers and *women*. Don't you enjoy women?"

"Used to."

"Well, you're forty-five. There are plenty out there waiting for you to find them. Use that as a motivation. Man, you deserve to be enjoying life. I ain't the most religious person, but God spared you. You're still here. Don't insult Him by *choosing* to not live."

I went into my wallet. I had a business card and handed it to him. "Todd, my cell phone number is on here."

I went into my front left pocket. I pulled out a roll of hundred-dollar bills. I peeled off ten. "This is a thousand dollars, Todd."

"What are you doing?" he said with panic in his voice. "You can't pull that kinda money out in public. People always looking."

"Here, take it. No one is looking now. This is enough for you to get a nice hotel room, buy some clothes and some personal hygiene stuff and get a haircut. After you do that, go somewhere nice to eat. Sit and order yourself a great meal and enjoy it. Then, you call me and I will get you a cell phone and take you to a counselor, get you some meds and see where we can go from there."

Todd held so tightly to that money, looking down at it in his hand. When he raised his head to look at me, tears were in his eyes. "I don't know who you are or why you would do this, but thank you."

He looked down at Moses. "You're a lucky dog. If he's doing this for me, I'm sure he treats you good."

"This is my buddy right here. I have my boys at home: Bradford, Vernon, Lawrence, Joe, Big Will. But Moses is my dog, as they say."

We laughed and Moses wagged his tail.

"Do we have a deal?"

Todd looked at me, eyes still watery. He nodded his head.

"OK, I will look to hear from you in the next day or so. You're going to do right, right?"

"Carpe diem," he said, as he walked away.

CHAPTER TWENTY-TWO: BIKER CHICK

I slept so hard that it took Moses' barking to wake me up at almost eleven. He had eaten the food I set out for him before we went to sleep. He was ready for a walk.

It was a beautiful morning, on its way to almost ninety degrees. There were beautiful white clouds scattered in the sky. It made me regret that I was dying.

"You're looking so much better than when I found you, Moses. Some good rest and food have done you good."

I felt invigorated by that. When I first saw the puppy he was somewhat battered and meek. In quiet moments, I wondered where he came from, whether he was sent to me by God. Until that moment, I had no idea that I needed a constant companion. But having Moses was uplifting because my attention was mostly on him and not what I was facing.

I checked my e-mails when Moses and I

returned from our walk and found one from my holistic physician, prepping me for my first treatment. Much of what she sent was a review of what coffee enemas do in helping alleviate toxins from the body.

I was not comfortable with the idea of something rammed up my butt, but I could not take another episode with my stomach in so much pain. If nothing else, if the enemas could alleviate that, or minimize that, it would make my remaining days much easier to deal with.

My daughter was not so sure, though. She had done her research, too, and found Dr. Ali. But there was dissenting opinion about coffee enemas. Maya finally came around to agree that if chemotherapy was not going to get rid of the cancer, why take my body through all that shock and torture?

"Daddy," she had said tearfully, "this is hard to say, but the reality is that at some point, the holistic treatments are not going to be of help. What then?"

I didn't have an answer. As much as I believed I came to grips with my situation, it remained hard to believe I was going to die. I comprehended all of what the many doctors told me. I embraced what Pastor Henson shared. But I could not conceive of dying.

"We have to deal with that when it comes, baby," I finally said to her. "We'll deal with it then."

I was excited she was coming that evening. It was funny: Being around Maya cheered me up because she was my blood, my offspring, my baby. But it made me sad, too, because I worried about how she would deal with my death.

Before I could get upset, my cell phone rang. I had spoken to my father briefly on the ride to Atlanta and forgot to call him to let him know we had arrived safely. I expected it to be him. Instead, it was Venus. My heart started pounding.

"This is a surprise."

"And hello to you, too, Calvin." I could feel her wide, toothy smile.

"Good afternoon; I'm sorry. This is still a surprise."

"Why? I told you I was going to call you today. What are you doing?"

"Hanging in today. Resting. My daughter is coming this evening. Gonna pick her up, but that's about it."

"Well, get ready then."

"Ready for what?"

"I'm going to pick you up. Let's go to Sunday brunch. I have the perfect place."

I really wanted to just relax with Moses

all day. My stomach did not feel its best, which worried me. Usually after an episode, the next day I felt totally fine. Not this time.

"OK. You know where the Residence Inn on Piedmont is, in Buckhead?"

"On my way. Can be there in about forty minutes."

"All right. Room 1906."

I showered, which made me feel better, got dressed in some Levi's, Kenneth Cole loafers and a plaid shirt. I shaved my head and sat on the couch with Moses until she arrived.

Moses rested across my lap as I gently stroked his back. "You may not want to hear this, but we're going to find a vet this week you get you checked out make sure you have all your shots."

That dog looked up at me as if he understood. It was amazing.

"If you can understand me, you should know it's going to be all right. I'm going to make sure of that. And if you can understand me, you know I'm sick. But I'm going to make sure you're taken care of. I promise you that, man."

I searched on my iPad for veterinarians and dog parks and found some prospects. Before I could click on them, Venus called. She was outside my door.

I rubbed Moses. "OK, buddy, I've got to run for a few hours. Your food is there and water. I have the TV on for you. You're going to be all right. Right? Oh, I'm leaving the 'Do Not Disturb' sign on the door, so housekeeping shouldn't bother you. OK?"

He just looked at me and wagged his tail.

I washed my hands and sprayed on some cologne and backed out of the door. "Be good, Moses. Be good."

I shut the door and turned around to a surprise: Venus was on a Harley-Davidson motorcycle. It was beautiful: black and gold, shiny and powerful. I stopped in my tracks, partly because I didn't expect that and partly because seeing her straddling that bike was sexy as hell.

"Been on one of these before?"

"In my dreams."

"Then this will really be fun for you."

She handed me a helmet and I acted as if I was not scared when inside I was nervous. But Venus calmed me when she told me to firmly take hold of her waist. "Just hold on tight. Don't try to shift your weight from side to side. Just move with the bike."

She revved up that machine and weaved through the parking lot with ease and grace. When she turned right onto Piedmont, it was open road in front of us, and she guided the Harley down the major street as the breeze wrapped around our bodies. It was exhilarating.

I could see over her shoulder that the bike was just like a luxury vehicle with the latest technology. It was an elegant motorcycle.

Before long, I felt like we were floating along. The Atlanta skyline was beautiful, and she pointed to sights as we rode through Midtown and alongside Piedmont Park. At a light, she turned around and said: "You OK? We're going to Murphy's. It's about three minutes away. One of the best places for brunch in Atlanta."

I gave her the thumbs-up. I wasn't that hungry, but I was going to enjoy the experience. I smiled to myself at that thought. I had been a person who was inflexible: If I wasn't hungry, I wouldn't go out to eat. Now I understood the value of an experience.

We arrived at Murphy's in the Virginia-Highland area of Atlanta. It was a lively section of town, with people walking to and from the shops and restaurants.

I felt a little lightheaded getting off the bike. I wasn't sure if it was the ride or my being sick. Anything that was off kilter concerned me. But it didn't last long.

We waited at the bar for a table. "You

didn't tell me you rode a motorcycle."

"You didn't ask me."

We laughed and toasted with my water and her mimosa.

"It's hot, but it's a beautiful day to be out on the bike," she said. "I've been riding for ten years. This guy I dated actually got me into it. My passion for riding lasted — he didn't."

"I hear you." My cell phone rang. I looked at it and it was Kathy. I wanted to answer so badly, but I thought I shouldn't. Then I quickly got a grip. "Excuse me one minute, Venus."

"Hey there."

"How are you doing today? Are you busy?"

"I'm good, I think" — I was not comfortable answering that, knowing my situation. "I'm about to have something to eat. You OK? Can I call you later?"

"Oh, yes, sure. I'm good. I was just checking on you. I've been looking at that check you wrote me. But we can talk about it later. Just call me."

"Was that your girlfriend?" Venus asked.

"That's hard to say. She's definitely my friend. We used to date a long time ago. Now she's going through a divorce."

"You still like her. I can tell. I could see it in how you smiled as you talked to her."

"I wasn't aware I was smiling."

"That's because it was so natural. She makes you smile when you're not even trying."

"What's your deal? Why are you taking me to brunch and your boyfriend isn't taking you?"

Before she could answer, we were directed to a table on the covered outside area. It felt like a new life, an unfamiliar life to be sitting outside at brunch in a different city with a beautiful woman perched across from me. I had created this box I was comfortable with at home, but it seemed so mundane and boring.

"I met someone who has potential. I like him. He's a college administrator at Spelman. He's smart and funny. But it's early. The real him has not shown up yet."

"That's pretty cynical."

"I've dated for a long time in Atlanta. Trust me, it's more realistic than cynical."

I nodded.

"How you doing? How you feeling? I have to be honest: I went to sleep thinking about you."

I was hardly arrogant enough to believe she meant that in a romantic way.

"Why do you think that was?"

"Calvin, I was taken by you, your story,

who you are. It's just so much stuff. First of all, I would be a wreck if I were in your situation. But you were just hanging out and having a good ole time. You seem so calm and clear in your thoughts. It's just really brave the way you handle yourself."

"Thank you. But, trust me, I wasn't always this way. In some ways, I don't believe it. I've seen all the X-rays and talked to some of the leading oncologists. So, I *know* it's real. It just doesn't *feel* real. I want to live, and for the first time in my life I've been forced to look at how I was living. I wasn't doing that much. In the last month, I have had more adventure than a soldier."

"You said your daughter's coming here today, right?"

"Yes. I'm looking forward to some quiet time alone with her. We hadn't done anything together, just me and her, out of town, in a while. At home, we see each other all the time. But we have not traveled anywhere. So with these treatments I will get, hopefully, we can spend a little time doing some things together — daddy/daughter — before she goes back."

"That should be fun. I can send you some things I think she'd might like."

"Cool." I did not give an extensive answer because I was too busy spreading apricot jam over homemade biscuits they brought to the table. Immediately, I liked Murphy's.

The service was attentive with a smile and efficient. The biscuits and muffins were delicious. They made me want to eat, which was a feat. She ordered the shrimp and grits and I ordered the strawberry pancakes, eggs and bacon. Murphy's felt like home.

The food reminded me of my grandmother, who made biscuits from scratch and pancakes that were melt-in-your-mouth good. She could cook anything. It also felt like home because the people were open and friendly. Everyone seemed was in a good mood, and that was pleasant to experience.

"There are a lot of great places to eat in Atlanta; this is one of my favorites," Venus said. "Brunch, lunch, dinner, you can't go wrong. That's why I chose it. I had to take you somewhere I knew you'd enjoy."

I was enjoying my time with Venus more than I had anticipated. Whenever I could engage people or a situation and forgot I was dying, it was a special time. I had it with Kathy longer than any other time. Walking Moses and caring for him took me away from my plight. It was during quiet time that I was overwhelmed with what was ahead.

"Do you mind talking about what's going on with you or does it bother you?"

"I have not told many people. I'm not trying to hide it. But I don't need to put it on blast, either. With you, it just came naturally with the conversation. I felt something about you that made me comfortable. It's hard to put a finger on."

"Well, I didn't tell anyone. I sensed that you hadn't told a lot of people. I don't think anyone would. But I — I don't know — I felt honored that you were open with me."

"What if I wasn't sick? Would we still be here."

"Yes, because we aren't here because you're sick. I have gone through some things in my life that make me cherish life and good people. One of my close girlfriends, Ladina, died from breast cancer last year. It was so sad because she didn't tell me she was sick. I had no idea. We were having a good time at homecoming that October. By January, she was gone. I didn't learn anything until she was in the hospital. By then, it was just a matter of days.

"So, for you to tell me, even though you don't know me, it meant a lot. I can't imagine what it was like for Ladina, so I can't blame her for not saying anything. Maybe I would do the same thing. I just wanted to know so I could spend that time with her and tell her how much she meant to me."

"That's definitely the dilemma that comes with this. The people closest to me — and you and a homeless guy I met late last night — know. But not everyone."

"A homeless guy?"

"Yeah, I was walking my dog around three in the morning and we ran into him and we just started talking. It was interesting because, basically, he was a guy — the same age as me — who had given up on life. I told him that I was losing mine and I have learned more clearly than ever that life is a gift."

"I looked at a woman who was like my second mother," Venus said. "She's older and losing the battle with Alzheimer's. Her mind is going and her overall health is deteriorating really fast, too. It hurts my heart to see her like this. And it scares me. It makes me think about my future."

"Be glad you have a future. A lot of it you can control by eating right and exercising. And getting rest. None of that matters when cancer comes calling, though."

Venus nodded her head slowly and sadly. "Venus, it's OK. I'm here now and I'm having a great time. And I appreciate you picking me up and bringing me here. I think I'll bring my daughter here before she goes back."

"What was your life like before all this?"

"You know what? It wasn't this exciting. It was good, but kinda mundane. I loved teaching and my students and that was my focus. I played golf a lot and I liked books, but I didn't travel much or have much adventure. I guess it was a safe existence.

"But lately, every day has been an adventure. It's like as soon as I decided to live my life, my world began to open up. If I had been living this way all along, no telling where I would be now or what I would have done.

"That's one of the things I will tell my daughter while she's here. We have one life. How we live it is up to us. But we have to live it in order to get something out of it."

Venus looked at me with sorrow in her eyes. "Don't feel sorry for me, Venus." She was the only person I knew named after the goddess of love, and I liked saying it. "I've accepted there's nothing I can do about what will happen to me in the coming months. I don't like it, but there's literally nothing I can do about it. So, I'm living and having the time of my life. But you'd better believe I struggle with it. Always will.

"I asked my pastor why this has happened to me and he said, 'Why *not* you?' And that made sense. It's about what I do while I'm here and not question God's work."

"But do you really believe it's God's will that you, you know . . ."

"If I believe that He watches over my daughter and that He wakes me up each morning and that He is the Almighty, then I have to believe that this is His doing. You know what I mean? Either you're in or you're out. That doesn't mean I didn't question Him or still say 'Why me?' But, in the end, He is above all and I embrace seeing Him when I'm it's my time."

"You're so brave. I couldn't . . ."

"You're stronger than you think. We do what we have to do. Also, I don't want you to get the wrong impression. Almost every night I cry myself to sleep. I'm scared to death when it's quiet and I'm left with my thoughts. I've made peace with it . . . most of the time. But I have broken things and cursed and cried. Inside, I'm petrified."

"Oh, Calvin. I'm so sorry. You seem like such a good man."

"I appreciate that. But you should take away that you have been a good part of my life, my new life that started several weeks ago. I'm thankful for that. I have a new friend."

Teary-eyed, she excused herself and went to the bathroom. I sat back in my chair and looked out onto Virginia Avenue. People held hands as they walked by. Some shopped. Others chatted on their cell phones. I was jealous. It seemed they did not have a care in the world.

CHAPTER TWENTY-THREE: UNPLEASANT SURPRISE

Venus took the scenic route back to the hotel. She went back up Virginia Avenue, to Monroe Drive and up Tenth Street, alongside Piedmont Park. I held onto her firmly and let the breeze cover my body.

I noticed the birds flying and the clouds above. I noticed the trees swaying and kites flying and people tossing Frisbees and the dogs running free in the park. My senses were aroused. Moses would enjoy all the open space, I thought.

At the light at Peachtree Street, Venus turned to me. "You OK back there?"

"Holding onto your waist? Yeah, I'm good."

She laughed. "OK. We're going to go up Peachtree so you can see more sights."

I nodded. I sensed Venus was not taking pity on me, but that she was a kind woman who liked me and wanted me to see her city. And the ride back was fun. The traffic reminded me of D.C., but the people seemed less stressed and more carefree. The city was full of energy. I loved it.

"I could live here," I said when we got back to the hotel. We both noticed the irony in that statement.

"Venus, that was a good time. Really appreciate everything."

"You're welcome. Let me know how the treatments go. If you're up to it, let's meet for lunch or dinner."

"No doubt. That sounds great."

We hugged and she kissed me on my face. "I'm praying for you."

"Thank you, Venus."

I watched her mount her Harley and ride away before I opened the door to see Moses. He was bouncy and happy, tail wagging. I didn't even close the door. I grabbed his leash and took him out.

I noticed that I was getting more fatigued quicker than before, so our walk only lasted a few minutes. Once he was done, I headed back to the room.

"Moses, man, I'm tired. All I did was sit up close and hold onto a beautiful woman, but I'm drained," I said. "I guess you know what's going on with me, huh?"

That dog made a sound I hadn't heard before, as if he were sounding out sadness.

"It's OK, man. It's OK," I said as I picked him up and played with him on my lap. "I'm going out kicking and screaming with you by my side. OK?"

Moses wagged his tail and I, again, was convinced he understood something. "Let's relax before we go to the airport," I said. I thought: *Maybe this fucking cancer has spread to my brain. Why do I continually talk to a dog? And ask him questions?*

The nap came and went so fast and I awoke feeling sluggish. I was ready for Dr. Ali's treatment. I didn't help myself by eating pancakes, but they looked too good and I didn't want to pass them up while I still had my taste buds.

Her pre-session e-mail indicated I should not eat after four in the afternoon and that I should have plenty of alkalized water, essaic tea and seasilver, a nutritional supplement. Together, along with the coffee enemas, I would be giving my body the best chance to stay healthy the longest. And if I was not too far gone, it would eliminate or cut back big time on the pain and give me energy.

I knew all this would be a temporary fix. The cancer had spread and was not going to stop. There would be a time when I would become emaciated and fade away looking much older than I was.

That was the talk I had to have with Maya. I wanted to warn her, prepare her, so that she would not be overwhelmed with what she saw. I was not sure how to have that conversation; wasn't sure how I would survive that conversation because I knew what my daughter's reaction would be, which would cause me to react in kind. Tears.

When it was time to head to the airport, I rubbed on Moses and carried him to the car. For some reason, I babied the puppy, which was a first. But I felt so connected to this little dog. I believed he would drive me home if he thought I needed him to. He'd figure it out.

I wondered if I would have cared for him had my situation not been the same. I wondered a lot about a lot of things because, in a lot of ways, I felt like a different person, someone I always wanted to be but didn't have the courage or the push to become.

I liked this me better than the pre-cancer me. I was bolder and more connected to the world and the people around me. I cared about more than just my family and my friends. That was the abject lesson in all this: Embrace life.

Before leaving for Atlanta, I told my

friends just that, even the ones who did not know I was dying. Even Maya's mother, Skylar, who I had no interest in seeing or talking to ever again. She likely felt guilty for all the drama she took me through and called to say she was sorry for my diagnosis. My first instinct was to tell her, *I wish you were the one dying,* but I held back and told her: "Appreciate that. Just take from me that you have one life to live and you should live it to the max. I know you disregard anything that comes from me, but I had to say that."

Skylar did unforgivable things to me, things that still make me angry, eighteen years later, which was the last time I actually laid eyes on her. I avoided her at Maya's high-school and college graduations for fear my rage would make me go off. I literally was in the same space with her but would not look at her. I knew it was hard for Maya, but I had no other emotion around her mother than rage.

I later learned to deal with it; Maya resembled her so much. But if there was such a thing as disliking someone to the brink of hate, that's how I felt about Skylar.

But she was a far cry from where my mind was as Moses and I pulled up at the airport. I was about to see my daughter, my soul, my lifeblood. I missed her the few days I was away. We had a daddy-daughter love affair that held both of us together.

It was amazing how something so wonderful could come from a relationship so toxic. My baby was pure and sweet and genuine — all the opposite traits of her mother.

I called her to let her know we had arrived at the airport. She was at baggage claim, retrieving her suitcase. "I'm at door N-three," she said. I was parked right there, ironically enough.

After a few moments, Maya emerged from the sliding doors, smiling a smile so wide that my world lit up.

We embraced long and tight, and Moses looked from the backseat window as I held back tears. I loved her beyond description, and all I had been through since leaving D.C. — helping save the bus driver, finding Moses, making love to Kathy, protecting the woman who was being abused, meeting Venus, helping the homeless man, riding the motorcycle — rushed to my heart. I had those experiences and moved on, but some were bigger than others and truly emotional.

But I composed myself. Maya looked at me with those eyes I loved. The look was strange, though. She said, "Now, Daddy . . ."

My attention was averted. I saw an image

over her left shoulder and glanced up. What I saw made me wish I were dreaming. The reality was a horror show. It was Syklar, Maya's mother.

I pulled away from my daughter. "What?"

"Daddy, I need you to be calm. Daddy . . ."

I didn't answer. I just stared at this demon walking toward me.

"What the hell is she doing here, Maya?"

"Calvin," Skylar interjected, "I'm here to help. I —"

"Help? Help what? Kill me? Maya? What's going on?"

"Daddy, calm down. Mom wanted to help, to be here for you."

"Baby, I love you, but this should never have happened. I have done my best to shield you from all the drama your mother took me through. The last thing I need, especially now, is to see her. Period."

"Calvin, that was a long time ago," Skylar said. "It does no good to hold on to so much anger."

"I'm not holding onto anything — it's embedded in me."

"Daddy, please."

"Please what?"

"Please give her a chance."

"She had plenty of chances, and all she

did was wreck my life, almost ruin my career and land me in jail."

"What?" Maya said.

"I'm telling you, I have tried to not expose her because she's your mother. But you're old enough to hear the truth. And I guess that's what she wants because there's no way she could have thought I was going to continue to protect her."

"Cal —," Skylar said.

"Don't call me that," I snapped.

"OK, Calvin, please. Can we just get in the car and talk about this in private?"

"I don't want you in my car, even if it is a rental."

"Daddy, *please.*"

I was disappointed in Maya, but she never knew the level of my animus toward her mother. I hated when parents would meet with me and bad-mouth the husband or the father of their children — right there in front of the kid. That was misguided and selfish. Misguided because it served no good purpose to belittle the child's parent. He was still her father. And selfish because it always seemed to me a way of the mother (or father, if that was the case) boosting herself by stepping on the man she laid up with to have this child.

But all gloves were off. Maya's innocence

and my love for her allowed me to open the door for my daughter, place her bag in the trunk and get into the car. I left Skylar's bag on the curb and didn't consider opening the door for her.

She struggled getting her bag in the trunk and then got in the backseat with Moses. I liked that because she hated and was afraid of dogs. "What's this? Can we do something about this . . . this dog?"

I immediately thought about Richard Pryor in his 1975 album, *Is It Something I Said?*, when he told the story of Mudbone entering the home of Miss Rudolph, the local witch. Mudbone asked Ms. Rudolph if she could do something about the three-legged monkey she had in the house. She said, "I don't have to do shit about the monkey. The monkey lives here, nigga, you're visiting."

"This is Moses' car as much as it is mine, nigga. You're just visiting," I said. "Deal with it."

"Daddy!" Maya said, mortified.

"The gloves are off. If she's going to be here, she's going to hear exactly what I feel. Sorry you will have to hear it. But I don't have time to be nice to people I can't stand."

"Oh, my God. Maybe this was a bad idea," Maya said.

"You think?" I fired back.

"No, it's going to be fine," Skylar said. "Just tell the dog to stop staring at me."

"Stop staring at her, Moses," I said. "You might turn into stone."

"Oh, boy. Is this how it's going to be?" Maya said.

"Bet on it," I answered.

"Well, can we go somewhere and talk?" Skylar asked.

"Don't talk to me."

"Baby, please ask your father if we can go somewhere and talk."

"Daddy . . ."

"Talk about what? I don't understand this at all."

Maya said, "I found a restaurant in Midtown we should go to and talk. It's called Negril Village. On North Avenue. You know where that is?"

"I don't and I definitely don't have an appetite."

"We can just sit outside and talk then. Please, Daddy. Can you do this for me?"

"Why am I doing favors for you? You came here to be with me."

"Daddy, we really need to talk as a family."

"Family? I guess she gave you some spiked Kool-Aid and you drank it."

"It was my idea, Daddy."

"Well, now I'm really messed up. You know what's happening tomorrow? You think I need her around?"

"We need each other, Daddy. I know there has been tension — more tension than I ever guessed — but you all came together to create me. That's enough reason for us to be unified, especially now."

My daughter was too rational for my anger. I didn't say a thing.

We went to Negril Village, the cool Caribbean restaurant with a great reputation. We got a table outside, and it pained me to sit across from Skylar.

They ordered and I had water. "So, what's there to talk about?"

"Well, Daddy, I have been doing a lot of reading and one of the things I read was that it is important, with what you're going through, to be at peace with the people close to you."

"She's not close to me."

"You're my parents and you *should* be close. That's the point."

"Actually, *what's* the point? In three months, six months, I will be gone. What good would being close to her — which wasn't going to happen — have on my situation? All it's going to do is make her feel

331

better about herself. Plus, I don't have that many acceptances of apologies to give."

"Ain't nobody come here to apologize," Skylar said.

"Then you should definitely go home."

"OK, Calvin, I'm really sorry — for everything. I mean it. But you've heard that before. You just have chosen to be stubborn."

"Don't come down here, where you are not welcomed, and call me names. Sometimes being stubborn is the best way to deal with ignorance."

"Again, I want to apologize."

"For what, Skylar? For what?"

"For everything."

"What's that mean, exactly?"

"You know what it means, Calvin."

"Yeah, but does Maya know? I guess it's time for her to know 'We just outgrew each other' was a lie."

"Daddy, do we have to do this?"

"I'm not a mean person — you know that, Maya. But I can't let her gallivant down here like she's saving the day, knowing her history."

"So what do you hope to accomplish, Calvin?"

"I'd rather be hanging with my dog and Maya. But since you decided you would come here, I have to deal with you being here."

"OK, go ahead. I can take it. Maya knows my heart."

"If you had one, that would make sense."

"Dad . . ."

"Maya, let's go back in time so I can tell you why I'm this close to hating her. I'll start when you were first born. I had already proposed to your mother. We were discussing wedding plans and living arrangements, everything. Then one day, I check my e-mail and there's a message from Delta Airlines asking about my experience on a trip to Chicago. She had used my credit card to buy a plane ticket, which I didn't mind. But she said she was flying to New York.

"So I asked her about the plane ticket. She insisted she went to New York. When I asked her to produce the boarding pass, she couldn't. We had had issues about her communicating with her old boyfriend in Chicago. So here she was engaged to me visiting another man."

"Mom . . ."

"Baby, I was young and uncertain of myself and about getting married." It was the same B.S. she said to me way back then. "It looked worse than it was. I wasn't going to see him. I was going to hang out with my close friend and her sister. I know what it looked like, but I didn't even see him that weekend."

"Yeah, right. You might as well had because in my mind, you did," I said. "And why wouldn't you just say that you were visiting girlfriends?"

"Because you wouldn't have believed me."

"You're right about."

But I wasn't done. "There were other guys calling. There was her stealing money from my account. From my *wallet.*"

"It was a rough time for me, Maya. Your father was already teaching and doing great and I was trying to find my way. It would have been easy to just ask for the money, but I was embarrassed."

"My mother used to say, 'If you lie, you'll cheat. And if you cheat, you'll steal.' And you proved her right."

Skylar looked embarrassed. "I never wanted this to come out. But you show up here like it's no big deal, knowing how I have felt about it all these years. But that's not the worst part."

"What? There's more?" Maya asked. "I don't know if I want to hear any more. Mom, I'm so surprised."

"Let's see if you're surprised by this: Your mother had me arrested."

Maya turned to Skylar, who lowered her head.

"After all that, I tried to forgive her and move on. It made me angry a lot of times, but I tried to forgive and hang in there because of you. I wanted us to be a family. I believed in that and that once we were together, she'd feel what I was feeling.

"But Valentine's Day came and I had planned us a nice dinner. Guess who was missing in action. She was nowhere to be found. Wouldn't answer her phone. So, I finally catch up with her and she's arrogant about it all. I say, 'Fine, give me my ring back. I'm done with you.'

"She starts talking about how she's going to keep it and I don't deserve it. She knew I was going to ask for it back because she had taken it off and hidden it. So I went out to find it. Once I threw a dresser drawer on the floor, she called the police. I kept searching. She finally got it but still wouldn't give it to me. So I took it from her, prying her fingers apart until I got it.

"I had some clothes there that I gathered and calmly took my stuff to my car, which was parked in her driveway. I was at my trunk when the police rolled up. She comes running out of the house, talking about I assaulted her.

"I said, 'Officer, as you can see, I'm calm and I'm leaving. Nothing happened to this woman.'

"He asked her if she was OK, and she said, 'No, he choked me. Look at my neck. You said you weren't going to hit me anymore.' There was nothing on her neck. And I had never hit her. But because she made the claim, the cop tells me to turn around and puts the cuffs on. It was a Friday. I was in jail for the weekend. Totally humiliating experience. If my job had found out, my career would have been over."

"How could you do that, Mommy?"

"Evil," I said.

"Evil?" Skylar said. "That's so mean."

"Hey, it is what it is. I gave you every chance, stayed with you when I believed you were cheating. And what I got was you sending me to jail? I had to spend thousands of dollars getting that thing off my record, go into a diversion program and basically pray that no one in the school system found out. It wouldn't have mattered if I hadn't done anything."

"Mom, we just talked about my friend doing something similar a few weeks ago. And you said nothing about what you did to Daddy."

"What did you want me to say, Maya? I

was young and hurt and scared. I didn't know what to do, so I tried to hurt him. I have apologized more than once."

"Yeah, baby, she apologized after she reiterated her story to the judge hearing my case. Because the police did not see any marks on her neck and because her story was not consistent, he gave me a break and put me into a diversion program. If she had her way, I would have been prosecuted for simple assault and battery and gone to jail for up to three years."

"Mommy . . ."

"You see why I haven't spoken to her but once in so many years?"

"That's a long time to be angry, Calvin," Skylar said.

"And it's going to be longer . . . until the day I die."

Seeing her did not lessen my rage. Actually, it only fueled it. Kathy was so important to me because she helped me get beyond it. I had dated and fallen in love with Kathy after Maya was born. When she moved to California, my friendship with Skylar grew into a relationship.

But I wasn't in love with her and my dad told me having a child with her did not mean I had to be in a relationship with her if I wasn't feeling it. I appreciated his voice because he was big on family. Years later, though, after Kathy and I fizzled out, I began thinking about my daughter growing up without me in her daily life and tried .to make it work with Skylar, although my heart was not fully into it. I shared my anger about Skylar with Kathy, and she talked me out of choking Skylar for real . . . and convinced me to move on with my life.

I did, but the disappointment, hurt and anger never left me. Now here I was trying to find some level of comfort at a critical time in my life, and she was in my face?

"So, we've talked and you can go on back to D.C. You're not needed here."

"We're going to eat our food and let you calm down some," Skylar said. She still didn't get it.

"If I haven't calmed down in eighteen years, why do you think I would now?"

"Because your daughter is here and it's important to her."

That was the most meaningful thing that woman said to me in eighteen years. My life was all about my daughter. Period.

"I'm going to the car to check on my dog. I'll be there when you're done."

Then I pulled out thirty dollars and handed it to Maya. "This is for your meal," I said before turning and walking away.

I had asked God for the guidance and strength to forgive Skylar. I prayed about it many times over the years, until I totally forgot about her. But I remembered the prayer Reverend Henson asked me to recite when I was challenged. So, when I got into the car, I had Moses hop onto my lap and I recited it:

"Father God, I know You have called me home. My time is coming. Give me strength and courage to walk in Your path in these final days. Thank You for the blessing of life. And thank You for the blessing of death, for I know the greatest gift is coming home to You."

The prayer work, inasmuch as I felt the burden was lifted off of me. I knew Maya would grill Skylar — another reason I left. My daughter was as sweet as they come. But when she wanted answers, she vigorously pursued them.

I could tell that they had a heated discussion by their body language when they returned to the car. And the silence. It wasn't right, but I was glad Skylar felt uncomfortable.

"So, you made a reservation at my hotel, right, Maya?"

"I did."

"And her?"

"She was staying with me, but I don't know now."

Skylar jumped in. "Why don't you know?"

"Because maybe we should spend some time apart. I love you, Mom. You know I do. But I learned a lot today."

"So I'm just persona non grata, huh?"

"Looks that way," I said with delight.

"And that's just what you want, isn't it. You claim I'm evil but you're the one who's evil."

"Hey, I went eighteen years and didn't say a word, even with all the contempt I have for you, contempt you knew I had for you. So, for you to show up here, uninvited by me, and to expect a warm and fuzzy greeting, you just fooled yourself.

"And that's what's sad: all this time later you're still making bad decisions. I ain't perfect, but I never tried to hurt you or anyone else. I never lied to have someone put in jail and I damn sure didn't cheat on you. So, you can continue to play the victim role."

"Mom, you can stay with me. Don't worry about it. I'm just disappointed."

We drove back to the hotel in silence, everyone trying to get his/her bearings. I still didn't understand why Skylar came to Atlanta, except that she was seeking some forgiveness from me before I passed on. I was not going to give it to her.

I passed on talking with my daughter and her mother that night. I wanted to get some rest, play with Moses and prepare myself mentally for my first treatment.

I did go over to Maya's room and hugged her tightly and kissed her all over her face like I used to when she was a little girl.

"That takes me back in time, Daddy. And it makes me sad, too."

"I know, baby. I know."

I hugged her and we both cried.

Chapter Twenty-Four: Can I Get an Enema?

I wasn't homophobic, but I knew taking an enema was not going to be easy for me. My anus had one purpose, and it was for getting stuff out, not taking stuff in.

At the same time, I was eager to get it. I kept it moving, but I felt a change in my body, in my health. It was not a dramatic change, but I felt less energetic and restless. Couldn't sleep well and I had lost almost ten pounds. It looked good on me — I had gained a few doing much of nothing over the years. But I was concerned about how I could stop the weight loss because I was afraid to consistently eat . . . and my appetite was diminishing.

Dr. Ali sent me much information on clean eating, and I had, for the most part abided by it. I was going to make sure I stuck to it starting that day because I wanted to stave off the real agony that was sure to come. That probably scared me more than death — the way I was going to die: a slow, agonizing deterioration as the cancer spread. My body functions would shut down, and eventually I'd just drift off. That was an ugly, ugly future.

I had to control my mind to not think of that as much as possible, as difficult as it was. That's what brought the tears most nights. Knowing I would wither away like so much dust. And that Maya would have to watch all that.

When it was time to go to the session in the Southeast section of Atlanta, Skylar was waiting outside my room with Maya. "You need to stay here or go somewhere else," I said. I left no room for interpretation or response. I simply walked to the car and held the door open for Maya.

She got in and looked back at her mom as if to say she was sorry. I drove off.

"Baby, I did not plan for her or anyone to be here but you. I know I'm being mean to her, but it's only because of what I told you and that she was not supposed to be a part of this."

"I understand, Daddy. You know I love you both so much. I can't believe how Mom was with you. I hope to God she's changed."

"Me, too. You know, it's bad enough that white law enforcement is out here across the country targeting black men. It seems worse now than ever. But when I spent a weekend in jail, all I saw were us — black men. Most were in for petty or trumped up charges. And I was in there for nothing. The only good that came out of it was that I got a personal look at the system at work against us.

"Black men, *young* black men, were so comfortable locked up. It was as if they were at a cookout or a reunion. They knew each other and the correction officers by name and what time we'd eat and what time lights would be out and what time they would count to make sure everyone was accounted for. They were at home and it was sad for me to see that. I taught kids who would end up where I was . . . or worse. That was the down side to teaching: Seeing kids that, no matter what you did, would end up in prison or dead."

"I know. I had some classmates that I knew were not going to make it. And the really sad part for me, Daddy, was that many of them were girls."

"It's a different time. But I wish I were in Baltimore to march after Freddie Gray's death. That got out of hand, and talking about it is just not getting us any results."

"I was going to go, but then I decided

against it. Some things came up."

"We have to march while we're here. I'm sure there will be other chances."

Our talk was just what I needed. It connected me to my daughter and it passed the time as we drove to Dr. Ali's. The GPS said her office was the yellow house on the right. It was an old Victorian that had a wraparound front porch. The yard was nicely manicured. The azaleas lining the house were beautiful.

"How you feel?" Maya asked as we walked up to the entrance.

"Like I'm about to be raped," I cracked, and she laughed. I did, too. Laughing at that moment felt good because I had a confluence of emotions that crashed together: anxiety, fear, anticipation, relief.

Dr. Ali came to the door after one ring, and she looked close to what I imagined: head wrapped in colorful print, African garb tunic, big hoop earrings. She smiled.

"Greetings, family."

"Hi. I'm Calvin and this is my daughter, Maya."

She welcomed us and walking into her place felt like walking into an organic oasis. The place smelled of fresh lavender and spice. There was some music that resembled a soft African drum beat and tambourine;

but it was peaceful. She sat us at a table with a mudcloth lining and went over the paperwork, the procedure, everything.

I liked her demeanor — she was calm but in charge, self-assured and empathetic.

"I'm sorry you're here. The only thing I can guarantee is that these treatments will clear out the toxins in your body that can pass through your rectum. Obviously, cancer has its own mind, especially at Stage 4. But you will feel significantly better and more energetic almost immediately.

"Coffee enemas properly detoxify the barrage of toxic compounds that we all acquire in our life. Coffee enemas help you make glutathione, an antioxidant that gets rid of the poison in your body. When you relieve your body of those toxins, you open up a new, healthy world. That's why people who don't have cancer have the coffee enemas. It's a healthy way of cleansing the body.

"But with our program, the enema is a significant part of the therapy, but not the total session. We have meditation and spiritual reading and introspective therapy. We go over clean eating, which is very important, and alkaline water. Our goal is to put body and mind in unison to create peace mentally, physically and spiritually."

The whole thing would take about two

hours, she said. And Maya could not wait there for me. "You can come back a little after noon," Dr. Ali said. I wasn't sure if she was a medical doctor, but that's what she went by.

Maya hugged and kissed me before leaving. Dr. Ali directed me to another room that had what looked like a hospital bed in it with a big pan at the end. She pointed out a room where I could undress and put on a robe. Dr. Ali said some things, but I hardly was listening.

My stomach began to churn, from fear and from whatever was going on in my body. It felt as it did before one of the severe episodes that put me in the fetal position. This session was coming at the right time.

Dr. Ali was gentle with me. Her calm soothed me and the actual execution of the enema hurt my manhood more than physically. I was tense and nervous — not a good combination. But she made it happen.

She asked if I had a poem or anything I'd like to recite as she did her job and all I could think of was the prayer Pastor Henson told me. So I said to myself, cringed and held my breath as the tube was inserted.

I felt humiliated, but I sucked it up because I needed to. And before long, the coffee did what it was supposed to do, and bile

347

began flowing like a waterfall into a Gerson Bucket, which was a product from the Gerson Theory, designed to activate the body's ability to heal itself through an organic, vegetarian diet, raw juices, natural supplements and the coffee enemas. I read that on its website.

The stench almost made me vomit. It overpowered the scented candles and fresh sage she had burning. It was so harsh that I didn't want to breathe. But Dr. Ali, wearing a mask, was the ultimate professional; she did not show any signs of distress. She handled her business, discarded the waste.

When it was over, after the cleanup, I felt better, stronger. I wasn't sure if cancer was in that bucket, but some stuff that was making me constipated and lethargic had to be in there. The main thing with coffee enemas was to cleanse the liver, which was important. The last CT scan I had did not show that cancer had spread to the liver. But I knew, based on all that medical mumbo jumbo the doctors said, that it would get there eventually. And that's when my demise would be on an accelerated countdown.

I survived the first session. The body and mind thing was OK, but I was all about getting that stuff out of my stomach. I felt better and energized, just as she said I would.

She said I could receive the enema twice over seven days; too much runs the risk of causing problems, which I could not afford.

By the time Maya came to get me, I was "feeling much better, but violated." She laughed. "Let's go to Whole Foods. I have a whole list of clean-living groceries to get."

"Do you really feel better?"

"I do. We have some bad stuff inside us, I'll tell you that. That was some experience. I have another appointment on Thursday and then every four days after that for a few weeks. So, we will see."

"Can I call Mom and tell her how you're doing?"

"If you wish. I don't think she really cares that much."

"Dad, Mom cares. Trust me. She cares because I care."

"Why is she here?"

"She really wanted to support you — and me. She knows how hard this is for both of us. I think it was a nice gesture."

"Yeah, nice if it were anyone but her. Wait, my phone is vibrating. It's your grand-father."

"Hi, Dad. I was going to call you, but I was talking to Maya. It went well. I'm still not a fan of enemas, but I tell you what: I feel a lot better. I didn't say anything to either of you, but all the adventure and lack of sleep had me feeling sluggish. And I couldn't consistently sleep at night. This is supposed to help with that and the overall cancer."

"Really?" My father did not get too excited about it, but he was the one person who refused to accept the doctors' prognosis. He lost my mother when she was young. When the doctors told him she would not survive the aneurysm, he cursed them.

He didn't bother cursing when he learned about me. Dad just cried with me and prayed that they were wrong.

He spoke to Maya for a while, too. "How is he? Really?" I asked my daughter about her grandfather.

"I don't know, Daddy. I was over Granddaddy's place on Saturday. He had out photo albums with all these photos of you and Grandma. He was very solemn. He told me I was stronger than him. But I was honest: I told him I cry myself to sleep every night. He said he did, too."

That didn't make me feel good. It was one of the reasons I was so upset about things: Other people, people I cared about, would be hurt. Skylar was not one of them.

"Dad, Mom came down here because she's scared. I know she did some really bad things to you. But she knows how much you mean to me and she's worried about both of us. So, she thought coming here would be a chance to mend the old wounds and we can talk and figure out some things, how to deal with all this."

I wanted to scream, but something else came out of my session with Dr. Ali. I needed peace in my life. For eighteen years, even if I didn't think about Skylar, the rage I felt for her resided in me. It was there, hovering. Dr. Ali, through the meditation and focus on cleansing the soul as well as the body, forced me to face that pain and anger — and to understand that it was weighing me down in ways I hadn't noticed.

Dr. Ali said, in a quiet, soothing voice as I sat on a mat with my feet together and eyes closed: "What we do here is help you to understand you can control your health and your peace. By clean eating (no meats, no dairy, just organic fruits and vegetables) and clean living (no people in your life who do not cheer when you win, no hanging on to grudges, no hatred), you can go about your daily life with the physical and mental and spiritual peace that satisfies your soul."

So, I told Maya: "You know what? You're right, baby. All these years, it has done me no good to be so angry. Of course, I *had* to be angry in the beginning. And confused as to why she would try to hurt me like that. But, in the end, she did what she did — I had to deal with it and let it go.

"I didn't. Telling her to her face and telling you felt good. I hated that you had to hear that, but her showing up here just brought back all the pain and anger that's been in me for *eighteen* years. But I see the light, so to speak. I understand that I have gotten way past that and have far more important life concerns to deal with than hating your mother. So, I have let it go, Maya. I will not bring it up again and I will treat her better. I won't be all hugs and kisses. But I will definitely let go of the hostility. This is a spiritual detox."

"Well, listen to you. I'm so happy, Daddy. That would make this whole experience so much better."

I shared my thoughts with her on my time with Dr. Ali back to the hotel. She wanted to stop by Atlantic Station, but I needed to get back to Moses. I was sure he needed to be walked.

When I got to the room, however, Moses wasn't there, and my heart pounded so hard I could hear it. *Where was he?*

I ran outside and scoured the sprawling complex, going between buildings, screaming his name. I was almost dizzy. I *needed* my dog. I had come to rely on him. He was a constant reminder that I did some good in finding and taking care of him. He was my comfort, my company. He represented life for me.

Sweat poured down my face, from the sun but mostly because the fear gripped me that I would never see Moses again. I ran to the front desk. No one there had seen him. I covered the entire property, but Moses was not to be found.

I went out to Piedmont Avenue, cars zooming by, but no sign of Moses. I was devastated. I took the longest walk back to my room, heartbroken. Instead of going in, I just sat there on the ground, head in my hands. I felt empty, as if I had lost a close friend . . . and it was my fault.

Just before I broke down, I saw an image through my peripheral vision. I didn't want anyone to see me in such despair, so I tried to compose myself and get up. When I turned to my right, there was Skylar . . . with Moses on his leash.

The relief was so strong that I actually had to hold back tears. She let go of the leash and he ran to me, bouncing like he did the first time I walked him in Charlotte. I fell back to the ground and let him jump into my arms. He was so happy to see me that he squirmed and wagged his tail as if it were a fan. "Man, I was so scared," I said to him as I held him in one arm and wiped my face with my other hand. "What happened? Where have you been?"

I looked up at Skylar. "I was scared to death. What happened? What were you doing with him?"

"I'm sorry you were scared. I was kind of devastated that you wouldn't let me go with you this morning, so I just hung outside right here, by your door for a few minutes, trying to figure out what I was going to do. Then the housekeeping woman came. She knocked on your door and when no one answered, she opened it.

"And your dog came running out. I had to chase him down. I'm not sure, of course, but it was like he was trying to catch you. I finally caught up with him and brought him back to your room; the housekeeper was in there cleaning. I didn't want to leave him, so I got his leash and took him to our room."

"Oh, my God. Thank you. Skylar, if this little dog had been gone, I don't know what I would have done. I was so angry with you that I forgot to put the 'Do Not Disturb' sign on the door. And if you weren't here, he would have just run off and gotten hit by a car.

"I know this is ironic since I'm dying, but you saved my life."

Skylar put her hand over her mouth. I had not said a nice word to her in eighteen years. Anything I had said was unpleasant. Hearing something pleasant from me shocked her.

"Calvin, I don't know if it's that serious, but I'm glad I was here, too. I knew he was important to you because you didn't like dogs. But Maya told me how you had grown so close to him so quickly. Anyway, I'm glad I was here. And thank you for saying something nice to me."

I gathered myself and stood up. I was so emotional and had so embraced letting go of our past that I put Moses on the ground and hugged Skylar.

At that moment Maya walked up. She was stunned, mouth open. Finally, she said: "Excuse my French, but what the hell is happening?"

CHAPTER TWENTY-FIVE:
BOMBSHELLS A FLYIN'

In my room, I watched Moses eat as Skylar and Maya gushed about how, in the finding of a dog, we were able to sit in harmony, as a quasi-family and talk to each other and not about each other — for the first time that Maya could remember.

"I thought I was going to faint when I saw you hugging Mom," Maya said. "I knew we had a good talk in the car, but my goodness."

"I know, right?" Skylar said. "I haven't felt any love from this man in decades."

I was not sure how to react, but I looked down at Moses, and I just gave them the truth.

"I was angry because I was hurt. That's not easy to admit, but it makes no sense to me to not be honest at this point in my life with my daughter and the mother of my daughter. We both were young. I shouldn't have been trying to get the ring back, to be honest. It made perfect sense to me at the time because I was looking to hurt you, and that was the only thing I had as my power. I didn't recognize that I was being petty. I didn't recognize that the best thing for me to do was to just leave. I couldn't accept what I didn't like and didn't know how to maturely respond to it. That doesn't mean it was OK to lie and say I choked you. It's to acknowledge that if I had been smart about it, I would have just walked."

"I'm sorry, Calvin. I am," Skylar said. "You said it better than I ever did: We were young and immature. I regret being who I was back then and I regret hurting you and lying on you. It has haunted me the last eighteen years. So, you don't know what it means to me to be able to sit here with you and have a real conversation. If we're going to be totally honest, I can say that I was acting out and afraid that you didn't love me as I loved you. I didn't know how to respond to being vulnerable. I never had been. Every guy I dated was just some guy. You were ambitious and doing what you wanted to do. I admired that. And I wondered: *Why would he want me? He doesn't really want me.* And those thoughts drove me to dark places."

"Did you know any of this, Dad?"

"None of it. I respect what you're saying, Skylar. I appreciate you saying it. In the end, I wish we were mature enough to have a real conversation and maybe we wouldn't have carried around all this stuff we have for years."

She took a moment before saying: "We weren't supposed to be together. We were good for each other for a time, but I think our coming together was to produce our child more than anything else. But I always wanted the best for you. I was proud that you were Maya's dad and proud of the way you always were there for her, as much or more than I was.

"So, learning about, you know, the cancer, it's been hard for me. It's been hard for me because you helped me bring this wonderful person into this world. *We* did that. *We* raised her — and look at her. Perfect. That's our special connection. So I would never want anything bad to happen to you. And I know how much you mean to Maya. I guess I'm just saying that we both need you around. And to think you won't be here is very hard to accept. Impossible to accept."

I had forgotten how talkative Skylar could be. I looked over at Maya, and she was crying. It became a sad scene, one I never would have expected. And I was at the center of it, which made it even worse for me.

I went to the couch and hugged Maya. "It's OK, baby," knowing it really was not OK.

Maya and I embraced, with Skylar looking on, and I tried to hold back tears. Right then, though, I thought about how silly that was, that notion that men don't or shouldn't cry. Was that saying men shouldn't have emotions? Was that saying that after he cried, he could not return to being the man he always had been? It was an archaic concept and a silly one, too. I cried most nights and I didn't feel less than whom I had always been.

I cried watching *The Pursuit of Happyness,* the part when homeless Will Smith and his son were barricaded in a filthy public bathroom and someone was knocking on the door. He hugged his son tightly, covered his ears and rocked him as tears flowed down his face. If that scene didn't ring emotionally to a man, then he was disconnected from his feelings.

Being a man had nothing to do with not crying. It had everything to do with *being* a man.

So when the tears rolled down my face, I was not ashamed. The emotion I had around my daughter always had been strong. Shoot, I cried when she was born.

Finally, we both composed ourselves — and Skylar wiped the tears from her face, too — and took deep breaths. I tried to ease the tension.

"It's time for a drink," I said. "Some vodka."

They laughed. "I don't think so," Maya said.

Plus, she said, "I don't drink anymore."

"Since when?" I asked. "We were at Ben's Next Door the other week and you were drinking."

Maya rose from the couch and stood in front of Skylar and me. "I drank water at Ben's. I drank water because I'm pregnant."

She covered her mouth. Skylar jumped up and hugged her. I was transfixed on the couch, shocked, confused, conflicted. I did not want my mixed emotions to spoil her moment, so I reluctantly got up and hugged my daughter, too.

"I'm so glad you're happy for me," she said.

"Well, let's talk about this." I sat back down. "For me, I won't say I'm happy. You're twenty-three, just getting your career started. You're *not married.* And who the hell is the father? On top of that, are you prepared to be a mother? You think it's a big responsibility? However big you think it is, multiply it by a thousand."

"Well, Maya baby, your father has some valid points," Skylar said. "Who is this boy who got you pregnant?"

"He's a twenty-five-year-old man, not a boy," Maya answered. "His name is Terrell Pickens."

I turned to Skylar. "Have you met this kid?"

"Never heard of him. Maya, who is he and why haven't we met him?"

"Dad, you actually met him."

"What? When was this?"

"That time about a year ago when you had to work at a basketball game at the school and I had that event at the Kennedy Center. I went with my friend, Maureen, instead, and we came out and my car had a flat tire. I called AAA, but it was taking a long time for them to get there. So, I called you and you came after the game. When you got there, there was this man standing and waiting with me. That was Terrell. He saw me waiting and asked if it was OK that he waited with me, that I shouldn't be out there by myself because Maureen had already gone in her car. You shook his hand and thanked him. You said, 'Now, that's a gentleman to wait with you.'

"Terrell and I started dating a little while after that."

"But you never mentioned him before," Skylar said.

"To me, either," I added. "And why is that?"

"Because you guys — I love you; you know I do — but you guys judge the men I have dated so hard. Even you, Mom, are tough. Dad only gave Omar a chance after he learned he was moving out of town.

"I wish I had told you, especially in the last few months or so when we got really serious."

"We don't keep stuff from each other, Maya," Skylar said.

"I didn't think we did. I learned a whole lot about you yesterday."

"Hey, don't get sassy," her mom responded.

"OK, OK. Let's all relax and take a deep breath," I said. I had never seen them at odds. I felt like I was back in the classroom, managing two teenagers arguing over a boy.

"We can get back to what's his name —"

"Terrell. His name is Terrell," Maya interjected.

"I'm sorry. We can get back to Terrell later. We need to be talking about our unmarried daughter being pregnant."

"You guys are so old school. People have children nowadays because they want children. Besides, you two weren't married when you had me."

"That may be true," I said, "but we did come together and try to build a family. Do you and this guy —

"Terrell, Dad."

"Terrell. Have you and Terrell talked about marriage?"

"That's the last thing they should be talking about if they're not in love, really in love," Skylar said. "They should not get married because they are going to have a baby. That's a bad reason to get married. We know that for ourselves."

"There are worse reasons," I said. "Look at our community. Having these broken homes is one of the pitfalls of the black community. I taught for all those years at Ballou and I saw time and time again how those kids with two parents behaved better, performed better and were less troubled. The foundation of our community has to change from the inside out, with strong families as the strength."

"I was one of those kids without two parents in the house and I turned out great," Maya said. "And so did Terrell. We turned out great. And we will make sure our child does, too."

"Yes, there are plenty of mothers who raised great children by themselves. And some dads, too," I said. "Maybe I've seen too much, having been a teacher. We have to start giving our kids the best chances to succeed. And having them out of wedlock is not it."

"Dad, this isn't the best scenario; we both know that. But we will take care of our child. Simple as that. The way you and Mom did me. Terrell's parents divorced when he was young, but they both helped raise him. So we both know what it's like and we're committed."

Skylar said: "The one thing we know about our baby is that she's focused. She got that from you. So you know she's going to be a great mother."

"When did you start having sex anyway?" I said. "I could have sworn you were a virgin."

"Mom . . ."

"Calvin, come on now: a twenty-three-year-old virgin?"

"But we taught her — well, I know I taught her about abstinence and waiting until she was married."

"Yeah, and your mother talked that same

unrealistic stuff to you," Skylar said. "God rest her soul."

I was torn: I wanted my daughter to have a child after she was married. That's every father's dream. I also understood the amazing gift that came with bearing a child. And the enormous responsibility. In the end, though, after I got over the shock and disappointment and excitement, I was scared. I wanted to see my grandchild and hold it and kiss it and spoil it.

But would I even be around to see my kid have her own kid? That became my prevailing thought.

"I just want everything to be perfect with you, Maya. Simple as that. But I know hardly anything is perfect."

"You both raised me right. I know that you'd rather I be married. I would prefer the same thing. But this is the hand I'm dealt. I want to win with it."

"One thing and I will let it go," I said. I always was forthright, but since cancer, I was even more expressive. "This is 2015, about to be 2016. Only people who want to get pregnant get pregnant. Is this what you wanted?"

I hit a nerve. She did not have an immediate response. Skylar said, "That's a good question, Maya. What's the answer?"

Our daughter got teary-eyed. "What is it?" I asked as delicately as possible.

"Daddy, I did not try to get pregnant. I promise you, I didn't. We used protection. But I knew what happened when I went to church last Sunday —"

"Wait. You went to church?" Skylar asked. "Where?"

"First Baptist Church of Highland Park in Landover. That's where Terrell goes. We went together because we needed some spiritual influence. So, the pastor, Henry Davis III, was preaching to us, it seemed. He talked about how every issue we have in life God provides something great. Then he says: "You know how I know? Because it says in The Bible, in Isaiah 66:9: 'I will not cause pain without allowing something new to be born, says the Lord.'

"And I just burst into tears. All I could think about was your situation and the fact that I would be bringing new life into our family. When I got myself together, I leaned into Terrell's ear and said, 'Our baby is God's gift to us, to offset the pain of my father.' "

And then I was just about in tears because I believed what my daughter said, that her baby — my grandchild — would be a gift from God. And I cried because I was not sure I'd ever be around to hold it or kiss it or spoil it. That uncertainty hurt deeply.

I was surprised when Skylar came over to me, tears in her eyes. She knew what drove my emotions.

"You're going to hold that grandbaby in your arms when he or she is born. I *know* this."

I couldn't speak. I just nodded my head. I already was determined to live out the rest of my life in a fulfilling way. This bit of news made me determined to extend my life more than what the doctors said. I needed to hold that baby.

"We're going to name it after you, Dad. Terrell and I already talked about it."

"If it's a girl," I said, "please don't name her Calvina or Calvinesha. Give her a conventional name, please. You kids with these hybrid names . . ."

We laughed, which was needed. And then we hugged each other and marveled at the gift of life growing inside my daughter.

Chapter Twenty-Six: In High Demand

Before I could get off the phone with my father, Kathy called on my hotel room phone. We hadn't had an extensive conversation since I left Charlotte and gave her the check. She wanted to know how the treatment went, and I filled her in and told her about Maya's pregnancy, too.

"And how's Moses?" She was slightly facetious, but I didn't care.

"My man is great. We've been hanging, enjoying Atlanta. I have another treatment in three days. So we're going to hang out, hit the park and the vet. Wanna make sure he has all the shots he needs."

"You are just taken by this dog."

"I was there when he needed me. And he was there when I needed him. No telling what would have happened to him if I were not. So we're kind of important to each other."

She said she understood, but how could

anyone really understand if they hadn't been told they are dying? It was a place I wouldn't wish on anyone. Besides Moses, Kathy was the person I talked more openly about what was facing me. And she was better because she could talk back.

"Sometimes, usually when I'm at my lowest point of that day — and every day, no matter what happens, there's a low point — I think about whether it would have been better to just fall out and die from an aneurysm or heart attack or even a police officer's bullet. That way, I wouldn't have this daily agony I have.

"The night I spent with you was one of the few nights in about two months that I did not cry myself to sleep."

"Well, maybe I should just be with you. I've thought about our night together a lot, Calvin. And it was a sweet night and emotional and important. I know you probably felt like I was comforting you, but you were comforting me. I needed to feel loved by someone who mattered to me. I am not proud that I'm married. But I'm not ashamed that I love you or about the time we had together."

"Me, either. But what are you going to do about your living situation?"

"I've already done it. I found a place. It's

not far from where I am now, but it's a great space and a great neighborhood. It will be ready in two weeks at the latest. I signed the lease. But the big thing is I told my husband that it was over.

"It amazes me that men try to straighten up when you tell them you don't need them anymore. He went through this long apology — and I let him go on and on so he could feel humiliated after he finished. But he said we just needed a fresh start and that we have a family and blah, blah, blah. When he was done, I said: 'You're right. We do need a fresh start. And that's why I'm moving out.' I got up and left.

"He followed me into the kitchen. He said, 'My boy saw you out with some guy. Didn't think I knew that, did you? What's up with that? Is he the reason for this?'

"I told him, 'He's the reason I'm leaving, yes. But not the way you think. He's the reason because he gave me hope that there is someone out there who will love and appreciate me the way I need and deserve. To make it crystal clear: I'm leaving because of you.' And he could not say a thing.

"So, thank you, Calvin — for the money, definitely. But mostly for loving me after all these years and showing me how good I should feel about myself and my future."

We talked for another thirty minutes about her kids and how she broke the news to them and how they were not as devastated as she thought they'd be. "Just be mindful that they could be holding things in because they love you so much," I said. "Continue to talk to them and encourage them to be open."

Before we said goodnight, I told Kathy something that I thought was important. "In my next life, you will be my wife."

"Oh, Calvin. I don't know what to say. Thank you."

We hung up and I looked over at Moses. "What's up with you? Want to get a walk in?"

It was close to ten and I was winding down. Figured I'd watch a movie until I broke down in tears and cried myself to sleep after I made sure Moses was good.

We walked out to Piedmont Road and took the same route from when we met the homeless guy, Todd Jones. I looked for him, but did not see him. I wondered, after giving him that money, if I'd ever see or hear from him. My instincts told me I would, but the reality was that he was a bipolar, alcoholic, drug-user. The odds were that he overdosed rather than tried to clean himself up. I tried, though, and that was all I could do.

The next day and a half were spent in the room with Moses. I was depressed. The grandbaby coming only magnified how messed up the little bit of life I had left was. I just wanted it to be over with. I felt like I was waiting on death.

I faked it enough for Maya and Skylar to leave me alone and explore Atlanta. They went to the new Civil and Social Rights Museum, to the King Center, to the outlet mall up Georgia 400, to the Woodruff Arts Center and even saw a Frankie Beverly and Maze concert at Chastain Park.

"Dad, I feel bad that you won't come with us," she said over the phone.

"Your dad needs to rest; that's what Dr. Ali said. I went to Whole Foods and got some smoothie stuff. I'm good. Moses and I are chilling."

She asked about what I was eating. "Smoothie with kale, spinach, carrots, ginger, apple, banana with flaxseeds maca, hempseed, moringa and peanut butter."

"Sounds interesting, but if it gives you what you need, then great. I will have one with you tonight."

"You don't have to torture yourself. I'm good with it. But this experience has made me think you should really look at your diet — especially now that you have a baby coming in about eight months."

"Yes, Mom and I have been reading all kinds of stuff. I'm on top of it."

By that evening, she and Skylar had done their running around and Maya came to my room. We hugged and I looked down at her stomach.

"What?"

"There's a baby in there. My grandbaby. That's something really special."

"I know. I can't wait until I start feeling him moving around and kicking. That's gonna be so weird."

"Where's your mom?"

"She's in the room. She wanted to give us our time together."

I made her a smoothie. She tasted it and made that face that people make when they ingest something disgusting. "Oh, my God. Dad . . . You *like* this?"

"I don't have to like it. I just have to drink it. It's full of nutrients and it's part of my clean-living deal."

We sat on the couch and chatted.

"So what's up with this boy — I mean, man? Terrell?"

"What do you mean?"

"Is he the real deal or what?"

"The only reason I think he's the real deal is because he reminds me of you. First of all, he's an assistant principal of a high school. Second, he's smart. He loves the English language. He appreciates words. He's probably too serious at times, but he's fun-loving, too. He's like, radical. Always looking at race and how it plays a role in what happens in the world."

"I like that about him."

"I figured you would. What I appreciate about you was that you lived a calm life; you didn't do a lot. But you always encouraged me to travel and open my mind and to be aware of how race and racism matters. That has helped me as I work in corporate America and deal with these people. Some of them are racist and don't even know it — or won't admit it. So, anyway, you prepared me for life. All I can do as a parent is take what you and mom instilled in me, and instill it in my child. That will carry her through."

"Her? It's a girl?"

"I guess that was a Freudian slip. We don't want to know what it is until he or she pops out."

I slid over close to Maya and hugged her. "You're going to be a great mom. I know that."

"Thank you, Dad. That means a lot. And I know you're concerned about us not being married. But I'll tell you a secret: I think Terrell is going to propose."

"Really? Really? Is that what you want?"

"I do. I believe he's the one. It's only been a year, but the connection is there."

"I know what I said, but do not rush into anything because of me or the baby. Marriage is a decision that has to be made purely based on what you believe is the thing to do. You should have your own criteria that you have to stick to."

"I will."

"And he'd better meet me and ask me for your hand in marriage before proposing. If he doesn't, we're going to have a real problem."

"I got you Dad. And he will. I know he will."

With that, we hugged and kissed and she made her way to her room as I stood there with Moses watching her. Something in her gait, the confidence, the youthfulness snapped me out of my almost two-day doldrums. "She's going to be all right," I said to Moses, who wagged his tail.

I left him in the room as Maya took me for my second appointment. The ride there was quiet until Maya livened it up.

"You know, if Terrell proposes, you're going to have to walk me down the aisle."

"I love your mind and optimism — about Terrell and proposing. I'm walking you down that aisle, by hook or crook."

I wasn't all the way in on her getting married until I spent some time with that joker and figured out his angle. If he had game, I'd be able to detect it. More than two decades as a schoolteacher prepared me for a lot, especially detecting B.S. I could sniff it before it was shoveled out.

We arrived at Dr. Ali's and Maya pulled off and I made my way in. She was just as welcoming and reassuring. I told her that I felt much better and that I had no issues around the enema or my stomach. Unlike the first visit, when the coffee enema was first, we did the spiritual component for about an hour and then enema.

I went through the process without issue. I enjoyed the meditation especially because I thought about my friend Kevin and my mother.

Kevin left me a charge to live my life, and I believed he would be proud that I had. I wanted to do some of the things he wanted to do, but, in the end, I believed I had to do what was natural for me while still honoring him. He was a unique friend, one who gave without hesitation of his time, resources, opinions, even, in my case, an organ.

I had a few people I called friend, but some of them were halfway in, halfway out. Call you when they were lonely or needed something. See you when it was convenient for them. Disappear when they think you need them. Kevin taught me how to be a true friend.

My mother? I missed her and her laugh. She would laugh about most anything and had an infectious spirit that filled a room. But it was her grace I most admired. Everyone loved her because her disposition was charming without trying. She engaged everyone. Anyone. And her dignity stood out.

When she passed, I was thirty-three and just grasping fatherhood. She was a big part of that, encouraging me through Skylar's drama to keep my focus on Maya. Mom said: "The baby is important, not her nonsense. You will come through this. But you have to hold on to your love for your child. That's powerful."

The emptiness left by her death could never be filled. My father raised me to be a man. My mother raised me to be a *gentleman*. While meditating, I could see my mother's face and smile and it made me feel good. I prayed that the afterlife would put me in her presence and we could laugh together again. That would make dying worthwhile.

CHAPTER TWENTY-SEVEN: AND SO WHAT HAD HAPPENED WAS . . .

I did not have another session with Dr. Ali until Monday, so I was determined to have fun on Saturday and go to church and relax on Sunday. Venus called and offered to take me on another motorcycle ride, this time to Stone Mountain. I accepted.

She showed up in white leggings and an orange top, which illuminated her dark brown complexion. Beautiful. We chatted in my room for a while and she met Moses and made an observation.

"That dog is so connected to you," she said. "He watches your every move, like a child would his father. He loves you."

"And I love him. Never understood how people were so connected to a dog. Now I know. I really understand."

Venus readied the bike after I took Moses down to Skylar to keep until I returned. "Our daughter has worn me out this week. I need a break, so hanging with Moses will be fine." I gave her my room key just in case he got hungry.

Venus guided the motorcycle about thirty minutes through the city and Atlanta's insanely busy highways to Stone Mountain. It was a prodigious site, but one that brought back all my knowledge of the Confederacy and the heinous crimes committed against black people. The South had come a long way since those times, but the slaughtering of young black men this year and last made us question how much more ground we had to cover.

It was hot, in the low nineties, but somewhat cloudy, making it tolerable. "It's a good day to take the lift up to the top of the mountain," Venus said.

And so we chatted and laughed about life and love while in line. Finally, we boarded the tram and made it to the top. The day was clear enough to see all the way to the Atlanta skyline. It was breathtaking.

"You can't help but feel closer to God up here. You see all that beauty out there and know it's His doing. I'm not that religious, Venus. Really I'm not. I'm more spiritual. But I know the power of God."

"I'm glad to hear you say that because, with what's going on with you, I would think it could be easy to lose faith."

"It hasn't been easy. But, you know, a pastor in D.C. told me: 'Why not you?' He said I was chosen by God because I could handle it and be a blessing to others. And as soon as I accepted it as that, all kinds of things began to happen."

Before Venus could respond, my cell phone rang. I was not familiar with the number, but I answered.

"Sir, this is Mr. Todd Jones. We met several days ago on Piedmont Avenue, in the middle of the night."

"Oh, wow." My heart skipped, I was so glad to hear from him. "I'm just calling to tell you that I have purchased a phone — I'm talking on it now. I checked into a hotel in Midtown. I cleaned up good, went shopping and even got a shave and a haircut. And I went to Negril Village and sat outside and ate a great Caribbean meal."

"I went to Negril Village, too. I'm so happy to hear this, Todd."

I asked him to hold while I told Venus what was going on.

"So, how do you feel?"

"Like a new person. Or, really like the person I was before, you know, stuff started happening."

"Todd, I'd like to see you. I told you I'd get you to a doctor to get you on the right meds and help any way I can. I'm going to uphold my end of that deal since you upheld yours."

"I don't know why you would do this for me, but I'm grateful. I'm really grateful."

He even sounded better. I told him my room number at the hotel and asked him to meet me there at seven. I gave Venus more details.

"Wow, Calvin, that's so great. The homeless problem in Atlanta is bad. It's bad everywhere. And I don't see any urgency locally or federally to do something about it."

"This is, like, the other side of being sick, of figuring out that we're here to live our lives but to also serve others. It doesn't have to be big, either. I extended my hand to this man and he was moved by that. Said he hadn't shaken someone's hand in years."

"I tell you, I'm so glad we met. I really am. I hope to God you beat this. I know what the doctors said. But, still, I hope there is another miracle out there because the world is better with you in it."

I was touched. "Thank you for saying that. That means a lot."

We turned away from each other and looked out across the land from the mountaintop. We walked around some and finally went back down the mountain. I asked Venus to stop by Whole Foods so I could pick up some items. She had a better idea: DeKalb International Farmer's Market.

I had not seen anything like it. Fresh fruits and vegetables from around the world. There were five different kinds of tangerines and peppers and anything else, for crying out loud. Just an enormous place with all the fruits and vegetables and spices I needed. And much cheaper than Whole Foods.

"I could live there," I cracked.

Since we were on her motorcycle, I could not buy but so much. But that was going to be my new shopping spot.

When we got to the hotel, Venus asked to come in to use the bathroom. I let her in with the intention of going to Skylar and Maya's room to pick up Moses. But to my surprise, Skylar, Maya and Moses were in the room — with a strange man.

I showed Venus the bathroom. "What's going on?" I asked with attitude. Why would Skylar have a stranger in my space? I looked at her for an answer, and she didn't respond.

"Sir," the man said, "good to see you again. It's me. Todd Jones."

I was floored. The homeless man had, indeed, cleaned himself up. He wore brand new jeans and a nice linen shirt. His face was shaven clean and his hair was cut into a nice fade. He didn't look ten years older than me anymore. And he smelled of cologne, not the streets.

"Oh, my God. Todd. You look great, man. I'm sorry. I did not recognize you."

"Well, to be honest, I didn't either, when I looked in the mirror. But your dog is special. I could tell he remembered me."

"Calvin, he told me how you met, what you did for him and I thought it would be OK to wait inside instead of out there," Skylar said.

"Yeah. Of course. It's fine. I'm so glad to see you. You met my daughter and her mom, I see. Thank you for honoring your word."

"Sir, I had no choice. You inspired me. And I did not do it because of other stuff you said you want to do. You've done enough. You got me off the mat. The rest is up to me."

Venus came out of the bathroom and I introduced her around. I noticed Skylar was not as warm as she could have been. *Women.* I hadn't been in a situation where I was at the center of woman drama in a long time. Only once in my life, in fact, when I was in college.

I hated it, but there was something empowering about a woman being jealous of your relationship with another woman.

"I was with Calvin when you called," Venus said to Todd. "So I'm really glad to meet you. Isn't Calvin great?"

"How long have you known Calvin?" Skylar chimed in with attitude.

"What's it been? A week."

"And you know he's great that fast? Hmm," Skylar said.

Venus looked at me. I was going to answer, but Todd said, "This man is different from other people, I'll say that. I hate that I have to run. But I contacted my daughter and she's coming over to my hotel to meet me. I just had to come here to see you and say thank you in person. We can catch up next week, when it's, uh, less hectic for you."

He and I smiled and I walked him outside; Skylar called an Uber car for him. When I got back into the room, there was no conversation among the women. So I tried to generate some.

"Venus, I didn't tell you, but my daughter is expecting. I'm going to be a grandfather."

"Oh, wow. Congratulations."

"Thank you," Maya said. "I'm so excited."

Then came a knock at the door. I thought maybe Todd had forgotten something. I opened it and then opened my mouth.

It was Kathy.

"Wow, what are you doing here?"

"Here to check on you. You didn't sound so good when we last talked."

She looked around me to see who was in the room.

"I'm sorry. Come on in."

The look on her face changed. She didn't know if I was about to have an orgy or a wild party or what. But she immediately got all territorial. She let go of her roller bag and turned to me and hugged me.

"I have missed you. I wanted to surprise you — but it looks like you already have company."

I scanned the room and the only happy face was Maya's; she knew who Kathy was. Venus and Skylar had looks of disappointment on their faces.

"Kathy, you haven't seen my daughter in a long time, but this is Maya."

Maya came over and they hugged. "You're so cute. Such a young lady, just as your dad said when we were together in Charlotte."

I shook my head. "This is Skylar, Maya's mother."

Kathy's head snapped around to me. "She came down with Maya to lend support. I'm glad she did. We got past some issues that have been there for years."

"Oh, you did?" Kathy said with sarcasm.

I ignored it. "And this is Venus, my friend from here that I met last week."

Again Kathy's head snapped around. "Last week?"

And again I ignored the question. "You know Moses."

The women began squabbling.

"So how do you know Calvin again?"

"Y'all met when?"

"And you're his baby mama or grand-mama?"

"How old are you?"

And on and on it went. I grabbed Moses' leash and put it on him. I stood back, near the door, and watched with a smile on my face. Listening to women squabble was as real life as it gets.

I was going to die. Doctor said so. But I wasn't waiting on death anymore. That day, in that moment, amid all that chaos, I felt alive.

THE CRAFT

The way many of us live our lives is not pretty. We plow on, handling one obstacle after the next, always grinding toward getting through the day. The next day offers much of the same. And before we know it, we're much older and we wonder where the time went.

Life and death are intertwined in this way: If you don't *live* your life, you might as well be dead. A less harsh way of looking at it is that death is inevitable for all of us, so why not make the most of life before it is over?

With this story, I hope you are forced to look at your life, what you have done, what you plan to do, how you want to be remembered. If you take that inventory and surmise that you are not living it, then *start* doing so.

That's the underlying theme — we control how our life plays out. Calvin Jones, unfortunately, did not come to this understanding until learning he was dying. The amazing part about that was that it was not *too* late.

With the specter of death hovering, Calvin focused on living and his world opened up, big and small. That's the challenge for all of us who carry a far smaller burden than Calvin did — making the most of our time here.

For me, the exploration of Calvin's unfathomable position was revealing, and took me to emotional places no book of the eight I've penned has. Thoughts flooded my brain about my mortality and living a life of purpose, accomplishment and giving. It also made me think of the sad eventuality of death of those I love.

Mostly, this project inspired me to maintain a mindset of enjoying life, of not limiting myself, of experiencing new things and places. We only live *once,* and so why not seize the day, every day?

— Curtis Bunn

DISCUSSION QUESTIONS

1) Do you know someone who was terminally ill and if so, how did their life play out?

2) How would you handle the news that Calvin received?

3) If you were gravely ill, would you reveal your situation to people or keep it to yourself? Why?

4) Did you agree with Calvin's position to forgo the doctors' recommendation? Why? Why not?

5) How would you/have you handled a situation where a loved one has been given a grim prognosis?

6) Have you experienced family bickering

after the death of a loved one? How did it resolve itself?

7) Can a pet be a comforting force in a person's life? How?

8) Are you living your life to the fullest? If not, what is lacking?

9) What is it you'd like to do that you have not?

10) What constitutes a full life to you?

ABOUT THE AUTHOR

Curtis Bunn is an award-winning sports journalist who transitioned into a best-selling and critically acclaimed author of novels that provide one-of-a-kind insight into the psyche of men. A graduate of Norfolk State University, he is a book club favorite who founded the National Book Club Conference, which hosts an annual event described as "Literary Bliss." Visit him at curtisbunn.com and on Facebook and Twitter @curtisbunn.

The employees of Thorndike Press hope you have enjoyed this Large Print book. All our Thorndike, Wheeler, and Kennebec Large Print titles are designed for easy reading, and all our books are made to last. Other Thorndike Press Large Print books are available at your library, through selected bookstores, or directly from us.

For information about titles, please call:
(800) 223-1244

or visit our Web site at:
http://gale.cengage.com/thorndike

To share your comments, please write:
Publisher
Thorndike Press
10 Water St., Suite 310
Waterville, ME 04901